Fatal Attraction

"**W**hat about Madelaine?" I asked. "Did you study her finances? She seemed to live quite well for a woman who didn't work."

"There's work and there's work, Paris," Claypole said, pointing his cigar at me like I was target practice. "We're both big boys. I can tell you where the money came from. First off, she modeled for a year. The agency's long out of business, but I collected enough to know she worked a lot." He rumaged through the file, removing a stack of magazine advertisements and handing them to me. "Here. A little present for you."

They were all of Madelaine . . . peddling cigarettes . . . peddling cars . . . peddling jeans . . . perfume . . . bras . . . panty hose . . . selling . . . selling . . . selling. The face looked up at me with haunting cat-eyes and lips that whispered secrets—of money and sex and other mysteries of life. I could feel those eyes sucking me in, teasing me, grabbing at my insides. . . .

MADELAINE

Bantam Books offers the finest in classic and modern American murder mysteries. Ask your bookseller for the books you have missed.

Stuart Palmer
THE PENGUIN POOL MURDER
THE PUZZLE OF THE HAPPY
  HOOLIGAN
THE PUZZLE OF THE RED
  STALLION
THE PUZZLE OF THE SILVER
  PERSIAN

Craig Rice
HAVING WONDERFUL CRIME
MY KINGDOM FOR A HEARSE

Rex Stout
AND FOUR TO GO
BAD FOR BUSINESS
DEATH OF A DUDE
DEATH TIMES THREE
DOUBLE FOR DEATH
FER-DE-LANCE
THE FINAL DEDUCTION
GAMBIT
THE LEAGUE OF
  FRIGHTENED MEN
NOT QUITE DEAD ENOUGH
THE RUBBER BAND
SOME BURIED CAESAR
THE SOUND OF MURDER
TOO MANY CLIENTS

Victoria Silver
DEATH OF A HARVARD
  FRESHMAN
DEATH OF A RADCLIFFE
  ROOMMATE

William Kienzle
THE ROSARY MURDERS

Joseph Louis
MADELAINE

M.J. Adamson
NOT TILL A HOT JANUARY

Richard Fliegel
THE NEXT TO DIE

Barbara Paul
KILL FEE
THE RENEWABLE VIRGIN

Benjamin Schutz
EMBRACE THE WOLF

S.F.X. Dean
DEATH AND THE MAD
  HEROINE

Ross MacDonald
BLUE CITY
THE BLUE HAMMER

Robert Goldsborough
MURDER IN E MINOR

Sue Grafton
"B" IS FOR BURGLAR

Max Byrd
CALIFORNIA THRILLER
FINDERS WEEPERS
FLY AWAY, JILL

R.D. Brown
HAZZARD

A.E. Maxwell
JUST ANOTHER DAY IN
  PARADISE

Rob Kantner
THE BACK-DOOR MAN

Ted Wood
LIVE BAIT

Madelaine

an Evan Paris mystery

Joseph Louis

BANTAM BOOKS
TORONTO • NEW YORK • LONDON • SYDNEY • AUCKLAND

MADELAINE

A Bantam Book / March 1987

ISBN 0-553-26400-1

Published simultaneously in the United States and Canada

Bantam Books are published by Bantam Books, Inc. Its trademark, consisting
of the words "Bantam Books" and the portrayal of a rooster, is Registered in
U.S. Patent and Trademark Office and in other countries. Marca Registrada.
Bantam Books, Inc., 666 Fifth Avenue, New York, New York 10103.

PRINTED IN CANADA
COVER PRINTED IN U.S.A.

U   0 9 8 7 6 5 4 3 2 1

To Kate Miciak.
Many thanks.

One

It was a sunny, windless Monday morning, the thirteenth of May. The sky was a soothing light blue, and the air was so clear off the Los Angeles coast you could see all the way to the islands in the Santa Barbara Channel. It was a perfect morning for being alone. I had every intention of being just that when I saw a car turn onto my driveway and pass through the lower gates, ignoring the no trespassing sign.

My old battered Bulova said it was only nine-o-five. I had been working since the early dawn on the side of the house with splints, wire, and sealing tar, trying to repair the trunk of an orange tree that had broken under the weight of its own fruit. My gardener had insisted there was nothing we could do but cut the old tree down. Against his advice, I was trying to save it. The ancient twisted tree had been one of Anne's favorites, and Anne had been on my mind all morning.

In a way, it was an anniversary of sorts for Anne and me. One year ago to the day, Anne's kidnappers had passed through the lower gates, driven up the last quarter mile of gravel driveway, cut the alarm, and entered our home.

Anne had been here alone.

She had gone to bed early to read and had fallen asleep with a book open beside her. Her assailants had tied her hands and mouth with packing tape and left a note for a million-dollar ransom. I would have paid without question, but before I could even begin to put the money together, her body was found in the surf off of Will Rogers Beach. She had been strangled.

Since then, most of my well-meaning friends have urged me to move. They insist the house has bad memories. Maybe. But there are many more good ones. Besides, the house wasn't to blame for what happened to Anne. Once her killers had made up their minds to get her, it wouldn't have mattered where we lived.

So I remain here—not out of stubbornness, nor to hold onto the past—but because it's a good house. It stands like a crown on the top of a sage-covered hill with an unobstructed view of the Pacific coastline for twenty miles in each direction. The house itself is big and yet intimate, a classical California-style Spanish adobe and brick hacienda with thick, whitewashed walls, exposed redwood beams, a red-tiled roof, and all the extras—pool, sauna, and greenhouse—that we had ever dreamed of. It is surrounded by a thick, fragrant garden of orange and lemon trees and tropical flowers, and it provided ample room for Zoot, our golden retriever, to run free.

La Casa Final, Anne had called it. The House at the End of the Road. It was a long way from the dingy apartment we shared over the merry-go-round at the Santa Monica Pier when we first lived together.

The only problem with La Casa Final had come right at the beginning. It seems almost funny now, but at the time, I grumbled that we'd made a serious mistake in buying it. We had only been here a month when someone printed up a "Map to the Homes of the Movie Stars" and erroneously included La Casa Final as the house where Carole Lombard and Clark Gable had honeymooned. When the first gawkers arrived, I wanted to sue or at least bash in the head of the idiot who'd made the mistake. But as usual, Anne made me see it in a different light. She rightly pointed out that we were still so far off the beaten track that only a dozen or so tourists a week ever bothered to make their way up to our little corner of the Santa Monica Mountains. Thanks to the large, handpainted sign that Anne put up saying, "Beware of Vicious Dog," the few who did drive to the top stayed in their cars, looking at the house, admiring the view of the Malibu coast and the Pacific, then driving off. Occasionally, someone would be brave enough to venture out of their car to pluck a few birds-of-paradise at the edge of the driveway, but Zoot's wild barking soon scared them away.

When the mistake was corrected on subsequent editions of the map, our uninvited visitors fell away to practically nothing. In the year before Anne was murdered, only a handful of star-gazers ventured up the driveway.

This past year, only two or three of the lost or curious

poked their noses past the bottom gate. All went away after a few minutes. That suited me just fine. Ever since Anne's death, I'd lost interest in seeing people. There was always the chance I might explode again like I had after they'd killed her. I was afraid of that.

The automobile now making its way up my driveway was taking the steep part of the hill slowly, no doubt afraid of the sharp drop off the edge.

Whoever it was had better take a quick look and just go, I thought, tying the last of the wires in place.

The car disappeared for a couple of seconds behind a stand of eucalyptus trees, then reappeared near the top of the drive. It was a twelve-year-old Plymouth, an ancient gas monster with dented fenders and great bald spots of rusted metal on the hood and roof where the sun had burned completely through the faded maroon finish.

I watched with curiosity as the battered old tank pulled to a stop on the lower parking level, directly in front of the upper gate to the house and in the very worst spot on the hill for sightseeing.

The driver was a woman with brown hair and sunglasses. A little girl of three or four with curly white-blond hair sat beside her on the seat. The woman slowly lowered her window part way and studied the "vicious dog" sign through the dark shades that hid half her face. Then, she looked up toward the house.

I was well hidden behind the foliage of the orange trees and had every intention of staying there even after she gave her horn several light taps.

"Hello, hello. Anyone home?"

It was a weak voice, thin and old. It barely carried the thirty feet to where I was standing.

"Hello. Anyone home?" she repeated, then called me by name. "Mr. Paris. Are you there?"

That surprised me. I was almost sure I'd never seen her before. I wondered how she knew who lived here. Way before Anne had been killed, our phone had been unlisted, and there had never been so much as a number on the lower gate. Even our mail was sent to a box number at the Malibu station.

She was still peering up toward the house and hadn't spotted me yet. When she took off her sunglasses, I saw that the face under the brown bangs was round and wrinkled with flat cheeks and heavy-lidded eyes. It was a kind face, but I'd never seen it before.

She honked again, more emphatically this time, but with a lingering reserve, perhaps hesitant to disturb the peace of the mountaintop. The little girl stood up on the seat and pressed her face to the half-opened window beside the old woman's. The woman said something to her and she quickly plopped back down again, then picked up the sunglasses and rested them coquettishly on her nose. The woman turned to the window and called out again.

"Hello. Hello, Mr. Paris. Anyone home?"

From the look on her face, she either knew I was home or was prepared to wait all day.

As much as I wanted to be alone, I couldn't let her sit there forever. It was much too hot in the sun for someone her age.

I walked down the path and out through the gate to the car. A thin patina of dust covered the roof and the hood like velvet.

The old lady was dressed in a white cotton frock with a prim collar and large daisies splashed all over. Up close, I could see that the brown hair was a wig that sat slightly askew on her head as if it annoyed her to be wearing it. Wisps of white hair poked out on the sides. Her cheeks were heavily rouged, and her lips were painted a brilliant red that clashed with the pasty hue of her skin and the dull watery gray-blue of her eyes. The tremulous smile that she gave me came with some effort.

"Can I help you?" I asked, rubbing the dirt off my hands. The interior of the car smelled of old plastic and lilac perfume— the sweet, inexpensive kind.

The little girl stood up in her seat again and watched me curiously out of large, blue, catlike eyes. She wore a white smock with white ankle socks and shiny black patent leather shoes. She was a pretty girl, the picture of good health. I thought I could see a slight resemblance between the old woman and the girl in the shape of their eyes.

"I'm looking for Mr. Paris," the woman said, eyeing me warily.

"I'm Mr. Paris."

"Evan Paris? Mr. *Evan* Paris?"

Her uncertainly was understandable. I hadn't shaved. My face looked and felt like cactus. I was dressed in cutoff shorts and a torn T-shirt and was barefooted and grubby from working on the tree. Even by California standards, I looked more like the help than the boss. I smiled. "I'm Evan Paris."

"Oh," she said, then, "oh," again. "I'm Arla Coltrane. I'm a patient of Dr. Baldwin, Elizabeth Baldwin." Mrs. Coltrane reached for her purse, pulled out a business card, and handed it to me with a shaky hand.

It was Liz's card. On the back, in Liz's handwriting, was my phone number and address.

She waited for me to look up before going on. "Dr. Baldwin said you might be able to help me." Mrs. Coltrane said the word "help" with a quick lick of her tongue across her dry lips. I got the feeling she found it distasteful.

Liz Baldwin is a professor of psychiatry at the Los Angeles County USC Medical Center downtown. I could only begin to guess why she'd sent me one of her patients.

I asked Mrs. Coltrane how I could help her.

She didn't answer me directly. She glanced at the girl, then back at me, then spoke with the force of an uncertain person on a definite mission. "It's rather long and involved." Her anxious look said that she wouldn't or couldn't tell me in front of the child.

Short of turning her away, there was nothing else I could do but invite her inside. "We can talk in the house," I suggested.

"Yes, thank you." She looked relieved, but when I opened her door, she hesitated.

"I . . . I'm scared of dogs," she apologized, glancing up at the "vicious dog" sign on the gate and keeping both feet tucked inside the car.

"I'm not," the child said resolutely, and wrinkled her nose at me. "I like doggies." She clapped her hands together and went, "Woof, woof," in the old lady's ear, startling her. The little girl giggled. Mrs. Coltrane affectionately put her arm around her and hugged her, then kissed her forehead.

"This is my great-granddaughter Trudy, Mr. Paris. I'm afraid she doesn't know the difference yet between a v-i-c-i-o-u-s d-o-g and a k-i-n-d d-o-g," she explained.

Trudy screwed up her face. The secret language adults used to talk over her head obviously intrigued her.

"There is no dog," I assured her. "It's just a sign."

I didn't explain that even when Zoot was still with us, he had never been vicious. He had been so gentle that he'd let

kids Trudy's size ride on his back. He was dead now a year.
Anne's kidnappers had cut his throat. It made my blood boil
just thinking about it.

I helped Mrs. Coltrane out of the car. She gratefully took
my arm as we began to climb the stone walk to the house.
She was a thin, frail woman who felt so light on my arm I had
the feeling she would blow away in a strong wind.

By contrast, her great-granddaughter was full of life, hopping and skipping up the flagstone steps and chattering away
to the disheveled, one-eyed rag doll she hugged to her bosom
like a life preserver. She raced ahead nearly to the front door,
then pivoted and darted back, dutifully taking her great-
grandmother's free hand and assuming a somber expression
to remake the trip. It was as if she were two different people—
the carefree child and the very grave miniature adult.

I had seen this same kind of behavior before in kids who'd
spent too much time with grownups.

The climb to the door was only twenty-five feet, but Mrs.
Coltrane was seriously winded by the time we reached it.
Her face had an unhealthy flush which began to worry me.

"Are you all right?"

She nodded, her eyes briefly flickering shut.

"Are you going to lie down and take a nap, Gran-Nanny?"
Trudy echoed after me, narrowing her intelligent eyes as we
entered the coolness of the living room.

"We'll take our naps later, sweetheart. Right now, Mr.
Paris and I are going to talk." She turned to me. "Is there
someplace where Trudy can sit and play with her doll?"

Someplace where she won't overhear us? her eyes added.

I had the perfect place. Anne had child-proofed one of the
small rooms off the living room for friends who came to visit
with their children, filling it with enough toys, books, and
games to amuse an entire nursery school. It hadn't been used
in over a year. I left Trudy there with a plastic Goofy mug
filled with lemonade, a child-sized doll of Kermit the Frog,
and the assurance that if she needed anything we were just
next door.

"Oh, don't worry, I'll be very, very good," she assured me
somberly.

I'm sure, I thought, and almost hoped she might be a little
bad. I had a feeling it might do her some good.

When I returned, Mrs. Coltrane was sitting with her eyes

closed. I thought she had fallen asleep, but she opened them and self-consciously sat erect as soon as I entered the room.

"Can I get you anything?" I asked. "Coffee or tea or something stronger?"

"Just plain water, no ice, if you don't mind."

I went to the bar and filled her a tumbler of water and looked around for what I should fix for myself. Normally, I don't drink during the day, but I wasn't feeling normal. Just being around strangers made me feel edgy. My eyes fell on an unopened crystal decanter of twenty-five-year-old Glenfiddich Single Malt Scotch Whiskey that Anne had bought me one Valentine's Day a couple of years ago. Pouring myself a stiff shot, I watched Mrs. Coltrane remove a large bottle from her capacious purse and shake out a handful of pills in assorted sizes, shapes, and hues.

She took all the pills, using the whole glass of water to wash them down. I brought her a second glass and sat down facing her, dousing my insides with booze and wondering how I was going to get this over with so I could get back to being alone. The mellow malt hit my empty stomach and rushed into my bloodstream like a dozen lukewarm swimmers.

Mrs. Coltrane studied the room acquisitively, searching the high-ceilinged walls from top to bottom as if trying to nail me down.

This room was all Anne—the dark stained floors, the specially designed windows and skylight cut into the old walls to let in the light but keep out the heat on hot days; the garden pastels—pinks, greens, and pearl white—of the sofa and armchairs; the pine monk's table; the antique Navajo rugs with their subtle blues, reds, and grays collected long before they became fashionable; the Ansel Adams prints hung along the front wall that she had picked up at an auction. Even the two Paul Klee paintings with their splashy red and orange motifs, which I had bought, had been presents for Anne because she'd adored them. About the only thing in the whole room that was mine was the Purple Heart in its small shadow box on the mantle that the War Department had sent my mother after my father'd been killed in action on Christmas day, 1944, two months before I was born.

When Mrs. Coltrane finished with her visual tour, she smoothed her dress and folded her hands neatly in her lap as if about to comment on the decor. Instead, she gave me a peculiar look similar to the one she'd given me out front when she'd doubted my identity.

"You know, Mr. Paris, I've read all your books, and I'm a great fan of yours," she began, "but . . ." Her hands squirmed in her lap. "Well . . . you haven't written anything in such a long time. I expected you to be much *older*."

Someone had once said "dead" to me in the same tone.

It had been a while since I'd managed a graceful smile, but she deserved one, so I tried. "I don't get much pleasure in writing anymore," I replied. No use in explaining any further. She wasn't here to discuss my books or my writing habits. "You said Dr. Baldwin thought I might be able to help you. Perhaps you could explain."

"Sorry. I didn't mean to get personal." She leaned forward in her chair with a sheepish smile and went on in a low voice, appearing worried that Trudy might overhear her in spite of the walls between us. "My problem is simple, Mr. Paris. I have cancer. The doctors have given me two to three more months to live at the most. Dr. Baldwin's been counseling me on dying."

"I'm sorry," I said. The words sounded lame. They always do. "But how can I help?"

"Oh, I didn't mean it that way." I'd flustered her again. "There's nothing you can do about *that*. There's nothing anyone can do. I didn't come here for me. I came because of Trudy."

She paused, twisting the broad gold wedding band on her left hand, nervously popping it on and off over a wasted finger that had probably once been plump enough to hold it firmly in place.

"You see, Mr. Paris, I'm the only one she has. When I'm gone, she'll have no one. I explained all this to Dr. Baldwin—we had our session at seven this morning—and she suggested you might help us. She gave me your name and address and promised she would call you and then call me back, but I just couldn't wait. So I drove straight up to see you."

She obviously regretted not waiting. She touched her hand to her wig to straighten it, sneaking a guilty peek at me as if expecting me to scold her.

"How exactly did Dr. Baldwin say I could help?" I meant to ask it gently. But I'd gotten out of the habit of polite conversation, and maybe the question came out a little harsh.

She wiggled uncomfortably. "I told her I needed someone

to try to find Trudy's father. My granddaughter Madelaine—
Trudy's mother—always claimed that Trudy's father was dead,
but I believe he may be alive. If he is, I want you to find
him. I could pay you. You're the only one who can help me.
Please?"

What on earth must Liz have said to her? I wondered.
Whatever it was, this poor woman had certainly misunderstood.

"I'd like to, Mrs. Coltrane, but what you need is a professional, someone in private investigations. I'm afraid I can't be
much help."

"But I'm sure you could do it. When Dr. Baldwin mentioned your name, I knew right away you'd be perfect. It's
just like a Jack Savage case." Her conviction was startling.

Jack Savage was the hero of my books. Back in the old days
when my novels sometimes made the bestseller lists, people
confused the character with me. It used to amuse Anne and
me, but now it only made me feel awkward.

"They were only stories," I reminded her.

"Yes, but they're wonderful stories," she insisted. "And
besides, you were an investigator and a professor of crime."

"A very long time ago, even before I wrote those books,
and my specialty was international banking and finance, not
domestic cases."

She eyed me levelly. The flattery disappeared. The glint in
her pale eyes was disturbing. She dealt her last card with a
totally open face. Though I could see it coming, there was
nothing I could do to avoid it.

"My granddaughter was killed . . . strangled, just like your
wife," she said accusingly. "And you found your wife's killers."

Her words landed like a kick to the gonads. Outwardly, I
held my temper, but inside I was suddenly seething. I belted
back the rest of my Scotch. Now even that tasted bitter.

What happened to Anne—what happened to me—was different, I almost shouted at her. If I went chasing after my
wife's killers and if I found them, it was because it was *my*
wife, and because what had happened to her was *my* fault.
How do you explain that sort of thing? How do you explain
that when it's someone you love, you simply act—out of
character, if necessary—but you act? How do you explain that
you don't owe the world for all the mistakes?

I pulled myself out of my tailspin with one quick look at her
face. It was written all over in every line, every crease. The
despair. The pain. The utter humiliation of what had hap-

pened to her. Only a fool would think he needed to explain
anything to this lady. Arla Coltrane was acting precisely as I
had. Out of character. For Trudy. Because she had no other
choice. I was being an absolute jerk.

Come on, Paris, listen to what she's trying to get off her
chest. Let her unload. It'll help her, and it won't cost you a
damned thing. You've wallowed in your grief long enough.
Give somebody else a chance. Just listen.

"Go on," I told her.

For a moment, she looked bewildered. I think she never
expected to win her point. When she realized she had, the
words spilled out. Maybe she was afraid that I might stop her
before she got it all out.

"I don't know where to begin. There's so much. I already
hired one investigator who turned up nothing. I could hire
another one, but I'm running out of time, and there's no way
for me to know who's good and who's bad. For Trudy's sake,
I can't take that chance. My granddaughter left some money
in stocks and bonds. When I die, Trudy'll have what little
money I've saved. She won't be destitute, but she will be
alone. I'm the last one alive on my side, and quite frankly,
I'm terrified of golddiggers. Besides that, the people in the
welfare department told me most couples want to adopt
infants. Trudy turned three in January. That means she'll
have to be placed in an orphanage or a temporary foster
home or with someone who just might want her money
unless I can locate her natural father or *his* family. That
would be best. I know it. I may not succeed, but I have to
try. You do understand, don't you?"

Sure I understood. I wasn't made of stone, but half of me
still just wanted her to go away and tell it to somebody else.
It wasn't the half I was proud of. So, I told her, I could
sympathize with her.

"Then you think you can help?"

I launched into another explanation of why I couldn't, but
she gave me such a desperately unhappy look that I simply
said, "Perhaps if you told me a little more, I might be able to
suggest something."

"What else would you like to know?" Her eyes clung to
mine like fingers grasping the edge of a cliff.

"Tell me more about your granddaughter." What she had
said lit up a couple of brain cells somewhere in the back of

my mind. "You said she was killed. When did it happen and where?"

"It—happened—six weeks ago, just down the road from here . . . in . . . Malibu." Her voice quivered and broke on her last words. "I'm . . . I'm sorry; I keep thinking I'm over it." She paused, looked up at the ceiling, and gnawed her lip. She tugged a tissue out of her purse and dabbed at her eyes, then returned to the purse and pulled out a newspaper clipping and handed it to me. "It's all here. It says it better than me."

The headline read: "Woman Slain in Malibu Cliffside Home."

I was right about the memories. The murder had made headlines for a couple of days. When I'd first read it, I'd thought of Anne and what she had looked like after they'd pulled her out of the surf and brought me down to the morgue to identify her. I felt the same surge of anger sweep over me again.

No, I told myself. That was the past. It was over. I was strong enough to fight it.

I shoved the images away and skimmed the article. Madeleine Lucie, twenty-three, had been knocked unconscious with a fire poker, then strangled. . . . Arthur Lannell, thirty, no permanent address, found at the scene of the crime by Los Angeles County Sheriff's Department deputies, arrested and jailed. . . . Lanell had hung himself in his cell the same day. . . . Lab tests showed large amounts of LSD and amphetamines in his blood. . . . Police labeled the case a random psycho killing. . . . No other suspects were being sought. . . . Arla Coltrane and three-year-old Trudy were listed as the only survivors.

It was one hell of a test for me to read through all that without getting the shakes, but I passed it—for now. I felt an absurd surge of relief. Stupid, what little victories we learn to celebrate.

When I looked up, Mrs. Coltrane appeared to be composed enough to go on again.

"What can you tell me about Arthur Lannell? Did you or your granddaughter know him?"

"I didn't. I don't know if Madeleine did. The police said he earned a living doing odd jobs in the neighborhood and sleeping on the beach. They said it's possible he may have worked for her. But if she did know him, it couldn't have been for very long. She'd only lived in Malibu six weeks."

"Where did she live before that?"

"San Francisco. She'd been there nearly four years. Before that, she'd lived for a year in Hollywood, and before that, she lived at home."

"Where's home?"

"San Pedro. My husband worked on the docks. We moved to the harbor when we were first married in 1935. My daughter Joyce—Madelaine's mother—was born there in 1943 during the war."

"What about Joyce? You said you were Trudy's only surviving relative. I take it Madelaine's parents are dead."

"Joyce died in a fire in 1963, when Madelaine was thirteen months old. My daughter was twenty. She was married to a man named Jimmy Lucie. They had gone to San Francisco, leaving the baby with us while they got settled. After the fire, my husband Vernon and I raised Madelaine by ourselves."

"What about your son-in-law? Is he still alive?"

"I don't know. Jimmy disappeared right after the accident. I haven't had any contact with him in twenty-two years. I hardly think he'd be much interested in Trudy." There was an old note of bitterness in her voice. "No, Mr. Paris, our only hope's in finding Trudy's father."

I didn't care for the way she used "our," but I was still looking for a graceful way to worm out of it. Liz would pay for this.

"Do you know if your granddaughter was seeing anyone at the time of her death?"

"You mean, like a boyfriend?" She scrunched her eyes in thought. "She might have been. The truth is, Mr. Paris, I don't know much about my granddaughter after she moved away from San Pedro. I never visited her in Hollywood, and I saw her only once in San Francisco. Even after she moved back here, I only saw her the few times she came by to pick up Trudy to take her back to Malibu overnight."

"Then Trudy was with you most of the time?"

"Yes, practically every night after Madelaine came down from San Francisco. Before that, I'd only seen the baby once. Luckily, Trudy was staying with me the night her mother . . ." Again she paused, kneading her hands together, trying to wash away any mention of death.

"Did Madelaine tell you why she was leaving the baby with you?"

She shook her head. "No, but Madelaine never liked talking about herself, not even when she was little. She was extremely independent. Vernon never liked it. He'd have been happier living a hundred years ago, when women did what they were told without thinking, but I liked it."

She sat tall in her chair when she said this, perhaps remembering the few times she had dared talk back to her husband. There was a feisty spark still burning in that wasted flesh.

"You really admired your granddaughter, didn't you?"

"Yes, I did. I admire the way young women are today. I admire their spunk. If I had my life to live over, I'd be more like them. But I've had a good life. Better than most. I'm not complaining." She smiled stoically.

I smiled back. I liked her. I liked her a lot. There was an honesty and spirit about her that I knew Anne would have liked, too. I still didn't think I could do anything for her, but I didn't want her to stop. There were too many loose ends. They were starting to get to me. Anne used to say I could never let a shoe go by that was untied.

"Do you know why Madelaine moved down here from San Francisco?"

"No, not exactly. But I always had the feeling it had to do with money troubles of some sort . . . though God knows she could have solved any she had easily enough. My granddaughter left Trudy more than a hundred and eighty thousand dollars in stocks and bonds. She didn't need to spend four thousand a month renting that place in Malibu." The figures were cited with reverence.

"Did your granddaughter work?"

She frowned disconcertedly. "No, I don't believe so. At least not recently. When she first left home, Madelaine wanted to do something creative with people, sick people, like dance therapy or something. She started working as a model to pay for school, and I guess she just got caught up in the glamour. She used to talk about getting into the movies. She could have, you know. She had the prettiest reddish-blond hair and green eyes, and the loveliest figure. The whole time she was in high school, she took dance over in Palos Verdes two times a week and piano lessons every Saturday. I can show you some pictures of her if you'd like." Her face lit up like a little girl's when she spoke. She touched her fingertips to her wig again to pretty herself.

"Yes, I'd like to see them," I said, as much to please her as to get a better handle on her granddaughter.

Her purse yielded a folded five-by-eight model's card. The photos were black-and-white. The front, lefthand side of the foldout showed a head shot of a very attractive woman with high cheekbones, full lips, and those same cat-eyes I'd seen on Trudy. Opposite were four smaller shots, showing the same woman in full length in a sequined evening gown, a bathing suit, a business suit with glasses and attaché case, and a tennis outfit. Madelaine Lucie had had one of those remarkable faces that could change from ingenue to sophisticate with a flip of a curl or a streak of makeup. This was a girl to dazzle and haunt the senses, no doubt about it. I flipped the card over. On the back was a striking shot of her draped on the bumper of a light-colored Jaguar in sweater and slacks with a mink coat thrown over one shoulder and looking like she'd always been right on the money. Her name, measurements, dress size, and hair, skin, and eye color, and the address and phone number for the Hollywood Regency Model Agency were printed in the bottom lefthand corner of the card.

"Those pictures were taken five years ago, right after she graduated from high school." Mrs. Coltrane brushed the photographed mink with a gentle finger. "She only modeled for a year. Vernon never approved of what she was doing, but she would call me once in a while to tell me she was all right She was a good girl, Mr. Paris. If only she'd been married when she got pregnant. It broke Vernon's heart that she wasn't. He had a stroke that left him paralyzed on one side. I think my husband felt he had somehow failed both girls."

"Both girls?"

"My daughter and granddaughter." Her eyes dropped to her ring finger. "My daughter Joyce became pregnant with Madelaine in her last year in high school. Being pregnant and not married was something everyone was pretty ashamed of back then. I think Vernon always felt she got pregnant because he hadn't been strict enough with her. That's why he felt he had to be stricter with Madelaine. When my granddaughter wanted to come home to visit after the stroke, Vernon swore that he'd die rather than see her. So she stayed away. When she moved to San Francisco, Vernon needed looking after twenty-four hours a day, but even if I could have gotten someone else to take care of him, he'd have never forgiven me if I'd gone. I tried to send her money a couple of times, figuring she might be hard up, taking care of the baby and everything, but she always sent it back with a fat check of her own. She wrote that she was just fine and that I should buy something nice for Vernon and me."

"But you did say you visited her once."

"Yes, about a year ago. After Vernon died. I only stayed a few days. She asked me to stay longer, but I'm used to my own bed, and I guess I just wanted to get back home. I could see she was fine, though. She was living in a very expensive house. I asked if she was still modeling, but she said she hadn't done that since she'd left Los Angeles. When I asked her how she could afford to live like she did, she smiled and said that she and Trudy would never have to worry and that I shouldn't either. Well, I asked her then if Trudy ever saw her father. For a moment, it looked like she didn't know what to say. Then she told me Trudy's father was dead, that he'd been killed in a car crash when Trudy was eight months old. He was trying to get a divorce from his wife at the time and had planned to marry Madelaine. My granddaughter assured me he'd left her and Trudy comfortably well off, even though he'd never married her. It upset her to talk about it. I wasn't there to nag her, so, I let it go, but I'll tell you, Mr. Paris, I never thought she was telling the truth. When Madelaine was a child, she didn't fib much, but when she did, I always knew. She had a way of avoiding your eyes. Vern used to call them her 'lying eyes.' And that's how she looked when she told me about Trudy's father. It didn't matter so much at the time, but now it does. Even if Trudy's father is dead, he must have had some blood family—a brother or sister or someone who might be willing to love Trudy after I'm gone. You don't think I'm being unreasonable, do you?"

"No, perfectly reasonable," I agreed. What I didn't say was that reasonable didn't necessarily mean possible. The granddaughter sounded to me like she'd been playing in the deep end of someone else's pool, probably playing more on her looks than her brains. On the face of it, there was no telling what was true and what wasn't. Nor was it clear whether Madelaine Lucie's death had been in any way connected to her life, or simply a random killing as the police said.

I needed hard facts. No, that wasn't true. I didn't need a damned thing. I should have let it drop there, but the loose shoelaces were getting to me. "Do you know what hospital Trudy was born in?"

"Yes, Mount Zion in San Francisco. I have her birth certificate. It was among Madelaine's papers. I made a duplicate for Mr. Claypole, the investigator I hired. Would you like to see it?"

"Please."

While she rummaged through her bag for the copy, I asked, "The detective you hired wasn't Donald Claypole by any chance, was it?"

"Why, yes, do you know him?"

"I've met him," I said, without going into the details. Donald Claypole was an operator of the old school who used to live high off of divorce cases when California laws were much tougher on cheating husbands. Rumor had it his billings had fallen way off in recent years and he was now running a very small shop.

"Do you think he's any good?" she asked, handing me the birth certificate.

"He's a professional," I told her.

Good is as much a matter of luck as anything in the business, I reminded myself as I glanced over Trudy's record of birth.

Trudy Jane Lucie was born on January 13, 1982. She weighed in at six pounds, seven ounces. The attending physician was a Dr. Martin Eisser. The mother was listed as Madelaine Kathleen Lucie. The space for the father had a line drawn through it. Not much to go on.

"How'd you get hooked up with Claypole?"

"I went to the police with my problem, but they said it was out of their jurisdiction. Lieutenant Blanche, who was handling Madelaine's investigation, recommended a private investigator and suggested Mr. Claypole. I made an appointment and went to see him three weeks ago. He seemed very kind and very understanding, especially after I told him about my condition and how little time I had. He seemed very sure he could do something for me. I gave him a five-hundred–dollar deposit and waited. Three days ago, he informed me that he'd done a thorough search of Madelaine's records. He had checked her old neighbors and even talked with models she had worked with five years ago. He couldn't turn up a single clue on Trudy's father. He explained that he could go on, but it would be a waste of my money. He was very nice about it;

I think he felt bad because he had led me to believe that he could do something. He even insisted on giving me back half of my deposit, which, I must admit, surprised me a little."

It surprised me, too. No one had ever faulted Donald Claypole for his generosity.

"Did he say why he gave you your money back?"

"He insisted it was his policy, but I think he felt sorry for me," she said dryly.

Strange, I thought, especially if he'd done all the legwork he claimed he had.

"Is there anything else you can tell me about your grand-daughter, Mrs. Coltrane?"

Her eyebrows went up, brightening her face. "She was a good girl, Mr. Paris. When she was little, she was always bringing home stray cats and birds with broken wings. Of course, Vernon never let her keep any of them, but she always tried to be good."

"What about her friends? Did she have many?"

She touched her fingers to the side of her head as if she were scratching out a thought. "I never met anyone in San Francisco. The only ones I know of would be in San Pedro, and I never knew many of them because Vernon didn't like her bringing any kids in the house. The only one that I know she did keep in touch with after high school was Helen Razkowski. Madelaine and Helen took dance classes together all through high school. Helen graduated a year ahead of Madelaine and moved to Hollywood to try to make a career as a dancer. Her mother moved away from San Pedro that same year to some place back east—I think it might have been Colorado or New Mexico, but I'm not sure. Madelaine and Helen stayed in contact though, and when Madelaine graduated, she moved in with Helen before she got her own place."

"Did Don Claypole speak with her?"

"Yes, but he said she wasn't very helpful."

"Did he speak to Trudy?"

"Yes. She told him she remembered a Mr. John and a Mr. Richer. Mr. Claypole asked her to describe them, but I'm afraid her descriptions weren't very accurate. Mr. Claypole thought Trudy might have simply made up the names."

"Is that what you think?"

"I just don't know," she said in a small voice. The whole

business had worn her down to the point where she wasn't sure of anything anymore.

I knew how she felt. There was a time when I'd been searching for Anne's kidnappers and butting my head against nothing but stone walls. I was hurting so much I couldn't see straight.

"Do you mind if I talk with Trudy?"

She hesitated, instinctively protective; then she relaxed and opened the last door to me. "Yes, you should talk to her. But please be gentle. I've told her that her mother's dead and won't be coming back, but I'm not sure she believes me. She keeps insisting her mother is only away on a visit. She's convinced if she's very, very good, she'll come back and take her to the beach house again. I wish there was some way to make my baby understand without hurting her more." Mrs. Coltrane dabbed at her eyes. "I'm sorry. God must have a reason for all this."

I couldn't help wondering if God had ever had a good cry.

"It's all right," I told her. "I'll be careful with her."

I refilled her glass with fresh water and left her alone in the living room, carrying refills of Glenfiddich for me and lemonade for Trudy into the playroom.

There was a sweet, little-kid smell in the room. She was sitting quietly on the floor beside her balding rag doll. The sun from the skylight overhead fell across her white dress, making it dazzle. She had arranged the other dolls and stuffed animals in a circle around her and was telling them a story about a little girl who lived in three different houses.

When she saw me, she gave me a studied smile and said, "We're having a party. Everyone's being good."

"Would you like more lemonade?"

"Yes, please." She came over and let me top her up, thanked me politely, then sat back down on the floor and sipped her drink from the red Goofy mug.

I sat down beside her on a bean bag chair and sipped my Scotch from a highball glass.

Trudy looked up and smiled. "When's Mommy coming?" Only her mouth smiled, though. Her eyes were weighing me to see how I would answer.

I already knew whatever I said would be no good. No one had been able to say a damned thing to me after Anne was killed, and I was a grown man. Even though I'd seen Anne dead with my own eyes, I still had trouble believing it.

Sometimes, I'd wake up from a dream so real that I'd swear she had been right there in bed with me seconds before. At times, I even thought I could smell her perfume in the house.

Jeezus, I thought, what's the best way to lie to a kid?

"Trudy, your mother's gone away. She won't ever be coming back."

She studied me skeptically, then said flatly, "That's what Gran-Nanny told me." It was impossible to tell whether she believed me or not. I suspected she was beginning to form the opinion that all adults lied. I'd been there, too.

"Trudy," I asked, "can you tell me about the people who used to come visit you?"

"You mean when Mommy and I lived in the other house?"

"Yes."

She frowned. "I don't 'member."

"You don't remember anyone ever coming to visit?"

"No one ever came."

"Do you remember a Mr. John or a Mr. Richer?"

Her look was wary. "Did Mommy go away with them?"

I felt like I'd just been backgammoned. "Mommy went away by herself, Trudy. I'm trying to find Mr. John or Mr. Richer. Do you know where they are?"

"No," she said, scooping up her rag doll. She was getting impatient with me. "They went away."

"Do you remember when you last saw them?"

"When I was a baby. When I was two," she insisted, holding up four fingers.

"How old are you now?"

"Three," she said, holding up three fingers. "Are you Mommy's friend?"

"I'm your Gran-Nanny's friend," I said. "Do you remember what Mr. John looked like?"

She pondered the question. "He was as big as a giant."

"How big is that?"

"Big," she said, holding her hand, fingers spread wide, as high over her head as she could reach. "He had funny eyes."

"Funny eyes?"

She covered her eyes and squinted between her open fingers. "Funny eyes."

"Do you remember what color his hair was?"

"Green," she replied matter-of-factly, "and he sometimes wore a red shirt."

"And Mr. Richer, was he also very tall?"

She nodded. "Even more taller." She held her hand over her head again and said, "Like that."

"Did he have green hair, too?"

"No . . . orange." She twirled the few remaining tufts of orange wool on the head of her doll.

"Are you sure, Trudy? It's very, very important."

She looked up with huge heartbreaking eyes and asked, "Will you tell Mommy I'm being very good so she'll come and get me?"

"I'll tell your Gran-Nanny," I promised.

"You go tell her. You go tell her, and I'll go with you."

She scrambled to her feet and tugged at my hand to get me to stand up. Her little pink fist clung to two of my fingers as we walked. Her hand was sticky from the lemonade.

It wasn't fair, I thought. What she was going through, what she would have to go through in the coming months after her great-grandmother died . . . it just wasn't fair.

Her great-grandmother sat with her head resting on the back of the sofa. Trudy released my fingers and darted to her side, tightly hugging her frail body.

"Your friend says I was a very good girl. Can we go home now? I have to see Mommy."

Over the child's shoulder, Mrs. Coltrane's face registered defeat. She pulled her closer, soothing the pale curls with a hand so thin it was almost translucent. "We'll go home now, darling. Your old Gran-Nanny has taken enough of Mr. Paris's time. Go get your doll, and we'll leave."

As Trudy trotted off to retrieve her doll, Mrs. Coltrane struggled up to her feet, using the arm of the sofa to steady herself. Her face went white from the effort.

"You've been kind to listen to an old woman's troubles, Mr. Paris. If you can help me, I'd greatly appreciate it. If not, perhaps you could suggest someone. I need to hire the best."

I could have recommended a dozen investigators who would give her her money's worth. I should have done just that. I had no business getting involved. But the old lady had gotten to me, and so had the kid. And damn it, so had Anne. I knew what she would have done. She would have rolled up her sleeves and pitched in.

"Why don't you leave it with me for a day? I'd like to do a little digging myself before I suggest anyone."

"I could pay you for your time," she said proudly.

"That won't be necessary."

"I don't want charity."

"It's not charity. I'm not taking the case. I'm just going to make sure you get on the right track this time and stay there."

I took her phone number and told her I wanted a detailed list of anything with an address on it that she'd found among Madelaine's belongings. In particular, I wanted a list of any bank or brokerage accounts. I also wanted written authorization to inquire into Madelaine's estate.

Trudy came back into the room, her one-eyed rag doll dangling from one hand.

"All set, Gran-Nanny," she announced. She turned to inform me: "I put everything back like I found it."

"Thanks," I told her. "Maybe you'll come back another time and play."

"With Mommy," she promised. She gave me a sweet, bright, meaningful smile that left me with a lump in my throat the size of a robin's egg.

Two

I was in. I could bullshit myself all I wanted to that I wasn't going to get involved. But I already was. I just hadn't admitted it yet to myself.

I called Lieutenant Blanche at the Los Angeles County Sheriff's Department headquarters downtown. I had a funny feeling it was the same Pete Blanche I'd known a long time ago. If it was, I wondered if he'd remember me.

"Of course, I remember you," he growled in a bulldog voice that brought back a flood of fifteen-year-old memories. "You're the rich, famous guy. What're you doing, slumming? How the hell are you, you prick?"

"I'm fine, Pete, just fine, thanks, and you?" He sounded

exactly like the old Pete who'd been at Berkeley doing a masters in criminology when I'd been doing my doctorate.

"I'm okay for an old man. At least, I thought I was when I woke up this morning. Now, I got you on the other end of the line. I don't owe you money do I?"

"No. We're all paid up." The debts he was referring to were very old ones. He and I had been part of a crew of once-a-week poker players during two school years. Pete had a habit of borrowing a few bucks from the night's winner and forgetting to pay it back. I'd once calculated I'd lent him just about what he'd lost to me during those years—which made us about even.

"So, how come you're calling me, Evan? You want some real ideas for one of your books? Maybe you got a part for a fat, ugly guy in a movie? What?" He sounded cheerful but also a little pressed.

I got right to the point.

"I'm looking into a recent murder—a woman by the name of Madelaine Lucie. I understand you handled the case."

"Yeah, Malibu murder. Ugly but open-and-shut. What d'ya want to know?" The question mark at the end was all cop.

"I'd like to come see you."

"Sure, but I'm just on my way to a meeting upstairs with the boss."

"How about an early lunch at the Bonaventure? That's near your office."

"You paying?"

"Of course."

"Okay, then you're on." He chuckled. "See you in an hour."

I smiled as I hung up the phone. Pete Blanche used to chuckle just like that on the rare occasions when he'd be lucky enough to win a pot.

I slipped out of my work clothes, took a quick shower, and shaved the bristle off my face. I put on a fresh pair of cords, a loose cotton shirt, and my best leather boots. I felt almost human again, and a bit strange. It had been the better part of a year since I'd gone out to meet anyone for anything that even vaguely resembled work.

It felt so strange, I almost forgot to leave a note for Carmencita, my housekeeper, telling her not to count on me for dinner.

I was locking the door when the phone rang. It was Liz. Before I could say a thing, she launched into an apology.

"Evan, I'm afraid I did something I shouldn't have. I gave one of my patients your address and phone number. I'm really sorry. She told me this terrible story, and all I kept thinking was that somehow you might be able to help her. I told her I'd phone you, but I've got this sinking feeling she'll beat me to you."

"She came by this morning," I explained as soon as she paused long enough for me to get a word in edgewise. "She brought the kid with her. They both left a half hour ago."

"Oh." Her voice was barely audible. "I'm sorry—" She seemed to begin her apology again, so I interrupted.

"No need to be sorry, Liz. I told Mrs. Coltrane I'd do a little digging and get back to her tomorrow with some ideas."

"Then, you're not mad at me?" she asked cautiously.

"For what, Liz? For deciding that I was hanging around the house too much and that I might need a shove to get me out in the real world again?"

"I-never-thought-that, Evan."

I laughed. "I know your therapeutic mind, Liz. Mrs. Coltrane was chicken soup. You're nothing but a meddler at heart."

"The thought had crossed my mind, but actually that wasn't the main reason I recommended you. I really thought you might *want* to help. I was quite touched by her."

"So was I. I was just on my way out to see what I could find."

"I'm glad. Will you call me and let me know how it turns out?"

"Sure."

She paused. She was waiting for me to say something more, and we both knew the "more" was the real reason she'd called. Liz and I had been on shaky ground with each other since Anne's death. We both also knew that I'd said all I could about what was bothering her.

Finally, she said, "I'd like to see you again sometime." She'd removed all the nuance with paint thinner.

"Is that an invitation?"

She hesitated, then sighed with genuine exasperation.

"I don't know," she answered softly, then added more emphatically, "No, it's not an invitation. I don't know what it is. Maybe it's best if we don't see each other. . . . Damn it, Evan, I don't know what I want. Just call me and let me know about Arla, will you?"

"I'll call," I promised and hung up.

Outside, the temperature had crept up another five degrees, cooking the last of the moisture out of the air. A breeze came up from the valley below, bringing with it the oily smell of the eucalyptus along the driveway. Anne used to say it made the place smell like cough drops. It did.

I left the top off the Jeep and let the wind blow through my hair. On the way down the hill, I caught a side view of myself in the mirror and realized how long it had been since I'd last seen a barber. I looked like a mountain man, tanned to bronze with a long mane of brown hair flapping behind me like the wings on Mercury's hat.

All I needed was to let my beard grow to look truly debauched, I thought. I hadn't had a beard now in over a year. The last time I'd had one, there'd been a few rivers of white on the chin. Anne had said it looked "interesting," meaning she didn't quite like it, but didn't quite hate it either. On the good side, she pointed out that it made me look like Rembrandt's King David. Liz, on the other hand, loathed it without qualification, mumbling a few unkind words about "aging hippies."

I turned onto the Coast Highway and headed south along the ocean front, sucking in the sweet ocean breeze. As I drove I reminded myself I didn't care what Liz thought. But maybe that was only partially true.

Liz and I went back a long way, even longer than Anne and I, by a few days. Nineteen years ago, she'd been Anne's roommate at Southern Cal. They were sophomores living in a pink stucco house on Thirtieth Street just off Hoover Boulevard. I was a junior and a placekicker on the football team—a specialist and lone wolf in a team sport—called in for the kickoffs, extra points, and panic-time field goals when the clock was running out. The status helped in lining up dates, which at the time seemed like the only good reason I had for continuing my education.

I got Liz's name from one of the linebackers, Joe Cleech, who'd met her through his girl friend at a ski party at Big Bear. Joe claimed she was the best-looking sophomore in school. Cleech was a man of refined taste, so on an impulse, I called and set up a date. When I arrived, however, I found I'd been stood up. Liz's roommate coolly explained that the old boyfriend from Stanford—the exfiancé, it turned out—had arrived in town unannounced and insisted on one last tête-à-tête with the woman who'd broken his heart. I was pissed off, but I also had two hockey tickets I didn't want to waste, and the roommate was about the closest thing to a date I was likely to scrounge up at ten minutes before game time on a Saturday night.

The roommate was no knockout. At first glance, she looked like the arty type—the kind who goes out of her way to look bad. She was dressed in old baggy pants and a man's shirt, and she wore a pair of large, unflattering horn-rimmed glasses that made her resemble some kind of noxious water bug. At second glance, though, I could pick out a nice figure under the oversized clothes and very pretty eyes under those glasses. But from the cool way she treated me, I was nearly convinced she hated men.

Later, she told me she thought I was a stupid jock. The only reason she agreed to go was because a guy she *really* didn't like had been bugging her for the last couple of weeks, and she was afraid he might stop by. So, I was the lesser of two evils.

As a couple, even for one night, we were like a bad case of diplopia. She was from the right side of the freeway, cultured and refined, already knowing what she wanted to do with her life. I came from money, most of it new, some of it tainted, and none of it had stuck to me after I'd left home. I was doing all right in school, but I was a punk and a drifter at heart who knew more about gang fights and rock'n'roll than Spinoza and Schweitzer.

As it turned out, none of that mattered. Somewhere under it all, something just happened between us. I got a kick out of the way she whipped out a biochemistry book during the hockey match and read it while snatching glimpses of the action between pages. I was also impressed when she picked right up on the rules and memorized the rosters of both teams with one glance at the program. She was equally impressed when I discovered after the game that I'd locked the keys in my car and had to pick the lock.

In a weird sort of way, we started to find things in common. She knew how to choose the right wines. I knew how to cure hangovers. She took me to my first ballet. I showed her how to hot-wire her Volkswagen. I took her across town to the barrios for real Mexican food. She took me to polo matches and introduced me to French cinema.

By the time I finally met Liz, Anne and I were a match.

Anne used to tease that if Liz and I had gotten together first, I'd have fallen for her. There was some truth to that. Liz was everything Joe Cleech said she would be. She was also Anne's best friend.

For the longest time, that had solved all the problems.

Now, there were more problems than Medusa had snakes.

Liz's problems, Liz's snakes; there was nothing I could do about it, I reminded myself as I nosed straight across town along the Santa Monica Freeway, past the suburban low-rise sprawl of America's third largest city. LA spread all around me. The smog—trapped in the basin by the mountains ringing the city to the north, east, and south—became thicker, dirtier and smellier all along the fifteen-mile run from the coast to downtown.

I exited onto the Harbor Freeway and headed north toward the intersecting ribbons of elevated freeways that knotted around the city center. On the few good days a year when the air cleared at this end of the city, the downtown core of buildings could be seen poking up out of the suburban sprawl like giant jagged teeth of steel and concrete.

Today, visibility was two blocks. A thick mustard brown cloud of stale car exhaust covered the core like the lid on a toilet.

Pete Blanche was already at the Bonaventure when I arrived.

The Blanche I remembered had been on the chunky side. The one who greeted me was a good forty pounds heavier, most of it right in the gut.

"Jesus, Paris, you look like a fuckin' movie star," he said. His face broke into a roguish grin as he offered me a beefy, freckled hand.

His grip was like iron. Pete Blanche had gone fat but not soft. His eyes checked me out coplike from head to foot, taking in details like he was snapping a series of Polaroids. "Jesus, you still got all your hair . . . and your teeth . . . and your waistline. Sonovabitch, you make me feel old," he grumbled. "I guess you wouldn't have recognized me." Self-consciously, he ran his stubby fingers through what hair he had left.

There were a few differences in addition to the new girth. I had never seen the mustache before. It was an uneven one that drooped more to the left than the right. And the mop of once curly red hair had suffered serious attrition, leaving a large freckled dome with a thin, closely cropped fringe of muddy-colored locks on the sides like a seedy Friar Tuck.

But his trademark eyes—the crafty deepset blues that snapped up the world in infinite detail—they were the same. Pete hadn't changed. Not really.

After the maitre d' had seated us, taken our drink orders, and left, Pete turned serious. "I heard about what happened to Anne. I'm sorry. I thought of sending a card or something, but somehow never got around to it. She was one of my favorite people."

"She liked you, too, Pete. Thanks." Anne used to help him with his term reports—she had helped all of us. I changed the subject before it got maudlin. "What about you? Still married?"

"Twice divorced and paying child support on five kids," he muttered, but there was also a touch of pride in his admission. "But that's another story. What's your business? How come the interest in the Lucie woman? You writing a new book?"

"No. I'm trying to help Mrs. Coltrane, the dead woman's grandmother." The waiter arrived with our drinks, and I waited until he took our meal orders and left. "She said she came to see you about the kid's father."

"Yeah, I remember." He knocked back half of his double bourbon and looked thoughtful as he coated a roll with two pats of butter. "Nice old broad. I was sorry I couldn't help her, especially after I found out how sick she was. But as far as I could see, nobody's broken any laws, so it's out of our hands. I told her to hire a private detective. I recommended Don Claypole. Hell, if I knew you were back in the business, I'd have sent her to you. When did you open up shop again?"

"I haven't. I'm doing a friend a favor."

He tipped the glass and eyed the ice cubes, then me. "This Coltrane woman's a friend of yours?"

"A friend of a friend." I told him the story Mrs. Coltrane had told me, including what Don Claypole had said and how he'd insisted on giving her back her money.

That gave Blanche a chuckle. "Sounds like he suddenly got religion."

"Think so?"

He shrugged. "Stranger things have happened. I heard he's been having a few problems with his ticker lately." Pete patted his chest. "Nothing too serious, as I understand it.

Just a friendly warning from the doctor to lose some weight and watch the diet. But maybe he started trying to make it up to the Man upstairs. Every time I get a gun drawn on me, God and I have a very nice rap. Then, I'm a pleasant bastard for about a month." Blanche stuffed the last of his roll in his mouth and began devouring a second one, buttering it between bites.

"Do you know Claypole well?"

"Not well, Evan. My oldest boy, Clive, the twelve-year-old, takes karate lessons at the same place as Don's youngest son. I run into Don . . . maybe . . . once or twice a month when I pick up my kid. Other than that, I don't see him."

"How's he doing businesswise?"

The blue eyes narrowed. "You got an angle on Don I should know about?"

"I don't have an angle on anyone. I'm rusty. I haven't handled a case in eight years. I'm just asking questions. Humor me."

He grinned slyly. "You don't fool me, Evan. You haven't changed. You're like an old dog with a bone once you get your teeth into something." We both knew if I did have an angle I wouldn't tell him until I was ready. Just the same, he filled me in on what he knew about Claypole. "Don's been kind of shaky lately. As you well know, the old private eye stuff is mostly history. The real money's in corporate work. Don needs guys with MBAs and accounting degrees, but he's not up to managing the new breed. At least, that's my opinion, for what it's worth."

He finished just as the food arrived. Pete looked askance when the waiter waved my grilled salmon in front of him. "The turtle food's for my skinny friend," he huffed, pointing at me.

He definitely looked more comfortable with the three-inch prime rib parked in front of him. The smile on his face was cherubic as he cut off chunks of beef, dipped the meat in mashed potatoes, sloshed the concoction in gravy, and shoveled the food in. The same look of contentment used to grace Zoot's face when Anne would bring him a bone from the butcher's.

We bullshitted about the old days for a couple of minutes, then got back down to business.

"What can you tell me about the Lucie murder, Pete?"

"What do you want to know?"

"Everything. Especially anything that might give me a lead on Trudy's father."

"You think we might have missed something?" Under the amusement, his look was challenging.

"Did you?"

For a moment he reacted like I'd just insulted him. Then, his face softened. "After what happened to Anne and you, I guess if anyone has the right to think that way, you have, Evan. But we're not all like Jarrish."

He meant Detective Robert Jarrish. Bobby Jarrish and I had grown up together, the two uncrowned princes of a loose gang of misfits, renegades, and juvenile delinquents who should have all ended up dead from the stunts we pulled. Bobby became a Detective III of homicide in the Los Angeles Police Department—that is, the city, as opposed to the county police, which is what Blanche belonged to. Jarrish had been in charge of Anne's murder case. If I'd listened to Bobby and left the investigation in his hands, I'd never have found out who killed her. Every cop in LA knew the story of the coverup.

"Look, Pete, I'm not questioning your integrity. I'm just trying to help an old lady. I love cops, especially you, but everyone makes honest mistakes."

He continued eating for a moment, then pulled at his nose. "Okay, Boy Scout, I admit it. We sometimes make mistakes. We're getting three homicides a day in the city and county combined. You could say we're overworked and understaffed, and half the time our state-of-the-art labs can't tell shoe polish from pig's blood. So, it's tough to be perfect, but I still don't think we missed on the Lucie murder. It was open-and-shut. But knowing you, I suppose you still want the blow-by-blow, right?"

"Indulge me. I'm paying for your meal. That's bribery. We could both go to the gas chamber on what you just ate."

He grinned. "Okay, okay, it's your dime." As he continued, he tore off bits of bread, dipped the bits in the remaining gravy, and popped them into his mouth one at a time like little brown gum balls. "The housekeeper arrived around eight in the morning, let herself in with the key Madelaine Lucie had given her, and promptly stumbled over the body on the living room floor beside the fireplace. The Lucie woman was dressed in a gray housecoat with nothing underneath. There was a stocking around her neck. The fire poker was lying beside her. The housekeeper called our substation at Malibu. They called us and sent over a deputy at the same time. He found the suspect, Arthur Lannell, sleeping it off in the crawl space under the back steps. He was a white, thirty-year-old male, about five feet nine, skinny, with scraggily brown hair and a beard. He was incoherent. He had a pair of woman's black silk panties stuffed in his back pocket. The panties had the dead woman's initials embroidered on the waistband.

"We brought him downtown for questioning. He admitted he'd taken about a dozen hits of acid. We sent him over to psychiatric. There was a mixup. They sent him back. Someone left him alone in one of the cells while they went to find me. Ten minutes later, he was dead—hung on his own goddamned shirt. At least he was thoughtful enough to save the taxpayers the court costs."

Pete grinned grimly, half at me, half at the Black Forest cake that the waiter brought for his dessert. It was the sort of grin I'd seen on a lot of cops' faces, especially the ones who'd seen more than they'd cared to of hate and death.

I swallowed black coffee. It wasn't as good as I remembered.

"What else did you find out about him, Pete?"

"Enough to convince me Lannell did it," he said, forking the chocolate and whipped cream into his mouth. "He'd been in and out of every loony bin in the county for drug rehab. He had an IQ of seventy-three, give or take ten. He did six months in Chino two years ago for selling acid to an undercover man. *And* he had four arrests for peeping in the last two years. If I'd had another couple of hours, I'd have gotten a confession out of him."

"He never admitted it?"

"What do you want, Evan, a written confession? He *hung* himself."

I didn't say anything, but he knew what I was thinking. It wasn't *quite* good enough.

He toyed with the cherry, suddenly unsure whether he wanted to eat it or not. We had been dancing the fine line between old friendship and professional pride for the whole meal. He knew as well as I did that one step over the line could spoil the reunion.

Since, as he put it, it was my dime, I took the first step. "And you're one hundred percent sure Lannell killed her?

You said he was on acid, and maybe a little dim. Maybe you guys scared him to death."

His eyes froze on me without blinking. "You mean us bad guy cops? You mean *we* might have strung him up?" he asked icily. Then he thought about it and relaxed a little and answered my question.

"Evan, since you want my professional opinion, I'll give it to you. I'm a hundred percent sure Lannell strangled Madelaine Lucie." His reply was all cop, official, sincere, and absolutely no help to me, which, I reminded myself, was why I had bought him lunch.

"What did the autopsy on the Lucie woman show?"

My persistence was beginning to irritate him. "Now, how's that going to help you figure out who the kid's father is?"

"Damned if I know." I shrugged. "What did the autopsy show? Any signs of a struggle?"

He shook his head in exasperation and pushed his half-eaten dessert to one side. "There were no signs of a struggle."

"Sexual activity?"

"No. Nothing specific, but you don't have to be Einstein to imagine what happened. Lannell saw her walking around the house in her peek-a-boo robe and went inside. He threatened her with the poker, but either she ran or she tried to go for him, and he hit her. He realized she'd seen him, so he finished her off with one of her own stockings, pocketing her panties as a souvenir. If he was peaking on acid like we think, he probably walked out the back door and forgot the whole thing by the time he hit the back stairs. We figured he crawled under the house and just stayed there until we found him. That's the whole shooting match. Take it or leave it, Paris."

I didn't quite take it, and I couldn't quite leave it.

"Sorry, Pete, but my brain's still a little fuzzy on one or two points. You said Lannell had been arrested four times on peeping charges. Did any stick?"

Pete was at peace with himself. He'd begun to poke at the cake again. He speared the lonesome cherry, gulped it down, then answered placidly. "The first three charges were dropped. The witnesses backed out. Didn't want to get involved. The fourth one earned Lannell a year's probation. He was still on it when he strung himself up. Stoned as he was, I think he knew we'd put him away this time. He had motive enough to kill her."

"What you're saying then is that Lannell had enough sense to kill her but not enough to clear out."

Pete eyed me like a bull moose who wasn't about to budge a fraction. "He was on acid, Paris, and he wasn't too swift in the first place, remember?"

"Okay, but one thing keeps bothering me. Peepers don't usually turn into killers. Peepers are the ultimate pacifists. I don't think I've ever seen a statistic on a violent peeper."

"Shit, Paris, I must've seen five hundred murders in the past fifteen years, and I've yet to see a statistic kill anyone. While you were out there investigating white collar crimes and winning book awards, I was picking through dead bodies and collaring killers. You know where I'm coming from?"

"I hear you," I told him, but that didn't mean I was through. "What about Lannell? Did you cross-check previous addresses to see if there was any connection between him and Madelaine Lucie?"

In spite of himself, a wan smile broke out across his moon face. "You sonovabitch, Evan. You're not going to quit until you have it all, are you?"

"Did you expect me to?"

"No, guess not." He chuckled. "Believe me, we checked it all out. As a taxpayer, you got your money's worth. Lannell grew up in Florida and came out here three years ago. The Lucie woman was in San Francisco the last four years. There wasn't a shred of evidence to connect them prior to her moving to Malibu."

"What about the housekeeper? Did she remember seeing anyone else around the place besides Lannell?"

"She was no help at all. She was from one of those fancy Beverly Hills maid services—Mrs. Rita Urchak, a little Ukrainian woman with a thick accent and so straight you could balance an egg on her head. She'd just been hired. She saw the Lucie woman for fifteen minutes the week before when she was interviewed and given the key. It was her first day on the job. She wasn't even able to positively identify the corpse."

"What about a Mr. John or a Mr. Richer? The little girl mentioned both names."

"Doesn't ring any bells."

"Boyfriends?"

"If you mean like guys hanging around who could have been the kid's father, then none."

"Even new boyfriends. Maybe she said something to one of
them that might help."

"We didn't find *any* boyfriends."

"A nice-looking woman like that with no boyfriends? Didn't
that seem strange to you?"

He stabbed his fork back into the cake and gave me an
indulgent smile. "Sure it's strange. Maybe she was gay. She
spent four years in San Francisco. She moves back down here
to Cuckooland and gets her head bashed in by an acid head.
It's not the kind of thing that happens to everyone, granted,
Evan, but it does happen. Even us poor, dumb, overworked
slobs in the Sheriff's Department get lucky once in a while
and get served up a case on a platter. Lannell's fingerprints
were all over the place. He had a motive. He had a history of
sex problems. He was a drug user. He hung himself after he
was caught."

"Were his prints on the fire poker?"

His smile fell like the blade of a guillotine. His eyes said,
you sonovabitch, you nasty sonovabitch.

"There were no prints on the poker. It was wiped clean,"
he muttered stiffly. "Probably with the panties. We did find
his prints on her shoes, if you're interested. They were lying
beside her."

"He could have picked them up after she was killed."

He drained the ice cubes from his water glass and chewed
while he talked. "Anything's possible," he sighed, wagging
his head to show he in fact didn't agree. "Listen, we could go
on like this forever, but the truth is, I gotta get back. I got a
pimp war brewing in West Hollywood. I gotta get out there
or there'll be blood in the streets. The boss's got a position on
this one, so I gotta make it look like I'm doing my job."

Pete was brushing me off, but I could tell by the glint in
his eyes that I'd planted a seed of doubt in the back of his
head. While I paid the bill, he kept running his hand over
the top of his bald dome like he was thinking hard.

"What the hell," he said, scooping up a big handful of
mints from the bowl beside the cash register on the way out.
"It was nice seeing you, and if I can be of any more help,
don't hesitate to call." He popped a half dozen mints in his
mouth and began to chew.

"Thanks. I appreciate it."

He looked like he was going to say something more, but

then changed his mind with a shake of his head. From the way he backed off it was something personal.

We were on the way out of the complex when he finally stopped and asked it. "You know, Evan, I read those books of yours, and I liked them. They were pretty fuckin' good for an illiterate bastard like yourself. But there's one thing that's been bugging me a long time. If you don't mind my asking, how come you didn't keep writing?"

I was silent for a moment, then asked, "Do you really want to know?"

"Yeah," he answered sincerely.

I told him the truth. "I ran out of things to say."

Three

I wasn't the real writer in the family. Anne was. I never intended to become an academic, a writer, or even a graduate student. Right after graduating from Southern Cal, I was called for my Selective Service physical. The Vietnam War was heating up at the time, and Johnson and Westmoreland needed a couple of hundred thousand more bodies for the fire. Good friends had already gone to Canada; others had joined up, and one of my best friends had died. So, my loyalties were split right down the middle. In the end, I was spared the decision. I flunked my physical because of too many old breaks that had never healed properly in my kicking foot.

For a while, I drifted. I worked as a short order cook in a mental hospital, as a social worker in an East LA youth club, and finally, as a researcher for a private investigator. By a happy coincidence, I found I had an aptitude for solving problems and actually liked the work. When Anne got accepted to medical school at Berkeley, she talked me into going to graduate school up there. I ended up staying for a masters and a doctorate in criminology, and ended up earning both only because of Anne's help in writing the theses.

After Anne finished her internship, we moved back to Los Angeles for her residency. I taught part time at UCLA and USC and consulted privately for a number of corporations on fraud and stock manipulation. Anne was on call most of the time at the County Hospital downtown.

As a doctor's husband, I had a lot of free time on my hands. One day I was telling Anne about a case I'd just finished involving three different governments, a ring of sophisticated mutual funds salesmen who operated throughout the States and Europe, and the disappearance of more than seven million dollars.

Anne suggested it would make a great book. Once she'd got the idea, she badgered me mercilessly until I sat down to try writing it.

I laid out the story on note cards, created Jack Savage to carry the narrative, shuffled the cards a couple of times until it all seemed to mesh, and began running pages through the old portable typewriter I'd used for my doctoral thesis.

Again it was Anne—or rather her absence—that kept me going even when I thought it wouldn't amount to zip. After a year, I had four hundred pages that looked about as long as a book.

Anne knew an English teacher at Southern Cal, a minor literary novelist, who introduced me to a reputable New York agent named Debra Jano, who was looking to expand her author list at the time. Jano found me an editor who knew more than anyone would ever want to know about enthymemes and rewrites. We signed a three-book deal and made a sale to a book club, then sold the film rights while we were still in galleys.

For a while, I had the touch. I bought a fancy microcomputer, learned how to word-process, and churned out the second book in six months. It got better reviews than the first. Anne and I took five months off and went around the world. When we came back, I thought I was really hot. I wrote the first half of the third book in two months, then I just stalled out like a car with bad plugs. It took me a year to finish the third one, but even with the additional time, it wasn't half the book the first two were. I spent another year writing the fourth book. It was so bad I burned it without showing it to anyone.

Meanwhile, the first three books went into multiple printings, and the movie opened. The money rolled in so fast I

was spending more time looking for tax shelters than new
story ideas. Using my computer to flip in and out of financial
data banks, I taught myself stock market programs. In a
couple of months, I was making my own charts and evalua-
tions and trading on the markets, lightly at first, then heavily.
To make a long story short, a run of good luck and a couple of
right guesses on a penny stock on the Colorado Exchange
made me a millionaire several times over. That was five years
ago.

In the meantime, Anne had finished her first book on
attitude and disease. The *New England Journal of Medicine*
called it one of the most important books of its kind. It was
the same year she had her first miscarriage.

It was a long time ago; more like a hundred years than five,
I thought, as I turned off the Santa Monica Freeway and
headed north up La Cienega. I wanted to stop thinking about
Anne, and yet I didn't.

I turned east at Melrose and began checking numbers. I
had decided to take a long shot and drop in on Don Claypole
without calling.

Claypole's office building was a three-story walkup, crouched
along a seedy strip of Melrose and a long, long way down
from the fancy address he'd occupied in fatter times. Claypole
& Associates occupied the second floor of the building above
a twenty-four-hour donut shop. I could smell sour coffee all
the way up the gray, sweaty staircase.

A patina of respectability had been slapped on the recep-
tion area. The walls were freshly painted a crisp white, and
the floor had been redone in beige indoor-outdoor carpeting.

The only body in sight was the receptionist, a nice-looking
redhead in her early twenties with a carload of freckles and
curly bangs that hung down so far over her eyebrows she had
to shake her head to see out. She shook her head eagerly
when she saw me, making me think she hadn't seen a new
face for days.

I told her my name and asked to see her boss.

"He's in. Let me see if he's busy," she said, batting cute
hazel eyes at me. She punched up a number with the end of
a pencil and waited. "Mr. Claypole, there's a Mr. Paris here
to see you. Evan Paris." She looked up to see if she'd gotten
the name right. I nodded. She listened, then looked at me
again and asked brightly, "The writer?"

"Yes," I told her.

"Yes," she repeated into the phone. She tapped the pencil on the desk like a drumstick while she waited, then finally hung up.

"Mr. Claypole says he's quite busy but he'll see you for a few minutes." From the snarky way it was delivered, I gathered "busy" was the office euphemism for goldbricking. "I'll take you back," she offered, getting up and coming around the front of her desk. "It's a little hard to find."

She was wearing something in dark pink that showed off a very nice figure and very long legs. She was nearly as tall as I was. As she walked by me, she made me think of a tall, cool, strawberry milkshake.

I followed her through a narrow maze of white halls with more beige carpeting, past newly painted offices with potted ferns, old desks, and battered filing cabinets. More than half of the offices were empty. This place was definitely not a beehive of activity. I counted six people in all, and half of them looked asleep.

At the end of the hall, we stopped in front of a closed door with a pane of frosted glass in its window.

"If you have any trouble finding your way out, just give a shout. My name's Shirley Bass," she murmured. Her breast brushed against my arm as she moved past me to open the door. She smelled like roses, like spring.

By contrast, Don Claypole's office smelled like autumn, like hot Santa Ana winds, like brush fires in the Santa Monica Mountains.

Claypole was sitting behind a massive oak desk chewing the end of a cigar the size of a monkey's forearm. A thick layer of smoke hung in the air despite the best efforts of the big noisy air conditioner in the window.

Shirley gave me a quick introduction, then exited. Claypole shoved himself up to his feet and extended a fleshy paw across the desk. His grip was tough but the rest of him looked sloppy.

He was medium height, stocky, and stood slightly tipped backward to balance the beachball-sized paunch that pushed out through the front of his brown sports jacket. His thin brown hair flopped from left to right in a futile attempt to cover the bald spot on top. Enormous gray bags beneath his dark eyes made him look at a quick glance like a clean-shaven raccoon. I guessed him to be in his mid-fifties.

Despite what Shirley had said about being busy, he acted

almost as glad to see me as she had. He offered me a seat, a cigar, and a drink. I sat down, accepted the drink, and turned down the cigar. He pulled out a couple of glasses, fastidiously ran a finger inside one, and then located a bottle of Johnny Walker Red in a bottom drawer. While he poured, I took in the room. The decor was what Anne would have called Modern Vanity. The walls were covered with plaques and awards on laminated boards. Right beside me was a stuffed sailfish with a brass plate beneath it that said, "Donald Claypole, Baja California, 1969." On the right wall was a series of pictures of a twin-engine speedboat. In a place of honor behind his desk was a framed picture of a much-younger-looking Ronald Reagan handing some kind of certificate to a much younger, much thinner Donald Claypole. I guessed it must have been taken when Reagan was still governor of California.

Claypole handed me my drink and sat down, smiling affably. "I think we met a few years ago at a conference in Frisco. You were giving a talk on international investigations, something about the thin line between what was legal and what wasn't. We were introduced in one of the hospitality suites afterward."

"Eight years ago. In the Mark Hopkins. You have a good memory."

He took that as a compliment and went on in the same vein. "It goes with the profession. You were still teaching then. As I understand it, you went off and made a big name for yourself as a writer. I'm not a reader, so I never had the pleasure, but I heard you made a bundle. You doing a new book?"

What appealed to him was the money. At least he was honest. Since I wasn't a paying customer, it was only fair to set him straight.

"I'm trying to help a former client of yours. Mrs. Arla Coltrane. I understand you ran a search for the kid's missing father and came up empty."

His smile drooped a fraction when I mentioned Arla Coltrane. He'd been expecting something more interesting. "I don't know what I can tell you, Paris. It was a real piece of hard luck, and one of the few times something like that actually touched me, but I couldn't do any more for her than I did. I ran down everything I could lay my hands on, even had a couple of guys check it out on the Frisco end, but we

struck out. I should have billed her for ten days, but I felt so
bad about it, I gave her half the deposit back. That's something I don't normally do."

"I was wondering about that."

He chuckled. Then, letting me in on the joke, he slid
forward in his seat and gave me the old man-to-man. "I still
don't know what made me give the old lady the break.
Business was so bad last year, I had to move into this dump.
Three months ago, I was beginning to wonder if I'd even be
able to meet the rent here. To tell you the truth, the old
lady's five hundred wouldn't have made any difference. I
figured if I was heading for the crapper anyway, at least I
wouldn't have her on my conscience." A long white ash fell
from the end of his cigar and splattered on the front of his
jacket. He rubbed it away, leaving a dull gray stain the size of
a silver dollar in its place.

"You mind answering a few questions on what you did
find?"

"I can't see why not. Shoot."

"What about general impressions? You must have had some.
Did you get any kind of a feel for Madelaine Lucie, the
person?"

His heavy eyelids dropped almost closed for a couple of
seconds, as if he were searching his mind for images, then he
hit me with those raccoon eyes of his and said, "Let's just say
I never had a good feeling about her. The two models I found
who knew her in Hollywood only barely knew her. Both said
she was big on the singles bar circuit, probably slept around a
lot—one-night stands, musical beds, that sort of thing. The
way I figure it, the Lucie woman probably wasn't sure herself
who fathered the kid."

"You get any names of the men she dated?"

His look said I wasn't paying attention. "We're talking
models, Paris. Dice without spots. Vibrators without batter-
ies. These gals can hardly remember yesterday, but"—he
began rummaging through a pile of folders on the corner of
his desk—"I can give you the names of the two gals I talked
to if you want."

I told him I did, and he put on a pair of half-frame reading
glasses to copy the names and numbers, then shoved the
paper across the desk at me. "Here, this is about as close as I
got to anyone who actually knew her besides the old Holly-

wood roommate, Kazkinski or Razpolski or whatever the hell it was."

"Helen Razkowski, the old high school friend?"

"Yeah, that's the one. A real tramp," he said sourly. "She goes by the name of Elena Rachel now and calls herself an exotic dancer. We're talking poor white trash, Paris. PWT. Got busted for dealing coke three years ago. Copped a plea and got it reduced to simple possession. Did a year's probation."

"Get anything out of her?"

"*Nada*. Nothing. Zip. She lived with the Lucie woman for six months. Didn't see anything. Doesn't know anything. Doesn't want to know anything."

"Think she might have been holding back on you?"

"I doubt it." He pointed the cigar at me like I was target practice. "You know, I don't like to brag, Paris, but I know my stuff. I offered her hard cash. She looked like she could use the money, but she couldn't come up with anything she could sell. Then, just for my own peace of mind, I told her I had friends in the police force who could make trouble for her if she didn't come clean. Still no dice. She insisted she hadn't seen the Lucie woman in over four years, and when they'd lived together, they hardly ran into each other. Said they were operating on different schedules. I take it the Lucie woman only used the place to park her underwear. That's about it. If this Elena Rachel was lying, I'd have smelled it."

"What about the Lucie woman? Did you study her finances? She seemed to live quite well for a woman who didn't work."

He rubbed his middle finger against the ash stain. "There's work and there's work, Paris. We're both big boys. I can tell you where the money came from. First off, she modeled for a year. The agency's long out of business, but I collected enough to know she worked a lot." He rummaged through the file again, removing a stack of magazine advertisements and handing them to me. "Here. A little present for you."

They were all of Madelaine . . . peddling cigarettes . . . peddling cars . . . peddling jeans . . . perfume . . . bras . . . . panty hose . . . selling . . . selling . . . selling. The face looked up at me with haunting cat-eyes and lips that whispered secrets—of money and sex and other mysteries of life. I could feel those eyes sucking me in, teasing me.

"That's only a small piece of the jobs she worked on, but

it's representative," Claypole went on briskly. "She must've averaged over a grand or two a week until she got knocked up. Her rent was a couple of hundred bucks when she shared with the Rachel woman and only four hundred a month when she moved into her own bachelorette on Beverly Glen. I don't say she didn't spend money, but a girl like her doesn't usually spend her own. The way I figured it, she took a fair bundle off with her to Frisco when she set up housekeeping there six months later. After that, I wouldn't rule out the possibility of a sugar daddy or two dropping a little honey in the pot for occasional favors, but that's only a guess. What I do know is that she started playing the stock market with her little nest egg. For a while she was a real shooter, piled up a small fortune. Then, in the last year or so, her luck changed, and she dropped a bundle. That's the story."

Was it? I wondered. It sounded a little too simple for my tastes. "Did she impress you as someone who knew how to pick stocks?"

He puffed on the cigar, sending up a noxious gray cloud. The laugh seeped out of the side of his mouth. "What the hell do I know about stocks? What does anybody know? It's all Lady Luck, Paris. I once had this woman client over in Beverly Hills who made a fucking fortune trading stocks on sunspots. You figure it out."

Maybe it had been luck, but I kept wondering how she'd been turned on to the stock market. Somebody had to introduce her to the game. "What about these sugar daddys you mentioned?"

"I said, 'I wouldn't rule out the possibility,' " he corrected me. "In fact, I wasn't able to turn up any boyfriends, rich or poor, period. If she was running around up north, she was pretty discreet about it."

Pete Blanche had said the same thing. "You said you thought she probably slept around a lot in Los Angeles, and yet when she went up to San Francisco, she appears to have led a celibate life. What do you make of it?"

He took the question personally. An offended look hung like a mask over his face. I was accusing him of not doing his job.

"The woman changed. She had a kid. Maybe she lost interest in sex. Maybe she was a born-again virgin. What can I say? Maybe you can find out something I couldn't." He said

it jokingly, but he bit down hard on his cigar as if he wanted
to hurt someone.

Before I could put him at ease, the phone rang and broke
up the fun.

"Excuse me." He grabbed the phone like the interruption
was more welcome than I'd suddenly become.

Receiver to his ear, his face brightened again as if a bona
fide paying customer had come on the line. "Maggie, how are
you? Good to hear from you. Hold on a sec, would you?" He
cupped his hand over the mouthpiece. "That's all there is,
Evan. I'd be glad to talk to you another time, but you'll have
to excuse me right now."

"Sure. Thanks for your time."

"Glad to help. Anytime, anytime," he repeated.

Somehow, I doubted it.

He waited until I was out of the room before going on with
his call. I could hear his muffled voice through the door as I
headed toward the front. The beehive was even more beeless
than it had been on the way through.

Shirley Bass was sitting at her desk, reading *Crime and
Punishment* and spooning out the last of a cherry yogurt from
a plastic cup.

She looked up at me from under her red shag of hair and
gave me a grin that could have sold toothpaste. "Everything
go okay?"

"Just fine."

"Coming back?"

"Maybe sometime."

She frowned with her whole face, but added cheerfully, "If
you do, bring one of your books. I'd like to read it." She
curled one of her red locks between two fingers.

"If you like to read, stick to Dostoevski," I told her.

My books were strictly for people who hate flying and got
stuck on airplanes with nothing to do. The last thing I wanted
on my conscience was the corruption of a serious reader.

She was unfazed. "Well, anyway, you know what I mean,"
she laughed. She had a warm laugh. A young, sexy, kid's
laugh. The kind that says, it's all right to make a fool out of
yourself if you like someone.

I smiled back and left. And yes, I knew what she meant,
although it had been a long time since anyone had put it to
me so succinctly. It had nothing to do with reading.

Four

Spring, I told myself as I headed north. Acacias in bloom. Vibrant yellow clusters of flowers hanging off branches like exploding fruit. Gardens bursting with whites, yellows, pale ice blues, purples, and pinks of cymbidiums, dianthus, and ranunculus. Electric green grass. That's what she meant. You could see it—*smell it*—in the hot, pungent air. Even in Southern California, where it can go to eighty or ninety in the dead of winter, there's something about the spring that's special. It's in the way people walk, in the way women change their fashions, their hair styles, their smiles. It's the good-to-be-alive feeling. A special kind of sap starts running in your blood.

If Anne were still alive, we might have taken a trip somewhere around this time of the year. Alaska, or Frobisher Bay in Canada to see the white nights. Or Paris. Or a canoe trip down some mountain stream, catching fresh trout for dinner and sleeping under the stars.

But she wasn't alive. I was, though you'd hardly know it. I'd been acting half dead from the knees up for a year now.

For the first time, I was glad to have Mrs. Coltrane's worries to distract me.

I drove up into West Hollywood and along Sunset Strip past billboard alley and the record shops until I found a pay phone and called Helen Razkowski, or Elena Rachel, as she now called herself. All I got was her answering machine. I didn't leave a message. I did manage to get ahold of Rita Urchak, Madelaine's maid. She told me just what Blanche had said. That she barely knew the woman. I hung up and dialed the two models Claypole had interviewed. Both were home, but neither remembered any of Madelaine's dates or anything else that might have helped me get a handle on her. They gave me a couple of numbers of photographers who'd worked with her, but again, I came up with zip. She was considered easy to work with, but she fended off all passes and apparently never mixed business with pleasure. No one she worked with seemed to know anything about Madelaine Lucie's private life. I was beginning to get the feeling I was dealing with some kind of shadow.

I headed back to Malibu. The only way I figured I was ever going to get a hook on the father was to get a handle on the woman.

I drove west across Sunset, away from the smog and back toward the beach, then headed up the Coast Highway for several miles.

Madelaine Lucie had rented her house along a short stretch of cliff overlooking the ocean about two miles north of the Malibu Colony and only a half dozen miles south of where I lived. A private gravel road serviced the score of homes along the ledge of the cliff. As I drove along the lane, I could smell the ocean spilling over the cliffs in the hot afternoon breeze.

The houses themselves were invisible from the lane, blocked off by thick hedges, stone walls, and vine-covered iron fences. "Private" or "Protected by dogs" signs hung on the gate posts of most driveways.

A black Saab was parked face in at the entrance to the driveway that hid the house Madelaine Lucie had rented. The trunk of the car was open, and the handle of a shovel stuck halfway out.

A tall, slightly stooped man in a Dodger baseball cap, T-shirt, khaki shorts, white socks, and sneakers was pounding a signpost into the ground with the back end of a hatchet. The sign said: "For Sale, Private." A phone number large enough to be read from the Coast Highway was printed on the bottom.

He stopped hammering as I pulled to the side of the road and parked. His face was weathered, with bushy white eyebrows that touched the peak of his cap. He gave me a long, hard look as I got out and crossed the gravel lane.

I was halfway to him when I realized I knew who he was.

"Professor Celli? Michael Celli?"

His eyes narrowed as he looked me over. "Why, yes. Who are you?"

"Evan Paris. I doubt if you'd remember me. I joined the faculty at UCLA as a part-time lecturer the year you retired."

"In my department?" he asked. Professor Celli was the Italian Renaissance specialist in the History Department.

"I was in criminology."

He studied me keenly but shook his head. "I'm sorry, I don't think I do remember you, but then you forget a lot of things at my age." There was a sparkle in his eyes that said his mind was as sharp as it always had been. He probably had never noticed me among all the others on the faculty.

"Are you interested in beach properties?" he asked as he gripped the stake holding the sign and pulled with his shoulders and back until it was straight.

"Not exactly, but I would like to see the house, if you don't mind."

His eyebrows lifted. "You're here about the killing, aren't you?"

"Yes."

I could sense him pulling back, not physically, emotionally. The sparkle went out of his eyes.

"Is it necessary?"

"I think it might help."

While he picked up his tools and returned them to the trunk of the car, I followed along, explaining about Trudy and Mrs. Coltrane.

"I'll show it to you if you want, but there's really nothing to see," he replied unenthusiastically. "I had it all cleaned up, locks changed, everything."

"I'd still like to see it."

"All right." His shrug was resigned. "I have a few minutes. Then I have to leave."

As we walked down the driveway, he seemed lost in himself, as if what had happened in the house had personally affected him.

"Do you live around here?" I asked, trying to dispel the gloom.

"No, I'm over in Brentwood, about a half an hour away. My wife and I have lived there since '47."

"How long have you owned this place?"

"It would have been twenty-five years this summer. I bought it for next to nothing." He spoke softly as we came into sight of the house. It was a small white Cape Cod with a shingled roof and a dark green door. A garden of yellow roses hugged the front and sides. "We planned to use it during the summer when the kids were out of school, but with camps and tennis lessons, we hardly came out here more than three or four times a year. I held onto it anyway, thinking maybe the grandchildren would use it, but now after what's happened, it's better to sell."

We stopped in the front yard under the shade of an old California sycamore that spread out overhead like a giant umbrella. From where we stood, you could see the edge of the cliff on both sides as it flared away from the house. Two other houses were visible on each side. North to our right were two small family homes—a large double A-frame of redwood and pine and a stucco house with orange roof tiles. Cheap houses—but the owners weren't to be pitied. Those were seven-figure lots under each one. The two to the south on my left each sat on triple-width lots, and the houses were huge and expensive compared to Celli's and the two to the north. The closer of the two on the south was an old wooden two-story monster with a veranda circling the back half of the ground floor. It looked like it had probably been built sometime around the turn of the century and was among the oldest I'd ever seen along the coast. The farther of the two appeared to be more a compound of houses than a single home. Five buildings on three different levels were built into manmade steps in the cliff. The buildings were modern and tall with cathedral ceilings, bare wood beams, and enough reinforced concrete and glass to build a small shopping center.

"Do you know your neighbors?"

Celli looked off in the direction I was looking and replied, "Not very well. I used to know the old widow, Haddie Pinfield, in the big white house. Her family once owned the whole stretch along here on both sides of the highway. I bought this place when she first started selling off the cliff frontage. The only reason I know she's still around is because I saw her out in her garden a few days ago when I was here fixing up my place."

"And the one next to it?" I asked, pointing toward the large compound of buildings.

He squinted into the sun. "That's the Cliff House. It was built by Simon Greeves about fifteen years ago."

"Simon Greeves of TEK Industries?"

"Yes, do you know him?"

"Only by reputation." Greeves was a major player in the West Coast conglomerate game. He'd founded TEK thirty-five years ago with a five-thousand-dollar loan from his wife's father and parlayed his nut into a Fortune 500 company worth billions. "Does he still live there?".

"I don't know. I only know him by sight, and I haven't seen him in years. I've seen a couple of people there—youngish people more your age than mine—but I really couldn't tell you if they're his grown children or new owners."

"What about your other two neighbors?" I pointed back toward the two smaller homes.

He didn't bother to turn, but dismissed them with a wave of a mottled hand. "Those other two have changed ownership so many times I lost track of who lives there ages ago. Before the murder, I hadn't even been out here in eight years. Can you believe that? Not even once." He sounded more perplexed than angry. "My gardener would come down twice a month to check the place over and tell me what needed fixing, and I'd simply write a check for whatever it cost."

"Did you normally rent it seasonally or all year around?"

He lifted his baseball cap and rubbed a hand over a thick white curly head of hair, then straightened the cap back in place. "I never rented it out at all. That's the funny thing." He fished a brass key from his pocket and led me to the front door and unlocked it. "I thought of renting it out, but I was always afraid of the headaches. Mrs. Lucie was my first tenant."

I stepped into the house behind him. The living room was spacious and ran the length of the house to the back. Sunlight streamed through the large windows that took up most of the far wall. The room had been recently repainted a warm peach with cream trim. The only furniture was a green metal stepstool in one corner.

"They found her right over here," Celli muttered, shaking his head sadly and pointing to a spot in the gray wall-to-wall carpet in front of the fireplace. "I had the old carpet pulled up and completely replaced." When he crossed the room, he stepped gingerly around the spot as if Madelaine were still lying there.

He took me on a quick tour of the rest of the house—through a large modern kitchen, a dining room, a den and a master bedroom with fireplace and bath, two smaller bedrooms, and a second bath—all of it repainted, recarpeted, and stripped. There was nothing of Madelaine Lucie left in the place.

I stepped out onto a narrow sundeck that stretched off the

back of the house overlooking the ocean. Professor Celli
stepped out behind me. A large pepper tree grew in the
center of the backyard. A hedge row of tall cyprus ran along
the property line on each side from the house to the edge of
the cliff fifty feet away and would have made the backyard
private enough for nude sunbathing if several of the cyprus
on the south side hadn't died or been cut down. Now, anyone
sitting outside could easily be seen from the two large houses
to the south.

Celli pointed out two bird feeders hanging in the pepper
tree. "That's about the only thing left from her," he said.
"She put them up after she moved in. She even thought of
the birds." Again, he shook his head sadly.

"What made you decide to rent the place?"

His bushy eyebrows knitted together. "I didn't really *decide*. I never even listed it," he replied sardonically. "I was
talked into it. My wife used to tease me, 'It's because of the
pretty face.'" He sighed heavily. "You know, she's right.
Imagine, a seventy-three-year-old man getting talked into
something by a pretty face." For a second, I saw the old
sparkle again as though the memory of Madelaine might have
excited him.

"What do you mean by 'talked into it'?"

He took a deep breath. "She said she just had to have it,
wouldn't take no for an answer. She practically got down on
her knees and begged me. What could I do?" His eyes
pleaded with me to tell him what he could have done differ-
ently. I was short on good answers.

"Did she ever say why she wanted the place so badly?"

"Sure, she did." He began counting off on his fingers. "She
said it was close to the Montessori School where she wanted
her daughter to go next year; she said it was on the ocean;
she said she had allergies and couldn't take the smog downtown; she said she didn't care what it cost; she said she had
fallen in love with the house; she said no one was using it; she
said it was a shame to leave a house like this empty when
there were people who would appreciate it; she said she
thought it would be the ideal place for her little girl." He
gave me a broken-hearted look when he finished as if to say
he'd gone over it a hundred times in his head, and he knew
why he'd done it, but he still felt guilty for what had happened.

I was more interested in what he hadn't said. "If you didn't
have it listed, how did she know about it?"

"She told me she'd heard about it from some real estate agent. I've been getting calls from agents all over the city for years. They're like flies. One fly hears about a dog taking a crap and he tells all the other flies. Real estate agents. Bah." He grimaced.

"Did she mention the name of the agent?"

He pulled at his chin with his thumb and forefinger. "If she did, I don't remember. I have a mental block against real estate agents. I don't trust them. I'm handling the sale here myself. I don't want anything more on my conscience. Whoever buys this place will know the whole story. I'm too old to have people cursing my grave."

I glanced back at the denuded house, then back at the backyard, where all that remained of her were two plastic bird feeders. I could sense her and even imagine her here, walking around, sunbathing, watching the birds, and maybe drinking coffee or tea on the back deck. Still I felt I was chasing a ghost. The only thing I really knew about Madelaine Lucie was that she seemed to provoke strong feelings—both good and bad—among those who encountered her.

"Did you see her often?"

"Only twice. Once when she came to my house to talk to me about the property. That was five months ago. And then once again a month after that when she signed the papers. She was a nice young woman. I make little jokes about pretty faces, but it's because I feel so bad about what happened to her. She was in fact a Madonna, a beautiful mother. So gentle with the little one you couldn't help loving her. Even my wife felt the same. Marie—that's my wife—she said, 'Michael, I don't blame you for being attracted to her. She's so alive; so beautiful; no man could not be attracted.'" He self-consciously hitched up his pants and managed to straighten his stoop.

"Did she have any trouble paying you?"

"No, none. She gave me postdated checks. I never even spoke with her after I handed over the keys. She was supposed to call my gardener if there were any problems, but she never had any that I know of."

He led me down the back steps and pointed to the crawl space under the house. "That's where the police found the fellow who did it. He was just sitting there." Professor Celli pointed without looking as if someone might still be hiding there. There was nothing to see but a gap under the steps.

No ghosts, no nothing. Celli started for the edge of the cliff; I followed and caught up.

"I don't like to think about it," he said softly as we walked until we came to the waist-high, white picket fence at the edge. Sixty feet down, a half dozen sun worshippers spread out on a thin strip of white beach, catching the last of the heavy afternoon rays. A path out the back gate twisted down the cliff and disappeared in the high weeds.

Celli stared out over the water.

"You called her *Mrs.* Lucie. Did she say she was married?"

He answered dully, without turning toward me. "She said she was a widow, that her husband died several years ago. The police told me Lucie was her maiden name. Perhaps she went back to it; I don't know."

"Did she give you any references when she took the place?"

He nodded. "Yes, and good ones, too—her old bank manager in San Francisco and the new one down here. I called them both and was assured that she could easily afford the rent. I don't remember their names offhand, but I could give them to you if you think they might help."

"I'd appreciate it, and if possible, I'd like to speak to your gardener."

"You'll have to wait a couple of weeks for him. He's gone deep sea fishing off Baja. But feel free to call me at home for Mrs. Lucie's references or anything else. My phone number's on the for sale sign out front." He glanced at his watch. "I'm afraid I'll have to get going. I'll lock up the house, but feel free to look around all you want, Professor Paris. I'm always glad to help out a fellow colleague."

"Thank you, Professor Celli." I smiled. No one had called me Professor Paris in years. "One more quick question. Does the path go all the way down to the beach?"

"Yes, but it also branches off in the middle and runs the whole length of the cliffs. I used to take my son and daughter on walks along it when we first came out here. Those were much pleasanter days. And simpler, too." His stoop seemed more pronounced as he turned and walked back to the house to lock up.

I looked back in the direction of the Greeves complex. A blonde in a fluttering white dress had come out of one of the buildings and was standing in the backyard. She seemed to be staring over in my direction.

Out of curiosity, I opened the gate and started down the back path.

Five

As I walked down the trail, the woman disappeared from view behind the high stone fence of the complex.

I found the path that cut across the cliffs and kept going, pushing my way through tangles of sea figs, ice plants, cow parsnip, and climbing milkweed that had greedily reclaimed the path in spots. I passed the white house with the veranda that belonged to Haddie Pinfield. The path up to the Pinfield house was so snarled with overgrowth it looked like it hadn't been used in ages.

I began to climb the steep path that snaked back and forth toward the Cliff House. A couple of gulls lazily circled overhead and drifted inland. My shirt was sticking to my back by the time I reached the top.

The monstrous high tech structures Greeves had erected towered above the walls. From head on, the buildings looked like the open jaws of five giant sharks, ready to swallow the entire Pacific.

The stone fence had an electrical sensor system on top and a sign that said: "Private property. Trespassers will be prosecuted." A heavy wooden door cut into the two foot–thick wall stood half open.

I had the feeling it had been left open for me. I stepped through to the other side onto a manicured lawn surrounded by impeccably trimmed gardens of pink and white azalias and rhododendrons. Several of the larger bushes had been sculptured into what appeared to be leaping porpoises.

The woman stood in the narrow shadow of the wall. She was barefoot and of medium height, small-boned, and boyishly slim. Her wispy, white-blond hair fell in tight curls down over her shoulders in front and back like rivulets of a waterfall. She wore a white, sleeveless cotton dress whose hem touched her ankles. Under the dress she was naked. The thin material revealed the faint shadows of nipples and pubic hair. She had a drowsy look on her small oval face as if she had just awakened. With one finger crooked against the side of her neck, she watched me like someone studying a lawn sculpture.

"You can come in." Her voice was so soft I had to hold my breath to hear it. She moved along the wall as if consciously keeping in its narrow shadow. Closer, I saw that her skin was a rich creamy white, almost translucent, as if she hardly ever went into the sun. Stepping out of the doorway into the shadow, I followed her along the inside of the wall, stopping when she stopped, maintaining about six feet between us, as though that was our prearranged margin of safety.

"I was watching you." She looked me over from head to foot, still trying to make up her mind about me.

I likewise took the occasion to study her more closely. Her face reminded me of an Art Deco statue I'd seen on display in the Hearst Castle at San Simeon. An ethereal face with an expression that somehow seemed out of time and place. Her eyes were a brilliant, sharp blue, like sparkling marbles that seemed to catch the light, smash it, and throw it back at you in a thousand tiny pieces. I guessed her to be in her early twenties.

She smiled in a way that suggested I'd met her approval. "I was hoping you'd come by. I left the gate open. I'm not supposed to." She laughed. It was a childlike laugh, not a seductress's.

"Why were you hoping I'd come by?"

"Because it's lonely here," she murmured, artlessly removing a curl from her face as she spoke and flipping it casually over her shoulder and out of the way. "I'm Laura Greeves."

"I'm Evan Paris."

Oddly enough, my name seemed to mean something to her. She raised her blond eyebrows fleetingly and cocked her head to one side. "The screenwriter?"

"Why, yes," I replied, a little surprised.

"You look amused," she insisted.

I had to laugh. "I am. No one recognizes screenwriters."

She frowned. My sin apparently was in comparing her to anyone else. "They don't, but I do. I read *all* the credits. I'm very interested in films. Besides, you were nominated for an Academy Award. I thought you should have won." She sounded like she meant it.

"Thanks, but it was enough just being nominated."

"Yes, I suppose," she remarked airily. "I was surprised to find out that you also wrote books. I don't read much. I suppose I should, but I never seem to like things that are good for me." She laughed again, dismissing the thought as irrelevant. "Are you thinking of buying Professor Celli's cottage?"

"No."

She didn't seem particularly surprised. On the contrary. She pointed at me and said knowingly, "Then, you're here about the murder." Her whole face lit up now, fully awake. "That's what I *first* thought—that you'd come about the murder. I'm psychic about these things. My husband says I'm not psychic at all, that it's just a matter of logic and good guessing, but I don't think so. I think it's more than that. I sometimes feel things *before* they happen. I have dreams that turn out to be true. And sometimes I just *know* things about people. Do you ever get feelings like that?"

I leaned against the wall. "Sometimes." I remembered a feeling I'd had—a premonition of sorts—just before Anne was killed.

She took a step closer and stared into my eyes. "Yes, you would understand. You're a writer. You even look sensitive. I was a witch once in a former life. I was burned at the stake in Salem in 1692. I bet you were Sir Thomas More, you know, like Paul Scofield in *A Man for All Seasons*, or someone like that who had his head cut off. You look like you've suffered."

She laughed gaily when I smiled and touched my neck to see if my head was still there.

She was definitely a bit nutty, but in a pleasant way.

"You think I'm crazy," she said flippantly, then answered for me. "Well, I am. A little bit." She glanced up at the sun as if it might burn her to a crisp even in the shade; she shivered at the thought, then looked back at me. "Why don't we go up to the arbor so I can sit in the shade? Then, you can ask me all the questions you want. You do want to ask me questions, don't you?"

"Yes," I told her.

"Yes," she repeated with her eyes half closed in thought. She slipped past me to the thick wooden door and closed and locked it.

"They get furious with me if I leave it unlocked, especially since the murder."

"They?"

"My husband, my husband's sister, her husband, my mother, my father-in-law—when he comes out here, which he rarely does—and even my psychiatrist, who *never* comes out here, thank God." There was more mischief than madness in her tinkly laugh.

She seemed lonely, one of those types who is just screwy enough to scare off most people but still sane enough to be perfectly aware of what she is doing. She smiled, seemingly both pleased that I'd stayed and surprised that I had.

"I take it you live here," I remarked.

"Yes, at least I have while my husband and I are separated. He stays in our house in Beverly Hills but comes out here to visit me. So does my mother, and my husband's sister, and her husband. I suppose it all sounds strange, but we all get on famously. Even Tom and I. We just don't sleep together. My mother and I have practically been a part of the Greeves family since I was a child. The fact that I married Tom and then separated from him has hardly made any difference to anyone—it's sort of like the Lords in *The Philadelphia Story*, you know, Katharine Hepburn, Cary Grant." She gave me a sweet smile. "I hope I'm not shocking you. My psychiatrist says I sometimes say things just to get people's attention, but I'm-not-so-sure." She measured her words carefully for the right effect. "I think I'm just explaining reality. Besides, as you can see, there's more than enough room here for everyone. My psychiatrist simply has no imagination. He hated *Annie Hall*." The grand wave of her hand showed off the monstrous complex and dismissed her psychiatrist in one gesture.

We walked to a vine-covered arbor in the middle of the garden. She dashed the last few feet into the shade of the arbor like someone getting out of the rain.

"I hate the sun. I'm a night person. This climate's totally wasted on me. You're tan. You obviously like the sun." She gestured toward the deck chairs scattered about. "Sit down. I'll fix you a drink. I bet you drink Scotch." She gave me a wink that was more awkward than seductive. She wanted to flirt but she didn't quite know how.

"Scotch would be just fine," I agreed, trying to remember how many I'd already had. It wasn't normal for me to drink so much in a day. On the other hand, it was an exceptionally unnormal day. The drink had definitely dulled the old anger.

"Without ice, right?" she asked, mixing the drink from a wet bar in the corner of the arbor.

"Yes."

"See? Psychic." She handed me my drink and settled down in a chair a few feet away in the shade with a Campari and soda and crossed her legs demurely.

"So, what do you think of this place?"

"It's impressive."

She laughed delightedly. "You're being kind. It's gross. Did you know that the architect who designed it actually convinced my father-in-law it would look like a giant sailing ship with the sails billowing in the wind. I don't know what you think, but I think it looks like a field full of nuns' caps. You know, Sally Field and *The Flying Nun*. Excruciating bad taste."

"I take it your father-in-law is Simon Greeves."

"Yes. I'm one of his extended litter. Did you know he was one of the original investors in *Cleopatra*? What a dummy."

"You don't sound as if you like him."

"I don't. He steps on people."

"Like you?"

"Me? I'm not even worth stepping on. I'm part of the decor. I meant like Tom, like others. Nothing Tom ever says, or thinks, or does is ever good enough for Simon." She shot me a sly glance. "Do you know what I'd do if I had all the money that my father-in-law has?"

"No, what?"

"I'd buy this place and tear it down to the ground. Then, I'd spend the rest of my life traveling around the world ripping down everything that was ugly." She eyed me intently, testing me again like a child.

"I don't believe you," I told her frankly.

She uncrossed her legs and recrossed them the other way. "Just kidding. Actually, if I could do anything, I'd rather be a man." She took a long strand of hair from the side of her face and held the end under her nose like a mustache. "Sometimes, I think I like women better than men." She paused and let her mustache drop off. "I don't mean sexually. I just mean as people. If I were a man, it would be easier to make friends with women."

"Don't you like men?"

She looked flustered. Maybe she figured I had her pegged all wrong. "I didn't say I didn't like men. Actually I like all kinds of people." She glanced back toward the house, then leaned closer to me and spoke in a conspiratorial tone. "I just don't seem to like the same people *they* do." She said "they" with a vengeance, giving me the impression she thought someone up there in the house was the real enemy, and I was part of her private resistance movement. "When I do find people I like, it scares *them* to death. *They* were all absolutely beside themselves when I made friends with Arty." She rolled her eyes to illustrate just how crazy it had made them. "We are talking Shirley Temple meets Frankenstein."

The only Arty I could think of was the one who had killed Madelaine Lucie. "You mean Arthur Lannell?"

Her face brightened. "Yes, did you know him?"

"No, but I know who he is."

The brightness clouded over. "Well, you've probably heard all the worst things about him. As a writer, you can read between the lines. Arty was a very sensitive man and very deep. You would have liked him. He didn't kill that woman, you know."

"The police think he did."

She pursed her lips contemptuously. "The police. They had to say something, but I think they're wrong. I can't prove it, but I just don't think he did it."

She was serious. She crossed her arms over her small bosom and glared boldly at me. I don't think she cared whether I believed her or not.

"Why do you think that?"

"I just *feel* it. I used to see Arty down on the beach, and sometimes I'd go there and talk to him or give him something to do around here just to have someone to talk to when I was alone. He couldn't express himself very well, but he was a truly caring person. I would have known if he had that kind of hate inside him."

"They say he was on drugs."

She laughed, then covered her mouth with her hand and apologized. "I'm sorry, that struck me funny. Arty was *always* on drugs. He used to chew acid tabs like Lifesavers. He offered me some, but I told him I wasn't ready. Maybe I should have done it; I don't know. He certainly never acted violent around me."

"Sometimes people we think we know very well are different people around others."

"Yes, that's what the police *and* my psychiatrist said, but I still don't believe it. Arty had plenty of opportunities to rape or murder me. He never even made a pass."

"If he didn't kill Madelaine, then who could have done it?"

"I don't know. Anyone." She shrugged. She avoided my eyes for a second, contemplating something, then seemed to brush that away. When she looked up again, she seemed determined to be helpful. "I had a dream that it would happen, you know. I dreamed that I was walking along the beach and I found her lying there with her eyes shut and her hair spread out like the rays of the sun on the sand. Very Fellini. I knelt down beside her to see if she was all right, and I opened her eyes with my fingers. But there weren't any eyes, just sand. Her mouth fell open, and it was filled with sand, too. In real life I would have been scared out of my mind, but I remember being more curious than frightened. I kept watching her face, and soon it started looking more and more like me. Then I woke up. That was two days before she was killed. My psychiatrist says it's some sort of envy and not a premonition at all. Maybe it's true. Did you ever see her, Evan?"

"Only in pictures."

Laura tilted her head back against the metal frame and spoke dreamily. "She was so beautiful, like a magnet pulling you to her. She had long, long hair and the most wonderful eyes. I would have liked to touch her. Just once." She glanced shyly over at me and murmured, "I would give anything to look like her." There was a sweet hint of envy in her voice, both naive and unsettling at the same time.

"But you're quite attractive," I told her candidly.

"No, I'm not. But thank you."

"Did you know Madelaine well?"

Again, she avoided my eyes, shifting uneasily on her chair like a child caught in a fib, changing her drink from one hand to the other. "To be perfectly honest, I didn't know her at all. I *wanted* to know her. I used to watch her from here when she was out on her back deck. I passed by her on the beach several times when I was out for walks, but I was too shy to say anything. I tried to send mental messages to her, but she never got them. I don't know, maybe I never sent them very well. Or she got them and decided to ignore them."

"Did you see anyone else over there with her?"

"Her little girl, but only a few times. Such a pretty child.

I'm very fond of children. I hope she's all right. Have you seen her?"

"Yes, and she's all right. Can you remember anyone else?"

"No. No one but Arty and the Mexican fellow who looks after the place."

"You saw Arty over there?"

"Sure. Lot's of times. Before Madelaine moved in, Arty used to sleep under her porch. The caretaker knew it. Sometimes, he'd pay Arty to help him fix things up around the house. When the place was rented, Arty moved down the beach somewhere where they were building a new house. He'd sleep there and come down here during the day to visit me or to collect bottles along the beach. Then, a couple of days before the murder, someone caught him sleeping over at the other place and chased him out. He didn't know where he was going to sleep. I told him to go back to Professor Celli's house. In a way, I'm to blame for what happened to him. If he hadn't been there, he wouldn't have been such a convenient scapegoat." She stopped and looked grimly over my shoulder at the house.

I turned to see what had attracted her attention.

Two women were strolling toward us along the garden path. They were both in their early forties and in what Anne would have described as excellent states of preservation.

The taller of the two had light brown hair with highlights of blond. Her right arm from the elbow to the palm was wrapped in a tensor bandage and carried lightly against her stomach. She was about five seven or eight.

The second woman was an inch or two shorter. She had small hips and a thin waist and disproportionately large breasts that gave her a slightly top-heavy look. Her hair was black and wavy.

I stood up as they neared the arbor. Between the two of them, they wore enough diamonds on fingers, wrists, necks, and earlobes to purchase a McDonald's franchise.

Laura smiled crookedly. I was almost certain I could see a glimmer of mischief in her eyes as she stood up to face the two women.

"Mother and Nicki, this is Evan Paris," she informed them. "Evan, this is my mother, Mrs. Patterson, and my sister-in-law, Mrs. Harold."

Laura's mother, the woman with the streaked hair, had a thin face with high cheekbones and small features very much like Laura's, though it all came out looking more severe than ethereal on the older woman. Perhaps it was the facelift with its telltale lack of skin suppleness which gave her a harder look than her daughter.

Mrs. Patterson stepped forward and gave me her left hand to shake. "Pleased to meet you. Sorry for the arm; it's an old war wound," she apologized, gingerly raising her right hand. Despite the handshake, I sensed that judgment was being reserved until she found out what I was doing there.

"Evan was nominated for an Academy Award six years ago for *Heart of the Hunter*," Laura announced.

Mrs. Patterson's eyes seemed to go from a cool to a warm blue as her smile widened.

"I believe I've heard of you," the other woman said, giving me an approving look as she shook my hand. The Harold woman's face was pretty, with round apple cheeks, plump lips, and large, perfectly white teeth.

"Of course, you've heard of him, Nicki," Laura pointed out. "You bought one of his books from the Book Club. You just never read it."

The plump cheeks reddened. She shot Laura a look that could have melted Buffalo in January, then turned back to me. "I'm sorry, Mr. Paris. I haven't gotten around to reading all the books I've ordered, but I certainly intend to read yours."

I was sure from the somewhat bovine expression on her face that she could remember nothing about me or my books.

"Evan was at Professor Celli's cottage. I invited him in for a drink," Laura explained, fingers testing the white fabric of her dress.

Mrs. Patterson nodded approvingly. "Are you thinking of moving to the cliffs?"

"He's not here to buy the house, Mother. Evan's a *writer*."

I was hoping she'd quit right there, but she didn't.

"He's interested in the *murder*. You know, *Psycho Comes to Malibu*? No more showers?" She grimaced.

Mrs. Patterson's warm blue eyes cooled off fast. Nicki Harold blushed as if Laura had said something obscene.

Laura's brilliant smile signaled that she had just scored a point against the opposition and was about to collect her reward. "Can I get you another drink, Evan? Anyone else? I'm ready for another one."

"I'm fine, thanks," I assured her. I tried to diffuse the

situation with the other two women, explaining about Mrs. Coltrane and Trudy. Both listened politely.

"That's very commendable of you, Mr. Paris, but I don't see how we can help," Mrs. Patterson replied coolly.

"He wants to know if we saw any people over there with the woman—anyone besides Arty and the little girl," Laura explained as she refilled both glasses. She was pure brat. She winked at me and poured Campari so fast that it fizzed over the top of the glass, splashing her dress and turning it transparent in front.

"I don't think you should be drinking, Laura." Nicki Harold's quiet voice barely concealed anger as she took the two glasses from Laura and deliberately set them down on the edge of the sink. "Mr. Paris said he doesn't want another."

Laura glared. "He was just being polite, Nicki," she sulked. "What would *you* say if someone like *you* showed up and looked so very unpleasant about *you* being here?"

Nicki Harold glared back. "You're just upset, darling. You like to upset everyone because you're upset. I wish I could make you feel that we're not all against you."

"What happened down the cliffs has been very unsettling for Laura," Mrs. Patterson said softly. "I'm afraid it's been unsettling for all of us. I hope you can understand that we'd rather not talk about it. Everything we had to say we've already told the police." What she didn't say—what I could see in her eyes—was that I'd offended her by invading their privacy and by taking advantage of Laura.

"I understand," I assured her. I did, and much more than she realized. The press had pushed my nose so far out of joint after Anne's death that I'd bodily thrown a couple of reporters off my property and ended up with two lawsuits against me for assault. "I'm sorry to intrude, but perhaps you could tell me one thing? Did either of you see anyone at the woman's house—any visitors, or perhaps a car? It could be very important."

"No one saw anything," Mrs. Patterson stressed, answering out of politeness, but her tone emphasized that I'd already overstayed my welcome by a couple of time zones. "I'm afraid we won't be any help at all, Mr. Paris. I was present when everyone in our household gave their statements to the police. None of us met or had anything at all to do with the poor woman. No one saw anyone other than her and her child, nor anything that could be of importance to you, I'm sure."

"I had the dream, don't forget," Laura piped in.

Nicki was making a vain attempt to sponge the Campari out of the flimsy cotton dress. The dress wasn't the issue at all. She was just trying to keep Laura occupied.

Laura's mother moved closer to me, positioning herself between me and her daughter. "Could I talk to you alone, Mr. Paris?"

"Certainly."

We began walking back toward the house as Laura called out, "Evan, if I don't see you again, good luck."

"Thanks," I called back, taking one last look at them. Nicki Harold had hold of Laura's skirt, reining her in like a horse. I had a feeling nothing would have made her let go.

"She'll be all right," Mrs. Patterson said soothingly as we moved out of earshot.

We walked past the concrete edifice which effectively knocked out the sun on that side of the house. A Japanese waterfall flowed through a mossy green pool surrounded by carefully tended bonsai of hemlock and pine. Mrs. Patterson toyed with her bandaged arm. "I'm sorry to have to be so frank with you, Mr. Paris, but I don't think your visit is doing anyone any good. I understand your motives, and I do think they're commendable, but I have Laura to think about. She's a lot more disturbed by what happened than she appears to be. I suppose she told you that she knew the fellow who killed the Lucie woman."

"Yes. She mentioned she used to talk to him all the time," I replied as we passed into bright sunlight again on the other side of the house. She subtly steered me onto the driveway leading to the front gate.

"I'd hardly call 'once,' all the time." She smiled faintly. "It seems Laura passed by this fellow on the beach two days before the murder and said hello. That's what's in the police report. Now Laura's gotten it into her head that she's somehow responsible for what happened to that other woman. Her doctor says it's a posttraumatic reaction—a complex guilt syndrome. She apparently feels that the fellow wanted to kill her and instead killed the other woman." She shook her head, all concerned mother now. "There's really nothing wrong with Laura. What she needs is a little time to calm down and forget what happened."

"I understand."

She looked relieved. We had reached the front gate of the complex leading out to the service road.

"I understand how you feel about your daughter, Mrs. Patterson, but surely, you'd have no objections to talking to me." For a second, I thought I had her and went on. "Do *you* remember seeing anyone over there—any strangers or anything unusual that you might not have mentioned to the police?"

Her back went rigid. Her cool blues glared contemptuously. "No, I don't think you do understand, Mr. Paris," she corrected me. "Our statements are all on file with the police. What happened up the road simply doesn't concern us, and I really think we'd all like to forget it. We have to live here. You don't. I'm sorry."

She opened the gate and held it open for me until I was out, then swung it shut.

Her face was bisected by the iron bars. "I do wish you good luck," she said genuinely, then added with equal sincerity, "but please don't call again."

She turned and walked toward the house without glancing back.

It was hard to outright dislike her, I reflected as I walked away. She did seem concerned and protective of Laura. On the other hand, I couldn't rule out the possibility that somewhere under her thin layer of protest was something more— something perhaps not terribly significant or incidious, but something that she or someone in that house had seen or heard or felt that she knew could wind up involving one of them in the dross of Madelaine Lucie's death. Of course, I also had not forgotten about Laura. I most definitely would have liked to find out just what parts of what she said were true and what she had made up. A gut feeling said that she had not fabricated everything she'd told me. Nor had I forgotten about Madelaine. The magnet, Laura had called her. She was there all right, hovering in spirit along the cliffs like a ghost who wouldn't let go.

Six

I couldn't let go either. I stopped in front of the driveway to the Pinfield house, hoping I could have a talk with the old lady before word got around the neighborhood that I was running loose, dredging up dead memories.

A high iron gate blocked my entrance and my view to the Pinfield place, but there was a call box on the gate post. I picked up the phone.

Mrs. Pinfield answered. She buzzed me in as soon as I mentioned the little girl next door.

An unpredictable jungle of ferns, vines, and palms led up to the Edwardian gingerbread mansion.

Mrs. Pinfield greeted me at the screen door in a faded lime green housecoat. She stood no more than five feet tall in her fluffy pink slippers. Each slipper had a rabbit's face on the toe. She was at least eighty, with snow-white hair tied in two little ponytails in back. Her skin was like a sheet of white paper that had been crumpled tightly then unfolded. Her cheeks and her nose glowed a warm red. I caught a whiff of sherry on her breath.

"I *thought* you were the one I saw on the path before," she said matter-of-factly, giving me the once over. Her brown eyes were magnified nearly twice their normal size by the thick lenses in her round, wire-rimmed glasses. "Come in. You'll have to excuse both old messes—me and the house. I keep promising myself I'm going to get around to cleaning this place up someday and make it livable, but I never seem to find the time."

I followed her through a living room crammed with Art Nouveau lamps, piles of books, couches buried under stacks of old 78 RPM records, a cello with no strings, three pianos, a zither, and at least four rockers; two dress mannequins in strange hats leaned precariously against each other like drunken sailors; and huge paintings of noblemen in large gilded frames stared down on the whole mess. It was all jammed so tightly together there was only space enough to pass through the room in single file.

"This junk's like family," she remarked. "Everything else is gone. Outlived three husbands. Three strong men." She dusted her tiny white hands together to emphasize the point and smiled wistfully, showing me a full set of pearly white teeth that all appeared to be originals.

The kitchen was less crowded than the living room but only by a shade. A rapid glance revealed that Mrs. Pinfield also collected tinfoil, rubber bands, brown grocery bags, plastic containers of any kind, jars (all washed with their labels scrubbed off), and candelabras of every size and shape.

"Sit down, make yourself comfortable," she murmured, gesturing toward the table that looked out over the back veranda and down on the beach as well as onto Professor Celli's cottage and the Greeves estate.

I had to remove a large empty clay flowerpot from one of the chairs to make room for myself beside the kitchen table.

"God, what an awful mess. I only realize how bad it is when I get a visitor," she clucked. "Now, what can I get you? I'm having sherry myself, but you look more like a hard liquor man to me. My daddy always kept a good liquor cabinet. I have bourbon, Scotch, rye whiskey, almost anything you'd care for."

"Scotch," I told her. "Straight, no ice."

"Good man. My daddy would have liked you." She brought over two glasses, a bottle of sherry, and a bottle of twenty-five-year-old Ballantine and poured us each a stiff drink before sitting down. "Now, what can I tell you?" she asked, looking me straight in the eye. We might have been about to trade horses.

She sat with her elbows on the table, chin resting on her hands, as I explained what I was looking for.

"So you're hoping maybe the child's father might have been hanging around and, as a nosy neighbor, I might have spotted him out of my window," she summed up, glancing out at Professor Celli's cottage, then back at me.

"Anything you saw might help."

She narrowed her eyes shrewdly. "First, what did those people next door tell you?"

There was obviously no love lost between the Pinfields and

the Greeves. I told her what Laura had said and then explained how Mrs. Patterson and Mrs. Harold had arrived and proceeded to give me the bum's rush. "Mrs. Patterson said they had all made statements to the police and that they had had no contact at all with Madelaine Lucie."

She followed this with her eyes half-closed. She perked up when I concluded, muttering, "Doesn't surprise me. They're not much for getting involved."

Hoping she might add more, I waited.

She slowly drained the last of her sherry from her glass with her head tilted back and her nose wrinkled like she was taking strong medicine. Then she poured herself another one. I moved to object when she attempted to top up mine, but she insisted. "Come on. Don't be shy. I got plenty where this came from. I must have two cases of the stuff in the basement somewhere. It's not every day I get to have tea with a good-looking fellow like yourself." She winked again like she was teasing me and held the Scotch bottle, poised and ready to pour.

I let her splash another three fingers into my glass, then gently steered us back to our original topic. "You don't sound like you believe what Mrs. Patterson told me."

She sniffed and glanced out the window. "I know what I see." So I didn't get the wrong idea, she added, "You have to understand, I don't spend all my time staring out the window. I'm not nosy by nature, but I do have a good eye and not much gets by me."

"What did you see?"

"More than they wanted me to, that's for sure," she said, her dark eyes shining behind thick lenses. "I saw Simon Greeves standing in the backyard of Professor Celli's house talking with the Lucie woman a week before she was killed. It was late; it must have been after midnight. I couldn't sleep, so, I went out for a walk in my back garden. That's when I saw them. The wind was going in the wrong direction, so I couldn't hear what they were saying, but he raised his voice a couple of times. I'm quite sure they were arguing about something. They stood there for about five minutes, then they both went back in the house together."

"Are you sure it was Simon Greeves?"

She tapped a finger against the frame of her glasses and said, "These old eyes are correctable to 20–20, Mr. Paris. I'm eighty-three and still driving. There was a good moon out that night. I know what I saw."

"Did you see him again?"

"No, just that once, but I'll tell you something else just as interesting. . . ."

She paused until she was sure she had my attention, then continued. "He wasn't the only one. I saw Simon's son, Tom, there twice. I didn't actually see him with her. I just saw him coming out of her back door on two different occasions. He has to cross right behind my place to get home."

"When did you see him?"

"The first time, about a week after she moved in, then once more, two, maybe three weeks later. And a couple of times in between that I saw that Patterson woman and also that Mr. Harold out there watching her place."

"Are you sure they were watching it?"

"Sure, I'm sure. They just stood there against the fence in her backyard and kept a lookout on the house."

"Together?"

"No. Separately. He came once; she came twice that I saw. They stayed maybe fifteen or twenty minutes each time. They might have been there other times when I wasn't looking."

She didn't appear at all offended that I was pumping her. In fact, she seemed to be rather enjoying herself. The thought crossed my mind that she might be making some of it up just to hear herself talk.

"Were there any others?"

"Not hanging around and spying," she continued cheerfully, "but there was one other fellow I saw over there maybe three or four times besides Arty Lannell. You know who Arty is, don't you?"

"Yes, the fellow the police say killed Madelaine Lucie."

" 'Say,' " she emphasized. Her tone was reminiscent of Laura's when she had defended Arthur Lannell.

"Then you don't think he did it?"

She shook her head. "He might have done it. I'm not saying it's impossible, but I just don't see it. Once in a while, Arty used to come up here to ask for work. I employ a couple of regular fellows to look after the grounds and what needs fixing up, but I liked Arty, so, I'd give him a job now and again—painting a fence or cleaning something up. One time, I had him do a little straightening out in the garage, and he found a whole nest of field mice. I was all for calling in the exterminators. But Arty wouldn't let me. He packed up those rodents in a cardboard box and moved mother and kids to a place down the beach where they wouldn't be in anyone's way. That's what Arty was like. If he did kill that woman, she might have been asking for it."

"Why do you say that?"

She tried to backpedal slightly. "I didn't mean that she *deserved* it. I just meant she was that kind of woman."

"What kind?"

She licked her lips. "The kind that drives men crazy. I never talked to her myself, but I watched her. She used to stand out there in back and feed the birds. Now, let me tell you something, Mr. Paris, I've fed the birds here since I was five and I never got one to come closer than a hop, skip, and a jump. That woman had them eating right out of her hands. Not only birds but squirrels and chipmunks. There was something about her. Something even animals could sense."

"You mentioned another fellow. Do you know who he is?"

"No," she replied, "but I used to call him 'the one with the funny eyes.' I saw him maybe three or four times and always late at night. He'd come out on the back porch and stare over at the Greeves' place next door like he wanted to eat it."

"Funny eyes?"

"Yes, strange eyes. His right eye was lower than his left," she explained, poking one finger against her cheekbone to indicate where the other eye would have been.

Trudy had mentioned that Mr. John had funny eyes. "What else can you tell me about him?"

"Let me think." Her brow wrinkled. "Except for the eyes, he was pretty plain. Middle-aged with ordinary features and a mustache trimmed close to the lip. Nothing to look at twice except for the eyes."

"What color was his hair?"

"Light brown and fuzzy, and he was bald in the front, but he wore one of those narrow-brimmed pork pie hats most of the time to cover it up."

"What color hat? Do you remember?"

"Dark green."

Trudy's man with the funny eyes and green hair, I thought. Bingo.

"How big was he?"

"Small and skinny," she said. "He smoked a lot and had a habit of flipping the butts onto the lawn in back without stamping them out. I was always afraid he'd start a fire."

"What about his clothes?"

"Flashy." She paused and closed her eyes to conjure up an exact picture of him. "He wore bright shirts open down the front, chains, sometimes a light leather jacket, and once a dark brown suit that didn't fit him very well."

I smiled. "You have a very good memory."

She grinned. "Sorbonne, 1922. Art major. My first husband always said I had a good eye for detail."

An excellent eye, I thought, if she were telling the whole truth and nothing but. "Did you ever see this fellow with any of the Greeves or with Madelaine Lucie?"

"No. The only time I ever saw him was when he came out alone on the deck or stood in the backyard. I can't even tell you if the woman was there in the house when he was around, but I had the feeling she was. The lights were all on."

Her memory and her reasoning seemed perfectly all right, but one point bothered me. Pete Blanche hadn't mentioned any of this.

"Did you tell this to the police?"

"Every last word," she assured me emphatically. "I was away the week of the murder visiting old friends in San Diego. When I got back and heard about that horrible business, I telephoned the police and told them just what I'm telling you, but they said they had solved the whole thing already. It doesn't surprise me—not with the kind of power the Greeves have. They've done it before, but I'm sure you know about that."

I didn't, but I definitely wanted to. "Done what before?" I asked.

She tugged at one of her pigtails in exasperation. "Why, swept trouble under the rug with their money. That Tom, Simon's son, was a regular hellraiser as a boy. There wasn't hardly anything he didn't get himself into—drugs, smashing up cars, even beating up girls. The Greeves had a maid, a cute little Mexican thing, half a dozen years back. They found her in the water with her head smashed in. Simon Greeves' money hushed that one up." Her eyes were on fire.

"Was Tom Greeves involved in the maid's death?" I tried not to sound too skeptical. I think she caught a whiff of it anyway.

"I don't know about *that*," she spoke more cautiously now, "but I do know he was involved in her *life*. I used to see him sneak off with the girl. After she was dead, the police questioned me, and I told them what I'd seen. They came back the next day and told me that Tom had denied ever having anything to do with her. Now, that's pretty funny, because I know what I saw, but as far as I know, no one ever did anything about it. It's the same this time."

"Are you suggesting that someone in the Greeves family was involved with Madelaine's murder and they've been able to hush it up?"

She put a finger up to her lips to stop me. "Don't you put words in my mouth, son. What I'm saying is that the Greeves might be more involved than they're saying. Now, that doesn't mean they're involved in anything, but if they were, they've got enough clout with Simon's money and the son-in-law's political connections to cover it up."

"The son-in-law's political connections?"

She grinned, obviously relishing the fact that she knew more than me. "Nicki's husband is *Neil Harold*. He's about to run for the U.S. Congress. They're already talking about him as possible presidential material. God help this country, is all I can say. Surely, you know who he is?"

"Neil Harold, the football player?"

She blinked uncertainly. "Well, I'm not sure, but I think maybe he did play football at one time. If Daddy were alive, he'd know. Daddy was a great football fan. I do remember someone saying something about Mr. Harold being an alumnus of UCLA. He ought to be in his forties by now. He's a big fellow with a round face. I call him the round-faced fool. He's always smiling. It worries me when people smile too much. You know what I mean?"

"I think I do," I told her. From her description, I was reasonably sure that the Neil Harold who'd married Simon Greeves' daughter was the same Neil Harold who'd played fullback at UCLA when I was playing for SC. He was two years ahead of me and would have graduated in '65. I didn't know him, but I knew of him and had played one season against him. The last I'd heard, he'd gone somewhere up north to Canada to play for one of their professional teams.

"We get a lot of crazy things happening round here," Mrs. Pinfield went on in an angry streak as she refilled both of our glasses. "Must have been a year ago, now, someone kidnapped a woman doctor living a few miles up the road. They found her body in the water down near the Getty Museum. The husband was a writer of some kind. Can't remember their names. I don't even remember if they caught who did it or not. You probably heard about it."

"Yes," I told her and took a long pull on my Scotch.

"It was really awful," she said shaking her head sadly.

"Yes," I told her again.

Seven

They say that time heals all wounds, and I suppose in a hundred years from now I won't feel a thing, but for the time being I'm still feeling it. The black moments. Most of the time I can fight them off, or do some little neat dance to sidestep them, as I'd been doing all day. But there are still times when I'm not looking, when the full impact of what happened sneaks up on me from behind like a shadowy beast, digging its teeth into the back of my neck and shaking me until my teeth rattle, and suddenly I'm back there and I could kill.

The whole thing had come crashing down on me from out of nowhere. Up until just over a year ago, I thought I had everything a man could possibly want: love, money, health, self-respect, and all the free time in the world. I had it all, and I never thought about losing it.

Then, one day, the beast showed its ugly head, only it was dressed in lamb's fleece and I didn't recognize it for what it was.

An old childhood chum named Eddie Kilgore showed up on my doorstep in the middle of February. I hadn't seen him since 1963.

He and I had been part of a gang back in high school. There were a dozen or so of us who palled around together, but the hard core was made up of four of us—Eddie Kilgore,

Johnny Sayers, Bobby Jarrish, and myself. We were all ref-
ugees from homes irrevocably broken by death, divorce, or
booze.

Eddie had been the clown, the one who played practical
jokes, bought cheap rubber imitations of puke and dog shit,
and constantly quoted *Mad* magazine. Sayers was the artist
and lover boy, with his duck-cut black hair. His older sister
was our ticket to parties. Jarrish and I were the tough nuts.
Jarrish was from mean streets—a drunk stepfather who beat
his mother and him until he got too big to beat. I was the
daredevil, the thrill seeker, the one who was always ready to
try anything once. Jarrish and I, being the biggest of the
four, vied with each other for the leadership. Sayers and
Eddie added their influence by playing us off against each
other.

It was a friendship that died a hard death one hot Saturday
night in our senior year. The four of us scored a couple of
cases of Coors beer off the back of a parked delivery truck,
got filthy drunk, stole a car, and drove it into an oil storage
tank, setting a block of warehouses on fire. Somehow we got
away unhurt, but two firemen who answered the call were
seriously injured when a wall collapsed. Though we were
never caught, we all lived with a murder rap hanging over
our heads for several weeks until the firemen came off the
critical list. Both recovered completely; and the statute of
limitations took care of the arson and grand theft charges.
Nevertheless, the immediate result of what happened at the
time was the disintegration of the gang.

We went our own ways after that. Sayers knocked up a girl
later that year and joined the army to beat a shotgun wedding. He was killed in Vietnam a few years afterward. Eddie
went off to City College for a semester, became a hippie and
got heavily involved in drugs. Last I had heard, he'd gone off
to India to find enlightenment.

Jarrish went off to Cal State on a baseball scholarship and
took night courses at Southern Cal so he could date the rich
sorority girls. I hardly saw him at all.

Then, by a curious coincidence, our paths crossed once
more. A few weeks after Anne and I started seeing each
other, she told me about a guy she'd dated before she'd met
me who was still hanging around. She mentioned it because
she had tried to let him down gently, but he'd kept after her,

and she was becoming a little afraid of him. The guy turned
out to be Bobby Jarrish.

I went to see him. We had a fight. It got mean. He broke
two of my ribs, and I broke his jaw and knocked out two of
his front teeth. In the end, there was a lot of swearing about
killing each other. I think we both felt bad that it happened.
At least I did, but when it was over, that was it. It was
finished forever between us. All that was left was pure poison.

Nine years later, he and I locked horns again. I had been
hired as a consultant to a large West Coast bank to look into a
fraud case. The Los Angeles police had investigated and
cleared the chief suspect. I did some digging and uncovered a
payoff and a lot of sloppy police work that led to an indict-
ment and the conviction of the original suspect and two
policemen. Detective Jarrish was never directly implicated in
anything illegal, but the two crooked cops had worked in his
department, and he was directly responsible for the careless
work that had allowed them to go undetected. I heard afterward that he apparently found his career drifting horizontally.

I never told Anne about Jarrish's involvement in the case
because I still had a bad taste in my mouth for him, but I did
use part of the story for my second Jack Savage book.

Then Eddie Kilgore, the third survivor of our original
quartet, showed up and began stirring up all the old memories again.

He arrived half starved and penniless, claiming he'd found
me by accident. He'd seen me drive by with Zoot in the Jeep
when he was hitchhiking in the other direction along the
Coast Highway, then spent three days wandering up and
down the hills until he found someone who recognized the
dog and the Jeep and pointed out where we lived.

In the twenty-odd years since I'd last seen him, he'd been
all over the world, in and out of the drug scene, the yoga
scene, and the back-to-nature scene. He had lived on an
Israeli kibbutz, in a mud hut in Peru, on an opium plantation
in Thailand, an ashram in India, an Alaska mining camp and
in a hundred other places. He spoke with a strange sort of
nostalgia about being busted and thrown into jails halfway
around the world or being chased or wanted by the police or
the army in one country or another. He'd picked up a working knowledge of seven different languages as well as a new
poise.

Eddie, the old practical joker, hadn't exactly become Thomas

Aquinas, but he'd developed enough finesse to charm Anne, who insisted he stay with us until he got his life together again. I was a little wary in spite of the old connections, or maybe because of them, but I went along, mainly because of Anne, but also because Eddie appeared in real need of help.

It was a mistake. Within a month, an army of low-lifers began besieging La Casa Final. It was plain to me that Eddie was setting up drug deals right under our noses.

I wanted to throw him out, but Anne voted to help him. We got in a fight over Eddie, and in the middle of it, Anne let it slip that she had seen Jarrish, my old nemesis, a few months before. He had run into her at the hospital while seeing a sick friend, and he had taken her to lunch. Afterward, afraid it might upset me, she hadn't said anything.

I saw red. I asked her if he'd tried to make a pass at her. She said no. He had asked her for a second lunch, but she'd turned him down.

I knew she was innocent, but I made her tell me all the gory details anyway. It wasn't much. He told her he'd divorced recently and was up for a promotion at work that he was almost sure he'd get. Anne said he asked a lot about us and seemed happy that things were working out for us. She and I patched things over quickly, but the Jarrish conversation deflected our argument over Eddie, and he won a reprieve.

Then, one morning about a week later, Anne couldn't find her watch. After she went to work, I went looking for it. I found Eddie in the guest quarters shooting up with one of the female scarecrows he'd dragged home. The watch was on the woman's wrist. It was definitely Anne's timepiece. It had her initials on the back. The strange part was that this woman didn't see anything wrong with taking it. "You got plenty of everything. Why should you care?" she had sniffed. "I should have just pawned it, like I was going to. Then you'd never have missed it." She laughed at me with genuine malice, daring me to do something about it.

I had visions of this slime crawling through our house. I'd had enough. While I was physically tossing her stuff in her bag, Eddie started screaming at me, calling me a cheap sellout and a bastard. I threw him out, too, packing them both into her car.

It was a strange parting. I had the feeling Eddie was glad that I was throwing him out and, in a way, sorry that he was making me do it. But in the end, he leaned out the window before they drove off and yelled, "I'm going to get you back for this, Paris. I'm going to get you right where it hurts."

For the next couple of days, I kept a keen eye out for Eddie or his friends, but no one showed up.

I thought we'd heard the last of him when a couple of weeks later Detective Jarrish of the LAPD showed up. I was home alone. Normally, the LA cops such as Jarrish cover the southern or city half of the lopsided sixty-by-eighty-mile hourglass that makes up the county of Los Angeles, while the Sheriff's Department covers the northern half of the county where I live, as well as scattered checkerboard pieces farther south like Marina Del Rey and West Hollywood and parts of the Sunset Strip. So, I figured Jarrish had come on personal matters, meaning Anne. I was wrong. He was all business. He was looking for Eddie in connection with a big drug bust in Boyle Heights. He wanted to know if I'd seen him since he'd shown up in town or knew where he might be.

I told him I hadn't seen Eddie and didn't know where he was. It was true that I didn't know his present whereabouts. I lied about seeing him for what I thought was a very good reason. He was out of my hair. I wanted him to stay that way. I didn't want Anne and me involved with Eddie or, for that matter, Jarrish. If Eddie returned, I told myself, I'd call Jarrish, but as long as he stayed away, I wanted to close off that part of my life, seal it into a jar, and bury it somewhere where it would never be found. Jarrish took my statement at face value. He left without even asking about Anne, which convinced me he really had come on official business.

I was half inclined not to say anything to Anne about Jarrish's visit, but I thought it was best that she knew in case Eddie showed up again.

Her face fell when I told her. She sat down and, without looking at me, told me that Eddie had come to see her several times in the past month to borrow money. The day before she had gone into her own account and lent him two thousand dollars.

I was mad but not at her. I knew why she'd tried to help Eddie. It was the same reason she'd become a doctor. She cared about people. She really cared. I blamed myself. It was my rotten past that kept driving the wedge in between us.

I blamed myself when Eddie got back at us like he said he would and kidnapped Anne.

I blamed myself for the way she died.

I even let Jarrish kick me around when he was investigating the murder.

His words seared me like acid thrown in my face. "You held out on me; you could have stopped Eddie; you could have put him behind bars, if you'd only told me the truth."

For a while, I believed him. I thought it was me they should have killed. I thought, I should be dead, not Anne. Me, not her.

Eight

It was dark when I woke up. The clock by my bed said two-ten.

I could vaguely remember driving home from Mrs. Pinfield's. I could remember thinking about Anne and why it had all come crashing down around me. I could remember going into the house and taking the bottle of Glenfiddich out of the liquor cabinet and finishing it off. I even remembered being too drunk to get up from the floor to go to the bedroom. I could not remember getting undressed or getting into bed.

Now, I was in bed, undressed and under the covers, half asleep, half awake. My mind was still floating from the Scotch. I hadn't drunk that much since the day they'd dragged Anne's body out of the water.

The moonlight came in through the skylight overhead, bathing the room in a soft yellow lustre.

Liz sat at the foot of the bed staring out the window. She was sitting so quietly I hadn't even noticed her. She still hadn't noticed I was awake.

She was dressed in a pair of faded jeans and a T-shirt with a short string of pearls around her neck—her favorite way of dressing when she wasn't playing doctor.

The moonlight threw playful shadows over her soft black curls and delicate heart-shaped face. Her dark eyes and soft, creamy skin always reminded me of some Biblical queen.

Fifteen years ago, she had won several national beauty contests. The years in between—medical school, psychiatric training, a marriage, a divorce, a dedication to work—had added more to her beauty, not less.

Some instinct warned her I was awake, and she turned toward me, but even when she looked at me, there was a sad, almost faraway look on her face.

"How long have you been here?"

She managed a half smile. "I don't know. An hour, maybe, two," she replied softly.

"It's 2 A.M."

She looked a little surprised. "Then, four hours."

"Four?"

She shrugged as if to say it didn't matter, but she tried to explain anyway. "When you didn't call, I thought it was because of the way I'd acted on the phone this morning." She stroked the quilt over my right foot as if she were petting a cat.

I felt a dull ache at the base of my skull that throbbed like an oil pump. "I was too drunk to call anyone."

"I know," she agreed, accepting my apology. She looked away from me and out the window again. There was enough moonlight to see all the way to the ocean.

"You thought I was Anne." There was a profound sadness in her voice.

I felt bad. Bad for both of us, but mainly for Liz. I hated to hurt her.

"She's been on my mind a lot," I gently pointed out.

"Mine, too," she said, talking to no one in particular.

I watched her and knew she was capable of sitting there and torturing herself for the rest of the night.

"Why don't you get some sleep, Liz? You're just letting it eat you up."

She ignored my suggestion. "You still love her, don't you," she insisted. It was more of a statement than a question.

"Yes." I hadn't said it out loud in a year.

She tried to make light of what I'd said. "Funny thing is, Anne always used to say that if anything ever happened to her, she wanted me to have you." She tried to laugh, but instead let her chin fall to her chest. "I miss her, Evan. I really miss her."

In a way, Liz was all I had left of Anne. I reached out and touched her back and rubbed it gently. I felt numb from the liquor, but the warmth and sweet perfume of her skin and her vulnerability began to arouse me.

She took both my hands and held them tightly in hers for a moment. Then she let go and got up from the bed.

"I should leave. You should get some sleep."

She didn't go, though. She walked over to the window and stood there, staring down the mountain to the ocean. I could hear the crickets outside, singing love songs to each other. I watched Liz in profile. The light threw a silver sheen over her long black hair. Her breathing was slow and irregular.

Just to say something, she asked me about Mrs. Coltrane. I told her I'd seen a few people but hadn't made much progress. She nodded and appeared satisfied, then, seemingly out of nowhere, she remarked, "She's really beautiful, isn't she?"

"Who?"

"Trudy's mother. Madelaine. I saw the pictures."

"Yes. She is." Liz sounded almost jealous. I knew it wasn't Madelaine who was bothering her.

She sat down on the window ledge and crossed her arms. For a long minute she said nothing. Then, she began, slowly and softly. "I know about Claire Roy. Anne told me. Were you in love with her, Evan?"

That threw me off. I wasn't prepared for a frontal attack on that part of my life.

Claire Roy had starred in the first Jack Savage film. She had just ended a very messy marriage and needed a shoulder to cry on. I was on the film set doctoring the script during most of the shooting. The film brought us closer and closer until I realized something serious was developing between us. It was the first time anything like that had happened to me since I'd met Anne. Anne had never told me she'd said anything to Liz, but it didn't surprise me. In some crazy way I now felt Liz deserved an honest explanation.

"I loved her," I said, "but we never made love."

"Yes, that's what you told Anne. She believed you." She sounded morose. "Is it true?"

"Yes." Liz wasn't doubting me. There was too much pain in her voice for that. I sensed she needed some sort of reassurance. "We went out a few times and once we almost ended up in bed at her place, and only didn't because someone showed up unexpectedly. I was relieved. I felt I'd somehow been saved from myself. That night I went home and told Anne the truth. I guess you know how she felt."

Liz nodded. "Yes, awful. She felt she had somehow failed you."

"I know." She never said it, but I knew.

"After that?" she prodded.

"After that, then, nothing."

"Because there was no point?"

"No. There was still a point. At least for a while. I still cared for Claire. I can't even say that I cared for Anne more. It was just different with Anne. In the end, it was enough to be with one woman. The other feeling went by like a storm and that was the end of it."

"Do you believe you could really love two women at once?"

It was a delicate question—the heart of the matter—considering what Liz and I had been going through over the past few months.

"I don't honestly know."

"If I'd been Anne, I'd have killed you, or walked out, or thrown you out."

"A lot of women would have. I'd probably deserve it."

"But Anne didn't."

"No. She didn't."

She let out a sigh like the sound of an animal in pain. "Do you know how that makes me feel?"

"Like hating me?"

"No, not you," she breathed unhappily and in a way that suggested I couldn't possibly understand anything that a woman could feel. "It makes me feel like hating Anne. *Because I can't be like her*. I can't be that *good*. I was jealous of her then. I'm jealous of her now—because she still has a part of you."

I didn't answer. There was nothing I could say.

She got up and took an indecisive step toward the door. I thought she would leave, but she turned back toward the window and stared out again for a long time. I lay there and watched her through lids that grew heavier and heavier until I dozed off again.

Sometime in the night I awoke to feel the warmth of her body and her soft smooth skin against mine. As she pressed herself against me under the covers, she whispered, "Just hold me. Tell me it wasn't my fault. Please tell me."

"It wasn't your fault," I assured her, kissing her lips, her cheeks, her eyelids. "It wasn't your fault."

"But I wanted something to happen. I imagined her in a car accident. I wanted her to just go away."

"It wasn't your fault," I whispered. "It was no one's fault." Her hair smelled like orange blossoms and wild cherries. Her skin smelled of dark spice. Her lips tasted soft and wet. She spread herself open for me. She sobbed as I entered her and filled her; she clawed at my back and hugged her legs around mine as if trying to pull all of me inside her. Afterward, we fell asleep, twined together like two shipwrecked survivors of a roiling sea storm.

Nine

The phone woke me at seven-thirty. Liz was on the other end of the line. For a moment, I was disoriented. Then, I realized she had already left and gone to work.

She was calling from the hospital to tell me that Arla Coltrane had checked herself into emergency but had brought the papers I wanted with her.

I hauled my carcass out of bed and checked the damage. The throb in the middle of my head was still there, and my mouth felt like sandpaper, but I felt a lot better than I deserved to feel after all I'd had to drink. A quick shower made me operable.

Liz was giving a lecture when I got downtown. She had volunteered to look after Trudy and had left her with her secretary. The poor little kid was curled up in a ball under Liz's desk, hugging her one-eyed rag doll like a life preserver and looking like a woeful ragamuffin. She wouldn't even raise her head to look at me when I said hello.

Arla Coltrane looked even worse. She was in an oxygen tent and having a hell of a time breathing. I stayed just long enough to have a quick look through her granddaughter's papers.

Right on top were stock statements from three different

San Francisco brokerage houses, showing that on at least two dozen occasions in the past year Madelaine had traded in TEK stock, buying and selling large blocks of shares in the company that Simon Greeves owned. Arla Coltrane had no idea who Simon Greeves was, but I was beginning to feel certain her granddaughter had. It definitely warranted a second look.

I took the whole bundle and drove to Matt Hecker's office to borrow a desk and a computer terminal so I could do some serious digging.

Hecker had been "Uncle Matt" to me during my formative years. He wasn't my real uncle, but I'd known the roly-poly white-haired old guy since I was a kid. As an investment advisor and business partner to my late stepfather Jake Lansky, Matt had been practically family. Matt and my mother had been an item for a couple of years after Jake died, and during that time I thought they might make it official, but in the end, my mother went off to Switzerland to marry her English viscount. That was almost thirty years ago.

Now, semi-retired, Matt still kept an office with a small research staff in one of the old brick high-rise buildings off Pershing Square and occasionally consulted for one of his old corporate accounts. When I'd first opened my investigations shop, I'd relied heavily on his data banks and communications links to track information for clients.

Matt showed no surprise when I appeared. Not a word about the long months since he'd last seen me. Somehow, he always seemed like he was expecting me, and I guess in a way he was because I'd been popping in and out of his life for years. He lent me a corner of his own office, and I set to work.

The Visa, Mastercard, and American Express statements and canceled checks from four different San Francisco banks and two in LA showed nothing exciting, and the only long-distance numbers on the old telephone bills were to Arla Coltrane.

The brokerage receipts were a different story. I began feeding the numbers into the terminal. On a straight line basis, Madelaine had had a cumulative net worth of more than nine hundred thousand dollars just over a year ago. She had steadily whittled that away to less than two hundred grand before she had died—mostly through what appeared to be a wide range of bad stock trades. I punched in a list of the stocks she had traded and started calling down charts, annual reports, 10Ks, newspaper articles, and general backgrounders on these companies. It didn't take long to find the thin thread running through all the transactions. TEK Industries. Only one in five of the transactions were direct trades in TEK stock, but three out of four of the rest were either major suppliers or customers of TEK, or had been linked as possible takeover targets during the past year. The remaining stocks were in businesses that competed directly with TEK or its subsidiaries.

The clincher was the timing of each trade, which almost certainly ruled out the possibility that Madelaine was operating on her own. Each buy and sell had come just before a public announcement of some kind—precisely as if she had been privileged to the information beforehand.

On the surface, that made it look like a clear case of insider trading—a clearly illegal pursuit. But it wasn't that simple, and Madelaine's trades actually raised more questions in my mind than answers. For starters, if she was getting advanced information directly from someone inside the company and illegally using this information to buy and sell, why had she made so many bad decisions over the past year? Clearly, she had picked her stocks to go the wrong way in many more cases than she'd picked them right. What then? Had she simply been picking up information incorrectly? Had someone been feeding her incorrect information that they thought was correct? Or had she been fed false information on purpose? If so, then who had fed it to her and why?

According to the latest 10K, the board of TEK Industries included corporate chairman Simon Greeves; his son-in-law and corporate vice-chairman, Neil Harold; Simon's daughter Nicki (no corporate title); Simon's son Tom, president; and Tom's mother-in-law, Margaret Patterson, who was listed as an executive vice-president. Laura Patterson Greeves, Tom's wife, was not listed on the board or as a corporate officer. However, Simon's exwife, Mrs. Amelia Greeves, was a board member. So were a dozen or so of the most prominent business and civic leaders in the county.

Matt snuck up behind me while the printer was spitting out paper. "I got a real crazy on my hands," I told him. "Outside takeover bids that sent the stock down. TEK moves that would have strained debt that set the stock hopping up a couple of points. Now, it's been plummeting again during the last two quarters despite the fact that it's earned more than it did in the two previous quarters. What the hell do you make of it?"

"Hard to say." He studied the printout I'd run off, then shooed me aside and sat down at the terminal. His chubby little fingers flew over the keyboard like a platoon of pink mice. "You got a definite yoyo play in the works. Let's see who's pulling the strings." His fingers danced on, punching in his own customized programs. For several more minutes, columns of numbers, data summaries, graphs, and charts flashed on and off the amber screen like brush fires. Finally, he stopped. "Look, here," he said, pointing triumphantly to an organizational chart of the company. "Most of the power rests with Simon Greeves. The top of the company is either family or hired guns. There's no real depth at the top, and now with the son-in-law heading toward the political arena, there's no heir apparent."

"What about the son, Tom?"

Matt swung around in his chair and faced me. "According to what I've heard, the son's a dunce. Can hardly walk and chew gum at the same time."

"So you figure the market is discounting on the basis of management?"

He nodded. "Most likely. Take a look at this." He turned back and called up one of the charts again on the screen. "You see these?" he asked, pointing to several breaks in a long wavy line. "They indicate bad decisions—bad moves— that the company made over the past year. It's nothing critical but anyone working with a similar program might conclude that TEK management is losing touch."

"Meaning Simon Greeves."

"Exactly. It's the kind of conclusion a good chartist might make," he agreed, smiling angelically and touching his fingers together in front of him like spider legs on a mirror. The devious twinkle in his clear blue eyes said he didn't necessarily agree with what anyone else might have concluded though. It was this devious twinkle that made very smart men pay hundreds of dollars an hour for Matt's counsel.

"Then, you don't think he's losing his grip."

Matt looked pleased that I'd taken his bait. "I suspect some of the brokers probably do and that could be why they've been discounting the stock, but I personally don't. Here, look at this." Matt pushed a few more buttons, and the screen scrolled backward for a couple of seconds, stopping at a similar chart to the one we'd been looking at with a pattern of breaks in the long wavy line. "See here, almost the same thing. This is TEK in 1961, when the company was still called Techno-Electronics, Inc. The stock was moving irrationally. Greeves had made a few small but potentially dangerous decisions, and the Wall Street Cassandras were out in full force predicting doomsday. That was exactly eighteen months before Greeves bought West Aerospace and doubled the market price of his shares."

"You think he's got something like that cooking now?"

"I never think what I don't know," Matt said firmly. "I'm guessing. Greeves is like the Lakers. It's only news when he isn't winning."

"Do you know him personally?"

"Just to say hello to. But I do know someone who's run up against him quite recently. You familiar with Lester Marko-vitch?"

"I know of him." Markovitch was one of the new breed of wheelers and dealers who'd made killings with junk bonds and leveraged buyouts in the last few years.

"Lester was part of a group that was talking about taking a run at TEK last year," Matt explained. "They started buying up small blocks of stock just to test the waters. Then, one day, while he's out in his boat in Tahoe by himself, two guys show up in an outboard. He knew them both. They were ranking generals from the Pentagon who said they'd flown out to Tahoe for a little fishing. Only neither of them had any fishing gear with them. The bottom line was some friendly advice about TEK. The generals told Lester if he went ahead with his takeover bid, TEK would lose all of its government contracts. Lester told me he had the feeling if he didn't let go he might find himself at the bottom of the lake someday with an AWAK missile up his ass. Of course, Markovitch does like to embellish at times." There was a warning note in his laughter that piqued my interest.

"You figure Greeves is that dangerous?"

He turned serious. "Look, Evan, I hear Greeves is a ruth-less son of a bitch. I think you should be careful, but I'm not going to tell you that. Hell, the last time I did, you jumped. Remember?" He gave me a crooked, affectionate smile.

I remembered. I was eight years old and had just discov-ered a wonderful tree in my backyard that grew higher than our house and was perfect for climbing. Uncle Matt had told me to be careful or I'd fall. Just to show him there was nothing to worry about, I'd jumped.

By all accounts I should have broken my neck. I got off lucky with a broken arm and three cracked ribs.

Ten

We weren't talking broken bones this time. This was beginning to smell like a hell of a lot more than a little lost orphan girl. Matt wasn't kidding me, and I wasn't kidding myself. But I wasn't about to hang back either. I jumped in with both feet. Somehow I had the feeling Arla Coltrane's side needed another good player to even things out. I hated an unfair fight.

I drove out to TEK corporate headquarters. The executive offices were in Westchester in an industrial park north of the airport. The building itself was a squat four-story box with gold-tinted glass surrounded by a couple of acres of neatly clipped lawns and an electrified fence. A burly guard in a military green uniform and mirrored aviator glasses took my name and called it in over his telephone. A moment later, he informed me he couldn't issue me a pass. If I wanted in, I had to call for an appointment. He gave me a name in the public relations department and allowed me to go through the gate to turn around, but only after he'd made sure there were at least two other security men inside the gate watching.

While I was turning around, one of the security men snapped off a few photos of me and my Jeep, presumably for the Greeves family album.

I called the number I'd been given from a nearby pay phone and spoke to a woman who explained that she was the press liaison for the corporation. Any questions I had should be put through her.

I hung up and called the main switchboard. I borrowed a

familiar name from the mayor's office that sounded impressive enough to get me through to Simon Greeves's secretary. She told me he was out and couldn't be reached, and it was uncertain whether or not he would be coming into the office that day. Ditto when I called the son Tom and the son-in-law Neil Harold. I called back several times using different aliases until I finally got lucky during the morning coffee break. One of the receptionists sitting in for Tom's secretary accidentally let it slip that Tom was out at the Santa Anita Race Track with his father looking over one of their race horses.

I drove out to Arcadia. It was still early, so the parking lot and race track grounds were nearly empty. There was an unattended limo parked in a no parking zone near the main entrance—a black Cadillac with personalized plates that read: "TEK-1." An avocado green Ferrari sporting "TEK-2" on its rear end was parked in front of the limo. There was a pile of mail on the passenger's seat of the Ferrari. The letter on top was addressed to Tom Greeves.

I headed through the stands and kept bumping into people who shrugged a lot and appeared to be pointing me in the wrong direction whenever I mentioned Greeves. It took me nearly half an hour of scouring the mammoth grounds, wandering up and down the long rows of stables, past fidgety racehorses, piles of manure, and grooms and stablehands plying their trade in the morning heat, before I finally spotted my prey down a long walkway between two back stables.

I already knew the elder Greeves by sight. I'd seen him in person on dozens of previous occasions at the Academy Awards, the ballet, and the theater.

He was attentively currying the rump of a sleek, white-faced chestnut colt. Casually dressed in a pair of white slacks and a green polo shirt, he was surprisingly muscled and slim-waisted for a man in his sixties. At a glance, he could have been someone half his age if not for the full head of silvery white hair combed straight back like a lion's mane.

His son Tom also wore his light blond hair straight back with no part, exactly like his father's. He was in his late twenties and tall like Simon, but thinner. He was dressed much too formally for the stables in a blue business suit, tie, and white shirt, making him look as if he had been called out to the track in a hurry.

Tom held the colt's reins and talked intently to his father

while the elder Greeves listened carefully and occasionally said something that I was too far away to hear.

A grizzled groom with a strikingly small head and an eye patch over his left eye stood out of earshot of the Greeves, leaning against the wall of the stable, hand-rolling a cigarette. He gave me a sideways glance out of his one good eye as I neared the other two, then looked down at his cigarette again and pretended not to notice me. Several other grooms and stablehands measured me from the sidelines.

The conversation between father and son came to an abrupt halt when the elder Greeves saw me approaching.

Simon Greeves continued to curry the horse's flank as he looked me over. His tanned face was clean-shaven and sharp like a hawk's, with a long, aquiline nose and intense gray eyes that peered out from under bushy white-gray eyebrows. His chin jutted out like the prow of a speedboat, reeking of power and arrogance, but his expression itself was impenetrable. He might have been looking through me rather than at me. Despite the heat, I felt a chill in the space between us.

By contrast, Tom Greeves seemed a dim shadow of his father. He was tanned and had the same gray eyes as the elder man, but his chin was receding, casting his face into a permanently weak, unhappy, chipmunkish look. He exuded nothing but a frail uncertainty when he folded his arms across his thin chest and tried looking me over like his father. Tom's eyes flickered as soon as I glanced at him. He turned away, seemingly dreading contact with someone he didn't know.

I focused my attention on Simon Greeves and began to introduce myself, but he cut me off in the middle.

"I know who you are." He continued to stroke the horse's coat. "You were at the house yesterday and spoke with Mrs. Patterson. She told you we had nothing more to say to you." He spoke softly but there was an edge in his voice like the bite of a snake.

Several of the stablehands stopped work and appeared to be waiting for some kind of signal. A uniformed chauffeur came out of the stall just to the right and stopped and stared at me as if he too were waiting for a go-ahead from the old man.

It had all the makings of an abbreviated interview, so I got right to the heart of the matter. I stepped closer so only Tom and Simon could hear me. The chauffeur shifted his shoulders to intervene, but a swift glance from the elder Greeves brought him to bay like a superbly trained guard dog.

I spit out what I had to say. "I have a witness who's willing to swear she saw you and several members of your family with the Lucie woman before she was killed. I didn't know that yesterday when I visited the Cliff House. I also have other information that could link Madelaine Lucie to TEK. I thought we might talk."

If the old man had any feelings on the subject, he kept them hidden. Tom took the news with a slight twitch of his small mouth, but curiously, his surprise seemed to be aimed at his father, not me. In any case, he managed to regain his composure before I could get a clear reading of what that might mean.

For a long moment, the only sounds were the slow steady scraping of the brush on the animal's hide and the occasional swish of the colt's tail, whipping through the still air, swatting at flies.

I was beginning to think I'd reached him and started to explain that my real interest was Trudy and Mrs. Coltrane when he cut me off for the second time.

"Mr. Paris, I don't care what you want or don't want. I don't care for you, and I don't care to be followed around. That goes for everyone in my family. You'd be wise to be on your way." He narrowed his eyes like someone putting me square in the middle of their rifle sights. All of the others except Tom seemed to be unconsciously drawing beads on me in imitation of the old man.

Tom was looking down at the ground, carving a line in the dirt in front of him with the tip of one very expensive shoe.

The elder Greeves took the reins from his son's limp hand, turned the horse, and began leading the animal away.

For a moment, Tom didn't move. Then he seemed to pop awake with a start when he realized his father was abandoning him. He gave me a jerky little smile as if I'd caught him playing with himself, then turned and hurried after his father.

As they moved away, several of the grooms and stablehands closed rank behind the departing royalty and stood facing me, challenging me to try to cross their line. The groom with the eye patch picked up a pitchfork, and the liveried chauffeur unbuttoned his blue coat just enough to let me see he was wearing a shoulder harness with a revolver tucked neatly under his left armpit.

It was pointless to try to start something. I turned and found my way back to the Jeep. The groom and several of his pals followed me at a distance, waiting on the edge of the parking lot to make sure I didn't try sneaking back around the stables another way.

Eleven

My luck with Amelia Greeves wasn't much better. Simon Greeves' exwife lived over in Brentwood in a big white Colonial-style house that sat on top of its own hill. Two LAPD patrolmen in a black-and-white were on their way up her driveway with their lights flashing by the time I'd parked near the front door.

I only got to see Amelia Greeves because one of the cops made her open the door to ask if she wanted to press charges against me.

She was a big square woman, more handsome than pretty, with high cheekbones, haughty hazel eyes, and a thick head of hair, dyed red-blond and fashionably shagged into a wild-looking mane. She called the cops "boys" and me "that man."

When she categorically refused to talk to me, I volunteered to leave peacefully. That seemed to satisfy everyone.

Afterward the cops pulled me over about a mile from the house on Sunset.

One of them ambled over to the side of the Jeep and told me he'd recognized me from Anne's investigation and figured I had a break coming. He warned me that his higher-ups in the department had put out an alert to watch the Greeves place—specifically for a black Jeep which fit the description of mine. "I don't know what the beef is, Paris, but make life easier on all of us and stay out of the area."

We parted on friendly terms.

At least I now knew that I was starting an itch. That was something.

I drove to Wilshire and made a few phone calls to contacts at the Securities and Exchange Commission and at the exchanges where TEK stock traded to check on any investigations in progress, but came up empty. I snagged a few pieces of interesting gossip locally about TEK money that had allegedly whitewashed an investigation into a chemical leak at a plant in 1974. There was also the story of an investigative reporter who'd stopped smack in the middle of a series on kickbacks on oil leasing on government land to join TEK as head of public relations. And one union boss broadly hinted that Greeves might have had something to do with the disappearance of former Teamster honcho Jimmy Hoffa. Unfortunately, with one exception, nobody I talked to had even gotten within talking distance of Greeves. He was a closed shop. No partners; no associates; no friends.

The one exception was Marvin Feldman, an obsessively fit, bald, fifty-five-year-old Beverly Hills lawyer. I got to his office on Rodeo Drive just after four.

I'd first met him in 1970 at the wedding of Anne's cousin, who was marrying one of Marvin's daughters. He had also represented me in the two cases involving the reporters I'd thrown off my property after Anne died. He'd won both cases. But then, in the last ten years, I doubt he'd lost more than a dozen cases.

Marvin was between appointments, working out in the private gym he maintained beside his own office. He was pedaling hard on a stationary bike. Several wires were taped to his hairy chest and bald pate, feeding lung capacity, pulse rates, and other statistics into a computer, which displayed the information on graphs on three separate screens hooked up beside the bike. A sign on the wall behind all this paraphernalia read: "When you quit, you die."

He had agreed to talk to me off the record about a paternity suit he'd handled for a young actress named Felicity Lane that involved Simon Greeves. The case had been news for a couple of weeks three years before, then had disappeared after an announcement of an out-of-court settlement for an undisclosed amount.

"It's a crummy story," he puffed, keeping his speed steady. "Young, gorgeous girl . . . arrives here from a small Texas town five years ago . . . determined to make it in movies. Lands few bit parts on TV . . . dates around . . . thinks she's got the world by the balls. One morning . . . Cinderella wakes up . . . discovers the glass shoe has been passed on to someone younger, fresher. She panics . . . gets lucky and latches on to Greeves. He springs for a Manhattan Beach condo . . . BMW . . . long string of credit cards. Poor, sweet, dumb Felicity figures on extending payments forever . . . stops taking the Pill, figuring on babies to nail the old goat. Presto, she gets herself preggers."

"So, Greeves did father her child," I concluded, recalling a rumor at the time that the settlement had involved a statement that the child was not Simon Greeves's.

Marvin's cynical guffaw set off all sorts of wild fluctuations on the pulse and lung monitors. He kept his eyes riveted to the screens. "I wish it had been . . . that simple," he rasped. "We had a good case. Greeves wasn't living with her . . . but spending lots of . . . money on her. It was perfect for palimony except for one thing." He threw me a grim smile.

"Which was?"

Marvin didn't answer right away. He sped up until he'd raised his cruising speed by five miles an hour. He held that for a full minute, then finally slowed down again and relaxed at a moderate cruising speed.

"Simple. Simon Greeves was firing blanks." He rolled his eyes toward the ceiling as if to say, how could anyone (read: Marvin) be so dumb? "As soon as we started the suit . . . Greeves sent his people to me with proof . . . he'd had a vasectomy in 1980. Felicity hadn't known it, of course . . . and on top of that, she'd told me one little, tiny lie. She said she hadn't been to bed with anyone . . . except Greeves . . . in a year. She conveniently forgot about a one-night stand with an old lover . . . which happened to coincide with the exact date she conceived, give or take a week. I think she almost convinced herself that it hadn't happened . . . and since she had been sleeping with Greeves . . . both before and after she'd become pregnant . . . she really believed the kid was his. Nice try, but no cigar. And you wanna know funny? The real father was a goddamn penniless actor." He laughed again with a miserable twist of his face that said he didn't think any of it was really funny.

"So Greeves *didn't* pay her off."

"No, that's where you're wrong," he corrected me. He was breathing normally now. "To my infinite surprise, Greeves acted the part of a real gentleman. Maybe he didn't want the history of his balls dragged through the courts; can't exactly say I blame him. On the other hand, he did come through with a settlement. Two hundred grand, which was pretty substantial, all things considered. The only stipulation was no more trouble from her. Felicity'd already blown the palimony suit with her little infidelity, so I told her to take the money and run—which she did."

"Any possibility the kid was his? That the vasectomy failed?"

"No chance. His people produced up-to-date tests. Not only that, we did the blood tests when the kid was born. No match."

"What happened to Felicity?"

He shook his head as he dismounted and toweled off. "The pregnancy was tough on her. Her looks went down the toilet. She tried dieting and exercise, but she couldn't bring it back. Finally, she started hitting the bottle, and then the pills. She went through all the money in two years. Then she tried to hit Greeves for more. I know because she tried to get me to intercede again. She said she'd tried to reach him but he wouldn't even return her calls. She drove up to his place in Bel Air with the kid in the car and parked in the driveway and just refused to leave. The police had to be called. She attacked one of the cops and ended up spending the night in jail before I could get her out. About a week after that, she turned on the gas and killed herself and her son. She left a note saying she couldn't take it. That was six months ago."

"What else do you know about Simon Greeves?"

"Personally? Next to nothing." He dropped the towel and began working his arms, curling a couple of twenty-pound dumbbells. He continued between grunts, the veins on his neck pulsing like fat worms. "All I know is the bare facts. . . . Greeves divorced his wife six months before he hooked up with Felicity . . . Amelia Greeves walked off with a bundle, leaving the poor guy with a measley couple of hundred million. . . . Rumor is—underline rumor, Evan, . . . rumor is he's muff crazy . . . always has been . . . the younger, the better." Marvin turned toward the mirror and watched himself as he worked his biceps.

"Any rough stuff? You must have dug around when you were making the case for Felicity."

He smiled. "We looked for the usual garbage . . . but either he's clean . . . or he's managed to keep a tight lid on it."

"What about the son-in-law, Neil Harold? What do you know about him?"

"Again, not much. A lot of talk. Political. He's been making moves . . . shaking hands . . . kissing babies. Don't know of any skeletons . . . yet." He grinned fiercely at himself in the mirror as he curled the last couple of reps.

"And the son?"

He put the dumbbells down and began toweling off again. "Now, that one's been in some trouble. Not serious trouble, but I know he's had brushes with the law, especially when he was growing up—smashing cars, drugs—kid's stuff."

"Ever hear talk of a possible coverup? A drowned woman, a maid of the Greeves?"

He shook his head. "Never heard that."

"If it did happen, do you think he could hide it?"

Marvin gave me a twisted, cynical grin. "Greeves could make the Statue of Liberty disappear if he wanted to. I'm not saying he did, mind you. I'm saying he could."

"Would he?"

This time he roared with laughter. "Evan, from what I've heard, if this guy saw you accidentally walking across his lawn in bright sunlight, he'd go after you with a lawn mower. That's his reputation, anyway."

Twelve

As I drove north into the hills above Sunset Boulevard, I reminded myself that only the day before I wanted nothing to do with the case. Now I was chomping at the bit because I still had nothing. Sure, I had innuendoes like Mrs. Pinfield's murdered maid and reporters who became PR flacks at triple their old salaries once they'd gotten close to the Greeveses, but all of it was like puff clouds on a summer's day.

I forced myself to keep an open mind as I headed toward Helen Razkowski's. Also a sharp lookout. Ever since I'd visited TEK in the morning, I'd had a feeling I was being followed.

Helen, or Elena Rachel, as she now called herself, lived a mile north of the Strip and a hundred yards off of Butterfly Lane on a dusty trail that was just wide enough for my Jeep. The trail ended at a turnaround in front of a thick jungle of snakeweed, blue palo verde, and giant coreopsis in great splashes of yellow bloom. A three-year-old pink Honda was parked in the narrow turnaround.

A large yellow cat with green human-like eyes lay sunning itself on the hood of the car. It jumped off with a fluid plop and headed straight for me, meowing loudly. Anne had once told me that cats only meowed at people, never at other cats. I meowed back. He meowed louder and began rubbing himself against my legs, then finally flopped over in the dirt on his back with his belly stretched out toward me.

I got the message. I knelt down beside him and patted his belly. He purred like a hummingbird with an amplifier. He was wearing a silver tag on his red leather collar that said his name was Mustard.

My new friend followed me down the winding flagstone path to the house, crisscrossing back and forth between my legs to keep my attention.

The house was a tiny whitewashed wooden cottage with bright red shutters, hidden from the world by an overgrown lawn and a tangle of vine-covered oaks.

Springsteen's "Born in the USA" was blaring out of the house as I approached the front door. There was no bell; I knocked and waited. Mustard made a couple of passes at my leg and meowed some more. I bent down and scratched his head. He purred appreciatively and rolled on his back, stretching lengthwise with an enormous world-weary yawn.

The music stopped and the door opened. I straightened up. A petite woman in bare feet, wearing frayed cutoffs and a white shirt, stood in the doorway, holding a thick artist's brush in one hand. Her shirttails were tied in a knot around her waist showing off the lean, well-defined stomach muscles of a dancer and a deep dark belly button. There were splotches of white, mauve, and cobalt blue paint on the front of her shirt, cutoffs, hands, and legs.

"My name's Evan Paris. I'm looking for Elena Rachel."

"I'm Elena Rachel. What can I do for you?" she asked crisply through the screen.

From what Don Claypole and Pete Blanche had said, I had
expected her to be hard. She was certainly that. Her voice
had the gritty rasp of a heavy smoker. Her hair was dyed jet
black and spiked on top, and her cheeks were lined with
deep pits that gave her a coarse look. And yet, there was
something soft and vaguely innocent about her sloe-shaped
eyes. She gave me a half smile to confuse the picture further.
One tooth in front stuck out at a peculiar angle, giving her
smile a lopsided look that was almost funny in an endearing
sort of way.

I tried acting friendly. "Can I ask you a few questions
about Madelaine Lucie?"

She shifted from one foot to the other behind the screen
door. Her face turned suspicious.

"You a cop?" She might have been asking if I was a turd.

"No. I'm a friend of Mrs. Coltrane's, Madelaine's grandmother."

She touched one hand to the top of her head as if testing
the sharpness of her spikes. "Then, I don't have to talk to you,
right?" There was a defiant glint in her eyes. We were
walking a thin line. She'd had her fill of police and private
detectives. On the other hand, I took it as a good omen that
she was still standing there.

"Not if you don't want to," I admitted.

She gave me a peculiar look with her head slightly cocked
to one side.

"Did Claypole send you?"

"No one sent me. I'm a friend of Mrs. Coltrane's," I
repeated. "I'm trying to help Trudy, Madelaine's daughter.
You might be able to help her."

"Gee, I don't know." She was still wary. She studied me
for a long minute, torn between talking and not talking.

Mustard scratched himself against my boots and purred. I
think the fact that he liked me finally tipped the scales.

"All right," she sighed. "Come in, but I don't think I'll be
much help."

She held the screen door open for me. Mustard tried to
slide in, too. She gently caught him under his stomach with
her bare foot, lifting him back outside. "Not when I'm
painting."

She gave me her slightly crooked smile. "He likes to eat
acrylics," she explained, as if she were talking about her

child. "Otherwise, he's really quite good." She spoke with a maternal mix of exasperation and love.

Her living room was tiny and immaculate with a futon rolled up into a couch in one corner. Two large speakers sat on each side, and a large Afghan rug covered the floor. The walls each had several large paintings of dancers in leotards and workout suits, signed "Elena Rachel" and dated over the past four years.

She walked ahead of me with that straight-backed, high-headed gait of a dancer, leading me through the living room to a screened-in porch in back that was nearly as big as the house itself. It was filled with large leafy ferns, yellow-green spider plants hanging from macramé slings, spilling their spindly tentacles toward the floor, fat-leafed avocado trees shooting up toward the ceiling, violets in bloom in shadowy corners, and at least a dozen different kinds of cactuses in various shapes and sizes growing out of an old claw-legged bathtub filled with dirt. A red lacquer Chinese card table and two black lacquer bentwood chairs stood against the far wall. The smell was damp and earthy and yet fresh.

In the very center of the porch was an easel with a four-legged piano stool in front of it and a small table beside it on which a paint-spattered pallet, paints, brushes, flat and straight pallet knives, and a can of water were neatly arrayed. The easel held a large unfinished canvas with a life-sized figure of a female dancer balanced on one leg on top of a ball with both arms outstretched into great white clouds that floated at shoulder height. The dancer's outstretched neck lifted her head above the clouds. Her long reddish blond hair seemed to be blowing in the wind like a flag, disappearing off the canvas on the right. The body was done in black charcoal outline with only touches of base color filled in. The only part that was nearly finished was the face. It was aloof, beautiful, haunting, and familiar.

"That's Madelaine, isn't it?" I felt a chill go up my spine as if I were confronting the woman herself when I said the name.

She gave me a benign look, then glanced at the canvas as if she were looking at it for the first time. "I don't know. I guess it could be," she said vaguely, turning her back to me and dropping the brush she'd been holding in the water can. "I never know where I get my faces. I suppose she's been on my mind."

She smiled sadly, leaving me with the impression that Elena had brought me in to see it on purpose. She wanted to share it with me but not talk about it.

She offered me one of the chairs at the red table, then excused herself and went to wash off the paint.

The painting hovered above me like a giant goshawk winging its way toward heaven and daring me to catch it. I wondered how many she'd dared in her brief lifetime and how many had tried.

In the middle of the table were the remains of a half-smoked joint and an empty matchbook in a black glass ashtray. The match book advertised, "Jay's Exotic Dancers, On Santa Monica, Open 24 Hours." Beside the ashtray was a half ounce of grass in a plastic sandwich bag, an unopened pack of Camels with filters, five soft pencils and a thick, spiral-bound, nine-by-twelve sketch pad open to the middle. The pencil drawing on the open page was the same as the canvas on the easel except there were several more arms and legs sketched in various other poses and extending out from the torso, reminiscent of Durga, the ten-armed Hindu goddess of war. I flipped back through the sketch pad and found detailed drawings of hands, feet, lips, breasts, eyes, and ears. A folded newspaper clipping fluttered out of the book and fell to the floor. I picked it up and unfolded it. It was the clip from the newspaper on Madelaine's death.

I refolded the clipping and placed the sketch pad back on the table beside the grass.

Mustard came around the side of the house and began beseeching entry at the back door. A few moments later, Elena reappeared, carrying a Chinese teapot and two cups on a red lacquer tray. She'd washed the paint off her hands and changed into a clean black blouse. The tails were tied together in front, leaving a two-inch-wide strip across her middle, showing off her deep belly button.

She rested the tray on the table, sat down opposite me, and began pouring the tea with precise movements. Mustard sprang up on the screen and hung by his claws like a Sherpa climbing Everest.

"He's just showing off," she said, ignoring him and handing me a cup of tea. "What would you like to know about Madelaine?" She caught my eye and deliberately held it. Somehow her interest seemed forced. She wasn't at all happy about talking to me.

I glanced at the picture of Madelaine behind Elena, both impressed with her talent and intrigued with her subject. "What was she like? You were good friends once, weren't you?"

She smiled wistfully. "Yeah. We were close. Like best friends. A long time ago." She looked down at her teacup. Mustard fell off the screen with a plop. She gave him a quick sideways glance, then smiled at me as if to say, See, I told you so.

"When did you first meet her?"

"About eight years ago. My mother and me, we moved out to San Pedro from Kansas City. My mother, she worked over in Marineland in the restaurant. I was a sophomore. Mad was a freshman. We took these ballet classes over in Rolling Hills. The rest of the kids came from families with money. We didn't fit, so we hung out together."

She tore off the cellophane on the pack of cigarettes with cool vengeance.

"Was Madelaine a good dancer?"

She smiled. "Better than me. But she couldn't handle audiences. In rehearsals, she'd be fine. Then we'd have these little recitals for the parents. Mad would get sick to her stomach. The few times she managed to go on, she froze. The other girls were nice to her face, but behind her back, they were always laughing at her. They called her the geek."

"Did she know they were talking behind her back?"

"Sure. She was smart. Funny thing was, she never liked dancing. She only put up with all the bullshit because she hated going home. The grandmother was okay, but the grandfather was totally zoned. Man, he gave me the creeps. I think he used to slap her around sometimes. She never said it, but I got the feeling."

She tapped a cigarette out of the pack, studied the end for a second, then lit it.

"Did she have any boyfriends?"

She laughed and blew smoke over my head. "Boyfriends? Mad didn't have tits until she was seventeen. That old man of hers, he made her wear these long funny dresses and socks. I mean like she looked weird, man. Creepy. The one time she got asked out that I know of, the grandfather said no anyway. When she finally split from home and found out what she looked like, wow. She just freaked and went nuts." She shook her head from side to side as if boogying to Madelaine's beat.

"Do you remember who asked her out?"

She squinted into the smoke. "I can almost picture him. I was a senior. He was in my class." She squeezed the words out like tiny drops from a tube of her paint. "He was fat. He wore glasses. He had zits. No one in the whole school would go out with him. His name was Stu . . . Stuart Whitelaw. A real jerk. You know, like ten pens in his shirt pocket and jabbering about computers all the time. He got some kind of scholarship to college back East. Got killed in a car accident about a year later. I think Mad told me that."

Stuart Whitelaw didn't sound like a good candidate for Trudy's father. "Did you ever hear her mention a Simon or Tom Greeves, or Neil Harold?"

Her face went blank. "I never heard of them."

"What about a Mr. Richer or a Mr. John? This Mr. John might have something wrong with one of his eyes, like a cataract or one eye lower than the other. Something like that. Ring any bells?"

She touched her face on the right side but shook her head. "No. Don't know anyone like that."

Despite her denial, there was something in that touch that made me suddenly uncertain of her.

"Are you sure?"

"Sure I'm sure." She gave me a level stare. "Like I told the police, I never knew any of the guys Mad went out with. I mean like I hardly even saw her when we roomed together. I was on shifts, waiting tables at Balthazar's on the Strip and taking art classes at City College or staying with my boyfriend in Marina Del Rey. Madelaine was modeling. She was always out on a shoot or away on location. I mean like we never slept under the same roof more than a dozen of times in the six months we roomed together."

"You never met any of her friends?"

"No."

"But you said when she finally left San Pedro, she really cut loose. She must have been dating. She must have talked to you about her friends."

She looked down at her hands and picked a speck of blue paint off her left thumb nail. "I meant like she started dressing nice, putting on makeup. Like just being herself. I don't know. I guess she went out. We just never talked about it." She flashed me a defiant look as if she really expected me to believe her.

"When was the last time you saw her?"

She shifted in her chair and impatiently stubbed out her cigarette: "Look, I already told the cops. Four years ago. She called me to tell me she was pregnant and moving to San Francisco. She said she was in love with some guy. If she told me his name, I forget. She said I should come up to visit. She said she'd send me her address, but she never did."

"She never called you after she came back?"

"Shit, man, either you don't listen, or you don't believe."

She was right. I didn't believe her, but there was no advantage in advertising it. She had already shut down on me. I tried to salvage what goodwill I'd already established.

"Madelaine was your friend," I reminded her. "Her daughter needs help."

She stared contemptuously at me.

"Would you take my number and call if anything comes to mind?" I asked.

She hesitated as if ready to fight me, then seemed to change her mind and smiled. "Hey, sure, why not?" She pushed the sketch pad and a pencil over toward my side of the table. "Write it in here. That way I won't lose it."

I wrote down my name and number. She read it back to me to make sure she had it right, then flipped the book closed.

At the front door, she gave me a quick warm handshake and held it for a second as if there was something more she wanted to say. Then the shadow fell across her face again, and she said a cool goodbye and let me out of the house.

Mustard walked me the rest of the way to the turnaround.

He slid back and forth between my legs as I walked, then flopped in the dust at my feet when I stopped by the side of the Jeep. I bent down and scratched behind his ears.

"She's hiding something, isn't she?"

Mustard meowed.

"I think she's afraid of something."

Mustard was silent.

"You'd really be helping her if you told me," I insisted.

Mustard meowed again.

He rolled over on his back and closed his eyes. I stroked his stomach. He purred like a windup toy.

Anne used to say the trouble with cats is they talk a lot but they never say anything.

Thirteen

I arrived home just as the sun was settling down for the night, disappearing like a fiery red gumdrop into a grayish pink ocean.

My gardener had come and gone, giving tacit approval to my handiwork on the old orange tree by putting several more braces under the damaged limb.

Carmencita had also come and gone, leaving a clean house, fresh laundry, and a big dish of cheese enchiladas and refried beans in the refrigerator.

I was still so wound up from the day, I couldn't sit still. Despite the fact that I'd spent the better part of a year here alone, it took me a half hour of rattling around in the house before I settled down enough to eat. Then, I quite enjoyed the solitude. I was halfway through the enchiladas, pondering Mozart's Violin Concerto No. 5 in A major when the phone rang.

The voice was unfamiliar. He identified himself as Neil Harold.

"I'm calling from my car," he said cheerily. It sounded more like Simon Greeves's son-in-law was speaking to me through the trans-Atlantic cable with a straw up his nose. "I understand you've been trying to talk to the family and haven't had much luck."

"I've had luck; it's just been all bad," I told him.

He found that amusing. "Well, if you can make do with me, I'd be glad to see you. I'm just on my way up to the Cliff House. I could drive by your place right now if you're not busy."

I told him I'd be happy to see him and gave him directions.

So, I thought as I put down the phone, I'd shaken one apple out of the tree. Fascinating. I scraped up the last of the enchiladas, finished off Mozart, and put the dishes in the washer.

Neil Harold arrived twenty minutes later, driving a dark green Lincoln. He was alone.

He was wearing a neat gray business suit with a quiet blue tie and pale blue shirt. As a concession to the late hour, he'd unbuttoned the shirt at the top under his tie. He seemed beefier by ten or fifteen pounds than he had been when he'd played ball against me twenty years ago, but he still seemed fairly solid, and he stepped with the animal lightness of someone who kept himself in good physical condition. He also had the politician's trick of taking hold of your arm behind the elbow with his left hand when shaking your right to give you that extra sense of intimacy. His warm blue eyes looked out from his boyish face with disarming sincerity.

"Thanks for letting me come up to see you," he grinned.

"Thanks for coming," I told him, fixing him a drink. We sat down opposite each other on the two couches in the middle of the living room, exactly as I had sat with Mrs. Coltrane the day before.

He positioned himself on the edge of his seat and smiled openly, trying to win me over.

"I remember you from Southern Cal," he began. "After I graduated, I went up to Edmonton to play ball for a year, then dropped out when I tore the cartilage in my knee. I came back down here and became a fan again. I saw you play in the Rose Bowl against Purdue in '67. Too bad about that one. They should have let you go for the field goal."

We lost that one by a point. I smiled appreciatively. I knew I was being flattered to death.

"I'm also a great fan of your writing, Evan."

He recounted enough about my three books to convince me he'd read them. Then he cut the crap and got down to business. "About yesterday and this afternoon—I want to apologize for the others. I've been in Sacramento for two days and only found out what happened late today when I returned. I'm not here to make excuses for the rest of my family, but I thought it might help if I explained a few things. That is, if you'll be willing to hear me out." He ran his big hand through his sandy blond hair and feigned embarrassment in requesting a favor.

"Go ahead," I told him. I couldn't deny I was curious.

He moved even farther forward on the couch, presumably

to let me in on his most intimate secret. "First of all, Simon Greeves is a very tough man with very strong ideas and opinions and very definite ways of seeing the world. The others—including Margaret Patterson and my wife Nicki—are following protocol—orders, if you will—set down as directors or corporate officers of TEK Industries and members of the Greeves family." He stopped. This was the point where he wanted some sort of acknowledgment that I followed him.

I nodded. "Go on."

He smiled. "With a business this size, the family and the corporation become vulnerable to attacks on a number of fronts. Simon is old-fashioned about public communications. He's of the 'no comment' school. I don't always agree with his methods, but I've worked closely with him for eighteen years, and I respect him. Deep down, he's a complex and sensitive man. He gave you a hard time today because he's been misquoted in the press whenever he's tried to argue his point."

"The point being?"

He smiled as if he enjoyed our repartee. "The point being in this case that he never visited the house where the Lucie woman was murdered, either before or after she moved in. Nor did Tom. Nor did anyone else in the family, despite what you may have heard. Simon is of the opinion that if you try to defend the truth, you open yourself up to all sorts of innuendo. That's why no one will comment, either to deny or affirm any rumors. That's company policy."

"But you're here."

He nodded. "Yes, I am. First, because I don't always agree with Simon over what's best for me, and second, because I've asked around about you and found out you're not likely to stop digging because you're told to go away. I was hoping I might be able to convince you to take the police report at face value—that no one in our family had anything to do with the dead woman."

"Why should I?"

"Because it's the truth." His smile said he truly sympathized with me, but he also acted like he definitely knew more than I did. "And because you're smart, and because I can guess who told you Simon and the others were at the Lucie house. Haddie Pinfield."

Okay, I thought, so he knows about the old widow and the fact that I'd been there. That hardly proved anything.

"The police could have told you that."

"They could have, but they didn't. If they had, it wouldn't have surprised me. I'll be blunt with you, Evan. Haddie Pinfield doesn't like Simon Greeves. From her point of view, she has a very good reason. Simon Greeves bought the property on the cliffs from the old lady years ago. At that time, he signed an agreement that restricted the size of the house he could build in return for first option on any other parcels that became available along the beach frontage. Mrs. Pinfield used a loophole to sell off two other properties without informing him. He sued and won a judgment of two hundred fifty thousand dollars against her. Then, he turned around and used another loophole to build the Cliff House. She tried to stop him and ended up losing again. To put it kindly, she's gone out of her way ever since to hit back at him by libeling the family. I wouldn't be surprised if she'd told you that my brother-in-law Tom killed one of our maids."

"She mentioned something about that."

He nodded, man-to-man. "That's one of her favorites. If you're interested, I'd like to explain that one."

"I'm interested."

He spoke soberly, his honest eyes riveted on mine. "There was a young woman who drowned in the surf on the beach below our property a few years ago. She was a student from Pepperdine who got hit on the head with a surf board and knocked unconscious and drowned. She was of Mexican American descent. She was with ten people from her class who witnessed the accident. No one at the Cliff House knew about it until the police came by to question us. The kids had parked on the service road in front of our place, but they'd gone down to the beach through Mrs. Pinfield's place. That's all there is to it. It had nothing to do with any of our help, and Tom wasn't even in town that day. He was up at the lodge in Big Bear. Needless to say, that didn't stop Mrs. Pinfield from inventing her story. I don't expect you to take my word for it. I'm prepared to give you the names and addresses of everyone who worked for us in the last ten years."

"Why? It seems like you're going pretty far out of your way to convince me of something that you feel you shouldn't have to defend."

"I am," he admitted. "Because I may need you at some future date." He spread his big hands over his kneecaps. "You see, Evan, I haven't officially declared that I'm running for Congress, but it's hardly a secret. False rumors about Tom and our maid and the Lucie woman have a way of surfacing sometimes in the heat of a campaign. It wouldn't hurt me to have a few people like yourself on my side who know the truth and would be willing to put their necks on the line for me."

He looked me over, measuring me from my chin to the crown of my head. I wondered what he thought he could see.

"I wouldn't mind taking a look at that list," I told him.

He grinned. "I thought you would." He reached in his coat pocket, pulled out two sheets of paper folded and stapled together, and handed them over.

I unfolded them. The first was a photocopy of the original newspaper article on the drowned student. According to the article, it had happened just as he'd said. The second sheet of paper contained a list of names and telephone numbers and dates of employment of the ten people who had worked at the Cliff House in recent years.

"The one you're looking for is Bonita Sandez. She's fourth on the list. She worked for us at the time the student was drowned. She's working for a psychiatrist in Brentwood now." He gave me a wry smile and then asked, "Just out of curiosity, did Haddie Pinfield say she'd seen me at the murdered woman's place?"

"No. She said she saw Tom and Simon actually at Madelaine's. She said she saw you and Mrs. Patterson standing by the back gate looking up at the house."

He raised his eyebrows as if letting me in on a bad joke. "That's good," he chuckled sardonically. "I was almost afraid she had forgotten about me. That would be a blow to my ego."

"Were you there?" I asked, trying to get a rise out of him.

He answered without taking offense. "No, of course not."

"If you were, you wouldn't tell me," I concluded.

His smile broadened. "If I were, I wouldn't be here."

I smiled agreeably. "Okay, fair enough."

He touched his hands together in front of him, forming a steeple with his fingers and stared thoughtfully over the top at me with a warm penetrating look that was meant to grab at my soul. "You have a good mind, and you have a reputation for caring about people. I'm running for Congress because I feel there should be more people who care about the health of this country. I plan to go all the way, Evan. I plan to run for the Senate after the House, and eventually, I plan to take a crack at the White House. I'm putting a team together, a team of strong men to help me. If you're interested—and of course, once you've finished your investigation—I could invite you out to the house, and you could meet some of the others. I think you'd find them interesting."

It was difficult to tell if he was trying to outright buy me or merely flatter me. I wasn't interested, but I wanted to keep the door open until I had finished my business.

"I'll think it over," I told him.

He looked pleased. "All right," he announced heartily. He stood up and gave me a confident nod of approval. "Thanks for hearing me out. I appreciate it. If I can be of any more help, don't hesitate to call. I won't suggest you not try to call any of the other family members. I know if you think you have to, you will, but it might be easier if you called me first. The rest of the family isn't running for office. They might not be as friendly."

"Does Simon know you've come to see me?"

"No. I was counting on your discretion." His conspiratorial look reminded me of the ones his sister-in-law Laura had given me the day before.

"I'll be discreet," I assured him as we shook hands. Then, with his hand still in mine, I popped it to him. "Has TEK ever had any trouble with insider trading?"

I felt his hand twitch, and his eyes narrowed a fraction of an inch as if I'd poked my fingers at them. I let his hand go, and he immediately appeared to recover.

"Insider trading? No. We've never had any trouble with the SEC or anyone else on our stock. Why?"

"Just a rumor I picked up. Probably just one of your enemies out to make trouble. That's politics for you."

"I expect it'll get worse." He grinned toughly to show me he was ready to take it. "But you be sure to call me if you do hear anything I should know about. You have my word, I'll look into it."

I told him I'd stay in touch. He gave me the thumbs-up sign as he slid into his Lincoln. We were old buddies already.

I stood in the driveway and watched him drive off to a full

orchestra of locusts working their wonders in the manzanita and sage. The red of his taillights grew smaller and smaller like dying embers of a fire until they finally winked out in the dark.

Fourteen

The next morning, the sun broke to the south in a ball of fire and climbed high in the sky over the ocean. There were no clouds and no fog along the coastline. The cool night air burned off in the first half hour, leaving behind a heat that grabbed at your throat like the thorny spines of jimsonweed.

I had been up for a couple of hours when Pete Blanche phoned. He sounded official and grim. "I want you downtown as soon as possible."

"What's up?"

"I got a body I'd like you to look at."

A knot formed in the pit of my stomach. "Whose?"

"Never mind. Just get your ass down here." He hung up.

I felt like calling him right back as a dozen faces flashed through my mind. I pushed them all out. I had to stay cool.

I hit the Santa Monica Freeway at the beginning of rush hour. It took me nearly ninety minutes to reach Blanche's office at the Hall of Justice.

He was on his feet, pacing the floor like a jackal. The state of his plaid double-knit sports jacket suggested he'd slept in it. He was sipping coffee out of a spattered styrofoam cup that looked like it had been used and reused several times. There was a large gravy stain on his tie and doughnut crumbs on his chin, and his face looked several years older than it had two days before. Even the left side of his mustache seemed to droop farther by a half inch. He was cool and reticent and scrupulously avoided eye contact, even when he said hello. He offered no explanations. I didn't ask for any.

He drove me over to the morgue in an unmarked maroon

Chevy. The whole way over to County General, he chewed
on the left side of his mustache and neither spoke nor looked
at me.

The body belonged to a small man in his mid-forties and
bald in front with thin, sandy hair and a deep scar over his
right eye that left a concave depression in his temple, making
his eye on that side appear lower than the left one. The
shroud was pulled down to his belly, exposing two dark holes
about the width of a pencil just to the right of his left nipple.

"Do you recognize him?" Blanche demanded.

I was willing to bet it was Mrs. Pinfield's man with the
right eye lower than the left *and* Trudy's Mr. John with the
funny eyes. But I wasn't willing to bet with Pete Blanche—at
least not until I found out what the stakes were. His brusque
manner made me cautious. I was being bluffed. I could see it
in his eyes.

"I've never seen him before," I told him truthfully.

Blanche's nostrils flared like a dog smelling shit. The brow
of his fleshy face wrinkled up. "His name's Johnny Sylvester.
Mean anything?"

"No."

His eyes became dark, nasty slits. "You sure?"

"I'm sure."

"That's funny," he commented, but didn't share the joke
with me. He just let it drop like an unpinned hand grenade.

Pete Blanche told the attendant we were through. We
walked back out in the hallway just as the refrigerator door
slammed shut on what was left of Johnny Sylvester.

"He was shot two times in the chest at close range with a
twenty-five-caliber gun, probably a pistol. We found the body
in his car behind a garage on Sunset just after three this
morning. No witnesses, no suspects, no nothing."

Blanche delivered the facts in a flat voice which told me
only that he hated death as much as any of us.

We drove back to Temple Street in silence, the only noise
being the steady crunch of salted peanuts that Pete fed into
his mouth one at a time from a bag hidden somewhere in the
depths of his right jacket pocket. I knew he was mad at me
because he didn't offer me any. I didn't care. After the
morgue, I wasn't particularly hungry.

We went straight to a minute interrogation room down the
hall from Pete's office.

The room contained three office chairs which had seen

better days, a pink plastic wastepaper basket, and a scarred oak library table with an ashtray and telephone on it. The calendar on the wall behind the table was two months out of date.

Blanche sat me down at the table, then left by the side door without excusing himself.

A large ugly fly buzzed the room and landed on the phone, then hopped to the ashtray. An empty packet of matches lay in the ashtray along with two stubbed out filter-tip cigarettes. The empty pack of matches said: "Jay's Exotic Dancers, On Santa Monica. Open 24 Hours."

The fly took off again when Pete came back. He was carrying a manila envelope and a fat green file folder. He sat down heavily on the chair on the other side of the table, pulled a rap sheet on Johnny Sylvester out of the file folder, and slid it across the table at me. While I began to read, he carefully unbent a paper clip and began using it as a toothpick to poke at one of his back molars.

The mug shots dated back eight years to when Sylvester had been booked for passing a bad check. In the two pictures of him, one head on, one in profile, the hair was a little lighter and thicker, and the jowls were a little tighter, but those were about the only differences. Under identifying marks was the contusion over the right eye which was referred to simply as an old wound without further explanation. It definitely made his right eye appear lower than his left. He had been arrested three times in the past fifteen years for writing bad checks, fraud, and possession of stolen stock certificates, had served a year on the fraud charge and two years for the possession charges. One charge had been dismissed on a technicality. His birthplace was given as San Pedro, California. He claimed to be a professional photographer. He had also been known to use aliases: Johnny Silver, James Selwin. He would have been forty-four years old in three weeks.

Pete tried to rebend the paper clip into its original shape, but the metal snapped. He dropped the pieces in the ashtray and added dryly, "He also pimped and dealt in drugs, mostly heroin and cocaine. We had him under surveillance a few times but just never nailed the bastard."

I said nothing.

He shook his head as if to say I never ceased to amaze him. Then he opened the manila envelope and peered inside until he spotted what he wanted. He removed a clear plastic envelope with two fingers. Handling it like it was something dirty, he set it on the table in front of me. Under the plastic was a scrap of white paper torn from a larger sheet and measuring about three by two.

On it was written my name and phone number in pencil—in my handwriting.

"We found it in his wallet." Pete's deepset eyes dug into me like fingernails. "Any idea why he might have been carrying your number around?"

"No, none." I did have a fairly good idea who'd given it to him, but Blanche had asked, "Why," not "How," and I didn't know why.

Pete dragged the phone closer to him and spoke into the receiver, "You can send her in now."

He memorized my left ear while we waited.

The side door opened, and a tall blond uniformed cop led Elena Rachel into the room. She was wearing a one-piece gray jumpsuit and a large purple bruise on her left cheek. Her inky eyes looked right through me.

Peter Blanche didn't invite her to sit down. He didn't even bother to look up at her. He watched me. "Do you know who she is?" he asked, nodding over his shoulder at Elena.

"Hello, Elena," I said. She ignored me. "Ms. Rachel and I met yesterday. We talked briefly about Madelaine Lucie. She told me what she'd told you."

"Did she tell you she worked regularly for Johnny Sylvester as one of his models, posing for girlie magazines?"

"No."

"Did you discuss Johnny Sylvester with her?"

"No."

"Is it possible she gave him your phone number?"

I glanced at her. Her face was the mask of someone who'd been through the system before, who had no love for it and was ready to go through it again, silently, without protest, without cooperation. The question was why? What was she hiding? What was she afraid of? What did she know? The only chance I had of reaching her was to appear to be on the same side as she was. The outside.

"I don't know. I don't see why she'd give him my number."

Pete pursed his lips. "Do you have anything you want to tell me that you haven't already told me?"

"No, nothing," I said, shaking my head.

His eyes locked on mine like a wolf eyeing a bunny. Nobody moved a muscle until he finally let out a deep sigh and turned with a disgusted air to the cop and snarled, "Take her away."

"Do you want me to hold her?" the cop asked.

"No, let her go." To Elena he added, "But don't leave town, sweetheart. We still might have a few questions for you." He gave her a small flat smile.

She returned him a dull, silent nod.

The cop put her hand on Elena's arm and led her out.

Pete sat across from me looking down at his hands and chewing the left side of his mustache.

Finally, he looked up. The glint in his eyes was half friendly.

"Let's go for a walk," he offered, getting up from the table. He took the papers from me and tucked them back in their folder. He dumped the folder and manila envelope off at his assistant's desk on the way out and snapped that he'd be back in ten minutes.

We went down the elevator and out on the street in silence.

Pete pulled a Mars bar out of his pocket and offered me half. I declined. My appetite was still somewhere back in the morgue. He munched, and we continued for two blocks until we were alone on the sidewalk.

"It seems kind of funny, you coming to see me on Monday about Madelaine Lucie, then you going to visit Elena Rachel on Tuesday, and then her friend turning up dead on Wednesday with your telephone number in his wallet. Kind of a lot of coincidences, don't you think?"

"Kind of," I agreed.

He took off his jacket and slung it over his shoulder. His shirt was soaked through with sweat. He squinted into the sun.

"I know that was your handwriting on the piece of paper," he said matter-of-factly, between bites on the chocolate bar. "I remembered it from all those times I used to borrow your notes during graduate school. I know you gave it to her. I had one of my deputies go over her place after we picked her up this morning. The paper came from a sketch pad she had on the table in the sun porch."

He turned and gave me a hard look, not angry, just serious.

"I also know you well enough," he went on, "to know that you probably have a damned good reason for not coming clean with me. I don't understand it, not yet, anyway, but I hope you're doing the right thing by keeping quiet."

I played dumb.

"Don't look at me like that," he growled. "I'm no fool." A couple of kids came up and walked along beside us for half a block. He waited until they crossed the street before he continued. "Some of the things you said the other day got me thinking. I took out the file on Madelaine Lucie and started going through it. There wasn't anything I could put a finger on, but there were a few things I thought were a little loose. It wasn't my top priority, but I figured I could take one of my deputies and have him make the rounds again, just to set my conscience at ease. I sent in my request at the end of the day. Normally, on something like that, I get a turnaround in a week or two. This time, my answer was on my desk when I showed up yesterday for work. It came in the form of a directive from the top. It called for an all-out push on all unsolved cases in the active files. That'll eat up every minute of slack time in the department. As you know, the Lucie case is *not* on the active list."

"You think there's a cover-up?"

Licking the last of the chocolate off his stubby fingers, he gave me an embarrassed frown. "Look, Evan, I don't even pretend to understand everything that goes on upstairs where the brass live. Maybe they know something I don't know and have no intention of telling me. Maybe it's all a coincidence and I'm just being overly sensitive. Anyway, I got my hands full enough without trying to buck the system."

"What do you want from me?"

"One, keep out of trouble. Two, anything you find, bring it to me first."

"How do I know I can trust you?"

"You don't." He smiled smugly, then added, "By the way, I had a little chat with a friend of yours about an hour ago. A white-haired old spitfire named Mrs. Pinfield. She told me to say hello."

So, I thought, he'd known all along that I knew about the man with one eye lower than the other. A funny guy, this Pete Blanche. A regular puzzle. "Was she able to identify the stiff?"

He scratched at his freckled nose. "She said it was the guy she'd seen."

"Then, why the hell *aren't* you taking it, Pete? That's a lead on your murder."

He grinned. "If I took it, I'd probably only muddy up the waters. You go bird dog it, good buddy. You're going to have to come back to me to close the deal anyway. Right?"

He was right. He could be easily watched and headed off if he did get too close to anything that might cause someone upstairs a headache. If he plowed ahead with the Haddie Pinfield angle, it would red flag his move. On the other hand, if he did nothing, and if there was a cover-up, those doing the covering would feel a lot safer. I was operating independently. No one could pull me away from what I chose to follow up. No one would be following my daily reports and anticipating my next move. And in the end, I'd have to turn it over to the police anyway. I also had to remind myself that if what he and I both thought was true, then it definitely wasn't kid's stuff. Two people were dead already.

"One more question," I told him.

"Shoot."

"Did you guys put that bruise on Elena Rachel's face?"

"No. We asked her about that. She said it was a date, which was probably a lie. That one's a born liar. Maybe you'll have better luck."

"Thanks. I hope so. By the way, I wouldn't mind getting my hands on a copy of Johnny Sylvester's file. I know a few people I'd like to show his pictures to."

"Yeah, I thought you might," he mused, stopping along the sidewalk in the shadow of a building that hid us from the foot traffic on the other side of the street. He turned and faced me, then unfolded his sports jacket in front of him as if he were getting ready to put it back on. Before he did, he reached into the inside pocket, pulled out an envelope, and using his coat as a cape, passed the envelope to me. There was no way anyone watching us from even a few feet away would have seen the envelope disappear into my pocket.

"It's a duplicate of Sylvester's rap sheet and arrest record. You're on your own now. I have to get back. Good fishing."

"Thanks," I replied.

I watched him slip his arms into his sports jacket and head back toward the Sheriff's headquarters.

A nice guy, I thought, and all cop.

Fifteen

I caught up with Trudy again at Liz's office. The kid took one look at the photo and positively identified Johnny Sylvester as Mr. John, the guy with the funny eyes.

Arla Coltrane wasn't quite sure. "None of these names fit," she insisted. She had put on her wig and some makeup and was able to sit up halfway to look at the pictures. She seemed to be struggling very hard with something when she did.

"He might have gone by another name," I suggested.

"Then, it could be." She turned the sheet sideways again. "Who?"

She stared down at the page. "My son-in-law, Jimmy Lucie. Joyce's husband."

"Madelaine's father?"

When she nodded, I felt as if a cool breeze had just swept through the room and uncovered a ghost.

"Are you sure?"

She hesitated. "I'm almost positive." She studied the pictures. "Of course, I haven't seen him in more than twenty years. Not since he left for San Francisco with Joyce. He didn't have that awful scar over his eye, but other than that, I'd swear it was him." She ran her finger over the scar. "If I could talk to him, I could tell you for sure."

She looked much too hopeful. For her, finding her lost son-in-law might solve everything. There was no way to let her down easy.

"I'm afraid that won't be possible. He's dead. He was killed sometime early this morning."

It took her a second to register. Then, she let out a deep sigh. "Poor Jimmy." She shook her head regrettably. "Were you able to talk with him?"

I explained what Mrs. Pinfield had told me two days ago as well as part of what Pete Blanche had told me about Sylvester. I left out what Pete had said afterward. The fewer people who knew about Pete's suspicions, the better.

Mrs. Coltrane wrinkled her forehead. "It's strange that after all these years, Jimmy should come calling on Madelaine. You think he was lonesome for family?"

"I don't think so. I think he and Madelaine were involved in something very unhealthy, something that probably got them both killed."

"Any ideas?"

"Nothing definite," I stalled. "What can you tell me about Jimmy Lucie and Joyce?"

"Well, now, let me think." She patted her wig down on top of her head with both hands as if readying a helmet before battle.

For the next five minutes, until she got too tired to go on, she spun out a tale about her unhappy daughter and Jimmy Lucie.

The daughter was a fat child who'd been physically and mentally beaten into submission by Arla's husband Vernon. In her last year of high school, Joyce discovered boys and got herself pregnant by a former schoolmate and high school dropout, Jimmy Lucie. Joyce refused to get married at first and apparently intended to give up the kid, but after Madelaine was born, she changed her mind. Six months later, she and Jimmy Lucie got married. They lived with Arla and Vernon for a while because Jimmy couldn't hold a job. Finally, he and Joyce left Madelaine with them and moved to San Francisco, promising to bring Madelaine up to join them as soon as they got established. It wasn't quite clear what went on there, but from the letters Arla received, she had the feeling that Joyce was supporting Jimmy while Jimmy worked on some deal.

Then came the accident. Lucie had called to tell the Coltranes that a blanket had fallen against a space heater and caught fire in the apartment hotel where they were staying and the whole building went up. Jimmy was out at the time and was uninjured. Vernon had refused to attend Joyce's funeral. Jimmy Lucie had sent Joyce's ashes back to Arla and right after that disappeared.

Lucie's father and mother were both dead, and the only one Arla could think of who might still remember him from San Pedro was an old widower named Fred Jessel, who ran the boardinghouse on Eleventh Street where Jimmy had lived after he'd dropped out of school and before he'd married Joyce.

I headed down to San Pedro to pick up a couple of pictures of Joyce that Arla said were in her old photo album.

San Pedro's the kind of place that people either don't know or like to forget. It's one of those checkerboard squares at the bottom of Los Angeles where the Harbor Freeway ends. Forty years ago it was a bustling port town with a red light district that rivaled Shanghai's, but the container shipping had since moved most of the sea traffic up the river and closer to the center of town, leaving a quiet, working class burgh on the west lip of the LA harbor, cut off from the mainstream of the city to the north by miles of oil storage tanks and shipping depots.

A sea breeze was blowing the last of a warm sticky fog off the streets when I arrived. It was five to eleven.

Mrs. Coltrane lived in a small frame house off Gaffey Street. A faded blue 1964 Corvair with no tires sat in the driveway on four cinder blocks.

The spare house key was in the can behind the bush near the side door just as she said it would be. The house was hot and stuffy inside. A hint of Arla's inexpensive perfume lingered in the stillness of the living room. The furniture was old and had not cost a great deal even when new, but the room was immaculately clean. A large, bloody painting of Christ on the Cross on black velvet canvas and out of the Tijuana school of fine arts hung over the couch. Christ with His Twelve Disciples stretched along the opposite wall over the plastic-covered loveseat. An old color television stood in one corner between two bookcases filled with paperback novels. All three of my books were lying in a pile on the edge of one shelf. None were new copies.

The photo album was on the bottom shelf. All the shots were captioned and dated. Joyce had been fat from day one, which was 1943. Arla looked pretty, like Madelaine but heavier. Vernon had the tough good looks of Errol Flynn. There was something mean in his eyes that stayed with him in every picture up to the end. In contrast, Joyce was so fat in most of the pictures that her eyes were little more than slits. From pictures of her standing next to Arla in 1962, the year before she died in the fire, I guessed she was about five six or seven. There was only one picture of Jimmy Lucie, taken the same

year. He wore the sullen look of a weasel—a weasel with a
slicked back duck cut and no scar.

I took the picture of Jimmy and one of Joyce and returned
the album to its spot and locked up. Then I drove over to
Eleventh Street to see Fred Jessel.

The sun was white hot now. Jessel's building was a four-
story structure with a roofed porch out front that looked
rickety enough to ignite from the sunshine alone.

A skeletal old man sat to one side of the front door rocking
himself slowly back and forth on a weathered rocker. His
egg-shaped head was completely hairless. He wore a T-shirt
that once said "Cal State." A woolly plaid blanket was wrapped
around his legs. Two naked, spindly ankles stuck out from the
bottom of the blanket into a pair of Nike jogging shoes with
the laces undone. The latest *Playboy* lay open in his lap to
the May centerfold.

He raised his head to squint at me through gold-rimmed
glasses. I stopped in front of him. The thick lenses magnified
his dark brown eyes to twice their normal size. He was
slightly cross-eyed so it was hard to tell exactly where he was
looking.

I gave him a friendly smile. From Arla's description I
figured he was Fred Jessel, but I asked him anyway.

"Who wants to know?" he snapped suspiciously. The chin
jutted up like a tough guy that he once must have been. The
hands turned into bony fists.

I tried to placate him. "My name's Evan Paris. I'm a friend
of Mrs. Coltrane."

The corners of his mouth wrinkled into a tiny smile. "Arla?"
he asked softly.

"Yes. She said to say hello."

That did the trick. He relaxed and sat back in his chair.
"Why didn't you say so? Pull up a chair, son, and sit down."

He gestured toward the open space on the veranda beside
him. I was in for a very strange meeting. There were no
other chairs on the porch. I leaned against the railing instead.
He took one last lingering look at Miss May, then flipped the
magazine shut and concentrated on me. "So, you're good
friends with Vernon and Arla. Well, how about that? You
know, Arla comes by and visits with me once in a while, but
never Vernon. What d'ya think's wrong with Vernon? You're
his friend. You think he's mad at me or something?"

I might have humored him if it had been a social call, but I needed facts. "Vernon's dead," I reminded him. "He's been dead over a year."

He squinted hard at me, or maybe at the post two feet to my right, which I suspected is where I must have appeared in his glasses. His long bony fingers came up and patted the top of his head like he was smoothing down hair that was no longer there.

"Gee," he muttered, "I guess I heard something about that. Must of forgot. Won't be no one left soon. Just me. Then what?" He gave me a baffled look. I could almost see him drifting off again.

I handed him the pictures that I'd taken from the Coltrane album.

"Jimmy Lucie used to live here about twenty-five years ago," I began. "He used to work in the gas station over on Pacific. He married Joyce Coltrane, Arla and Vernon's daughter. I want you to tell me what you can about Jimmy or Joyce."

Birdlike, he tilted his head and held the photos close to his right cheek, studying them out of the corner of one eye.

"Sure is an ugly cuss, ain't he," he said, holding the picture of Jimmy up in the air.

"Do you recognize him? He used to live here." I repeated.

"I don't remember names so well," he said, holding Joyce's picture closer and studying it. "Now, this one I remember. The Coltrane girl. Now, what the devil is her name?"

"Joyce," I said patiently, realizing he'd heard hardly a word I'd said.

He looked skeptical. "Maybe. Not sure." He closed his eyes, concentrating hard, then opened them and shook his head. Then he looked more hopeful. "She's a real wild one. Comes over here and disappears upstairs with that football player. I should probably say something to Vernon, but what the hell, it ain't no business of mine. Seems to me that feller got her in trouble. Don't know what happened to her. Used to see him all the time on the television though. Now, what was his name."

"Jimmy Lucie," I interjected. I held up Jimmy's picture. "He used to live here. He married Vernon's daughter, Joyce."

He studied the pictures again. "Can't remember."

"You said he played football," I coaxed, trying to catch the elusive thread of his thought. "What did he look like?"

"Can't remember," he repeated stubbornly. "Just can't,

but my wife's coming home in an hour. If you want to wait around, she'll probably remember. She's much better at names than me."

Arla had said his wife had been dead ten years. I was spinning my wheels.

"I'd like to wait, but I can't," I told him, taking the pictures from him.

"Well then, come back again sometime," he offered cordially, then went back to reading his magazine. He didn't even look up when I said goodbye.

As I drove away, I wondered if he'd even remember that I'd been there.

Sixteen

Two and a half hours later, thanks to light traffic on the San Diego Freeway and the wonders of modern air travel, I was in San Francisco.

The Paris of North America sits on a misty peninsula of solid rock, pointing north like a sore finger between the San Francisco Bay and the ocean. Chilly sea breezes maintain autumn temperatures all year round despite the hundred-plus degrees of the mainland at summer's height.

Downtown San Francisco is choked with modern skyscrapers and older stone towers, clinging precariously to steep hills that climb straight up from the waterfront.

By two-thirty I was sitting in a quiet bar on Fisherman's Wharf, a pleasant tourist area on the bay, having a drink with Detective Sergeant Abel Hobbish, of the San Francisco Police Department, Bureau of Homicide.

Hobbish is a big black man in his late thirties with protruding eyebrows and piercing brown eyes. There's a thin white scar in the shape of a Y on his left cheek that he got from a knife in the face when he was twelve.

He was leaning over his ginger ale, eyeing me with more

chagrin than amusement. "Let me get this straight. You want me to personally go crawling around in the basement of the department archives to look up a twenty-two-year-old case of a woman killed in a fire?" His nostrils flared.

"I need a favor."

"Yeah, fine, you need a favor, but why me? We got junior clerks to do that sort of thing."

Abel Hobbish was one of the old gang from the weekly poker sessions at Berkeley. Unlike Pete Blanche, he had not gone to seed. He looked as fit, trim, and physically menacing as he had fifteen years ago. For anyone on the wrong side of him, his innocent-looking smile was about as friendly as the grill work on a Mack truck bearing down on you at a hundred and ten.

Hobbish had come up the hard way from the streets of San Jose to Stanford on scholarship. He'd graduated from the masters program at Berkeley at the top of our class, then had gone straight into the SFPD. He had a wife named Evelyn and two teenage daughters, and he lived in a ranch house in Hillsborough that was half paid for. He'd phoned the day they found Anne's body and had flown down for the funeral. He was like a brother.

"I don't want anyone except you knowing I'm looking," I said casually.

"The last time you didn't want anyone to know something, you almost got me busted."

"Seems to me you got a citation after the dust cleared," I reminded him.

"Yeah, sure, but now I'm nine years closer to my pension, man. I got two kids to send to college. One wants to study medicine."

"You worry too much."

He folded both hands on the table in front of him and studied me. "I don't suppose you're going to tell me what you want this information for."

"No, but while you're at it, there is something else."

He was about to protest, but I waved him down and explained. "It shouldn't be much trouble. I need the file of a woman named Madelaine Lucie. L-U-C-I-E. She was murdered in LA six weeks ago. She moved down from the Bay area about a month and a half before that. Someone up here did the background check on her for our Sheriff's Department."

One eyebrow curved quizzically upward. "That was Pete Blanche's case, wasn't it?"

"That's the one. Who handled it on this end? You?"

"No. A friend of mine, Frank Esposito. He mentioned Blanche. Does Pete know you're messing around in his case?"

"The case is closed, and Pete knows, but that's off the record."

He shook his head disdainfully, finished off the rest of his drink, and set the glass back on the table. "You got any more work for me?" he asked sarcastically.

"No, and thanks. I'll be at the Mark Hopkins at six."

He left ahead of me. I paid the bill, collected two dollars in change, and retired to the phone booth in back to line up a few appointments.

Fifteen minutes later, I nosed my rental car into one of the underground lots off of Market Street and headed up the elevator to the offices of Miles, Bannan and Meeter, one of the brokerage houses that had handled Madelaine's money.

Madelaine's broker at MB&M was a dapper fellow named Colin Smythe, about fifty with horn-rimmed glasses, a navy pinstripe suit, and a bow tie. He was the nervous type. He sat at his desk and fiddled incessantly with his clothes and his nails and grinned through a set of small, even teeth while he talked. "Ms. Lucie was one of my best customers. She made several very large trades a month. For a while, she had an awfully good run of luck. Then, she just sort of petered out."

"Any idea why?"

He scratched the tip of his nose with an index finger. "Not really. No."

"Did she impress you as knowing much about stocks?"

"We didn't talk much. She told me what she wanted and I filled her order. I asked her a couple of times where she got her information. She said from books."

"Did you believe her?"

He folded and refolded his slender hands on the desk in front of him and studied his Ivy League ring. "I always wondered," he admitted. "You know, in the beginning, if I'd listened to her, I might be rich."

"But not in the end."

"No. In the end, if she'd only listened to me. . . ." He shook his head. "Hindsight. An invention of fools."

"How did she become your client? Someone recommend her?"

He pulled on one side of his bow tie for a second as if that might help him to think better, then shook his head. "As I recall, it was a cold call through the front desk."

"Did she give you any references when she opened her account?"

"Let me look." While he rummaged through a thick file containing a couple of inches of loose papers, he rambled on. "I was sorry to hear about her death. Tragic. I understand they caught the fellow. I never met her, you know. All our transactions were over the phone. Ah, here it is. Her references."

Smythe handed them to me. I looked quickly and saw nothing new. Both references were bank managers I already knew about.

Smythe chattered on as I handed the sheet back to him. "You know, it may sound funny, but I always pictured her as a mousy little thing with glasses. The first time I saw her was when her picture appeared in the LA paper. She was pretty."

Pretty and dead, I thought. It was one hell of a combination.

I told Smythe if he thought of anything else he could leave a message at the Mark Hopkins that night. After that, he could reach me in LA.

"By the way," he said as he walked me to the door, "I read all of your books. So did my wife. She'll get a kick out of hearing that I met you like this."

I shook Smythe's sweaty hand, which seemed to startle him, and left.

I called on one more broker and two of Madelaine's bankers and spoke to the rest on the phone. Most had a lot less to say than Smythe. Madelaine had never borrowed money, so no one had paid attention to where her money came from.

I made a quick call on her pediatrician, whose office was just down the street from my hotel. He had no knowledge of who Trudy's father might have been. Madelaine had never discussed it with him, even in confidence.

Picking up a quick change of clothes at Stanley's on Maiden Lane, I arrived back in my hotel room just before six. There was a message that Hobbish had called. I dialed back.

"Good of you to call," he grumbled. "Another five minutes, and I'd have gone home to the wife and the kids."

"How'd you make out?"

"I'll let you decide," he informed me mysteriously. "I'll be there in twenty-five. Don't move."

While I waited, I grabbed a quick shower, changed, and ordered up a couple of sandwiches and a bottle of Scotch.

Hobbish showed up carrying a battered black leather attaché case in his hand and a curious look on his large square face.

He opened the case and handed me a dusty file folder marked "Lucie, Joyce."

Now that he was off duty, he accepted a shot of Scotch, then tuned in the news and munched on a sandwich while I checked out the file.

Many of the pages were discolored and brittle, but the file looked complete. The investigation report said the blaze had been presumably started by a blanket that had fallen off the bed into a space heater, spreading quickly to the rug and walls. The building had collapsed during the three alarm fire, destroying most of the evidence. The only victim had been Joyce Lucie. Her husband, James Lucie, of the same address, identified the remains by a watch, a necklace, and the wedding ring.

There was no suspicion of arson or foul play.

The officer in charge of the investigation was Lieutenant Michael Costa.

He had written a footnote at the bottom of the page. It said: "Fifteen thousand dollar life insurance policy, payable to husband. Double indemnity. Jack Starch, adjuster, Bay City Insurance Company."

The coroner's report went into more detail. It listed the victim as Caucasian, female, age 20, approximate weight: 170 pounds, height: 5 foot, 6 ½ inches. Cause of death: smoke inhalation; third degree burns to one hundred percent of body. Identification: by jewelry. Other identification: not possible. Teeth recently extracted. Upper and lower plates destroyed in fire. Pathology report: excess amount of alcohol in body. Victim likely unconscious at time of fire. Liver showed signs of cirrhosis. Chronic alcoholism suspected." The coroner's report was signed by Richard Hew, M.D.

An envelope was attached to the back of the file. In it were a set of very unpretty photos of the corpse plus a series of X-rays. I couldn't see anything in the photos that might help me. I took a quick look through the X-rays. An old break in the left femur showed up clearly.

"How'd you do in Criminal Pathology 512?" I asked Hobbish.

"I aced it," he said, glancing up sourly from the television. "Why?"

"Have a look at these."

"What am I looking for?" He took the X-rays and held them up to the lamp beside his chair.

"History," I told him. Old breaks had a way of showing up on X-rays forever.

He studied the X-rays carefully, going through the whole sequence three times. "You got one break. Left thigh bone about three-quarters of the way up."

"Nothing else?"

"Nothing." He handed the film back to me, then added offhandedly, "By the way, I did a little poking around on my own. The only one from the case still alive is Jack Starch, the insurance investigator."

"Did you speak to him?"

"No. Figured I'd leave that pleasure to you." His smile was syrupy. He was still offended that I wouldn't let him in on the story.

"What about the Lucie woman? Were you able to get her file?"

He poured himself another drink and rolled the glass in his hand, studying the ice cubes, then me. "That presented a bit of a problem, Evan. It wasn't in the records room. I talked to my buddy Esposito, but Frank said his boss requested the file about four weeks ago. It went upstairs and hasn't come back yet. Seems to have gotten lost in the shuffle somewhere."

"Interesting. You guys lose stuff often?"

One eyebrow went up. "We get our share of misfiling around the office. Frank thinks it'll turn up sooner or later."

"I guess that's that," I shrugged.

Having set me up, Abel gave me a wily look and pulled another rabbit out of his brief case, this time in the form of a jumble of note pages.

He grinned. "Not to worry, Evan. Frank said I could look over his original notes. You're lucky. Most of our guys throw them out once they've finished a case. Frank's a nitpicker. He likes to save things. He also takes damned good notes."

"Did you mention me?"

"I told him I was doing some cross-referencing on a sex murder inquiry from Los Angeles."

"Sweet."

"Yeah, un-hunh," he smiled blandly, then turned serious. "Listen, Evan, I may be able to cover your ass for a day or two, but I wouldn't count on keeping any secrets downtown, if I were you. That place has a funny way of leaking when someone upstairs has their eye on something."

"You think someone's got an eye on this one?"

He held up a finger to correct me. "I'm saying if they did, I doubt you could go poking around too long without someone hearing about it. If you're messing around in the deep end, you ought to have a few friends on your side. Friends who can backstop in a pinch."

"Meaning you?"

"Meaning me."

"What about your pension?"

"Fuck the pension."

"You want me to call your daughter and tell her no medical school?"

"Chicken shit."

I began reading through Esposito's notes. I could trust Abel with my life, but if he was right about people looking over his shoulder, it was best for all concerned to keep him out.

Abel played with the channel changer, switching from one news broadcast to another and finally settling on a rerun of *M*A*S*H* and the last half of the last sandwich.

Hobbish was right. Esposito kept good notes. Madelaine had lived downtown in an expensive townhouse on Russian Hill overlooking the Bay. None of her neighbors had noticed any guests, either male or female. Several had remarked that she had been distinctly chilly when they had tried to talk with her. One woman ventured that she might have been a hooker or a porno star. Esposito's conclusion was summed up in the word "gossip" in the margin beside the "hooker" comment. The only thing that looked vaguely interesting was the name of the neighbors across the street—Richard and Cathy Silliphant. It was the closest I'd come to a Mr. Richer since I'd started. I wrote down the address.

The rest looked like a waste. Boutiques where Madelaine had shopped. Trudy's day care facility. Two parking tickets, both paid on time. And a maid who had gone back to Mexico two weeks after Madelaine had moved, current address unknown.

I packed up the folder and handed it back to Abel. "Thanks," I told him.

"Any help?" he asked, eyes on the TV set.

"I don't know yet."

He let out a big sigh and leaned forward in his chair with his hands gripping his knees. "Look, I don't know what the hell you've gotten yourself into, but I'm getting bad vibes."

I knew what he meant. I'd been having the same feelings myself. They had been with me ever since I'd seen the body of Jimmy Lucie down at the police morgue.

"I'll be all right," I assured him. "I'll call you tomorrow."

"Yeah, tomorrow. Don't forget. Good to see you out again."

"Nice to be out."

I let him go first. Five minutes later, I was down in the street in my car, heading toward Russian Hill.

Seventeen

Three months ago, Madelaine had lived in a narrow brick two-story frame house on Vallejo Street. The short space between the sidewalk and house was filled with lilies, brodiaeas, poppies, and tulips in brilliant fire colors that glowed warm in the subdued early evening sun. Richard and Cathy Silliphant lived directly opposite in a wood-frame three-story townhouse with a skinny front lawn. The front walk to the Silliphant house was guarded by a monkey tree on each side, each carefully pruned into a small lollipop of bushy green monkey tails.

I rang the Silliphant doorbell. It chimed the first three bars of Shubert's Unfinished Symphony.

A tall man with a full head of bushy red hair and a pudgy face came to the door.

Trudy's giant with red hair, I thought.

He had a drink in one hand. His ruddy complexion suggested it wasn't the first of the day.

"Nice bell," I told him.

He looked amused. His smile showed off two rows of expensively capped teeth. "Yes, it's digital. It comes with fifteen different tunes, but I haven't figured out how to change it yet." He shrugged with the easy air of a social drunk and asked pleasantly, "How can I help you?"

"You're Richard Silliphant, aren't you?"

"Yes, and you're . . . ?" He raised his eyebrows slightly as if he had my name on the tip of his tongue.

"Evan Paris."

The name didn't appear to mean anything. "If you're here to see Cathy, you're out of luck. She's at some kind of meeting for the Symphony. I don't know when she'll be back."

"Actually, I'd like to talk to you." He looked startled. I had the feeling no one ever came to see him. "I have a few questions about Madelaine Lucie, the woman who used to live across the street."

His smile slipped a notch. "I thought that business was all taken care of. They found the killer, didn't they?"

"They found a fellow they *thought* did it. The original investigation overlooked a few things, Mr. Silliphant. I thought we might talk."

He changed his drink from his right to left hand and tried sounding casual. "Well, I don't think I can be of any help. I never met the woman. I don't know a thing about her."

"I think Madelaine's little girl might be able to identify you as a caller," I suggested.

What was left of his smile crumbled.

"Madelaine's little girl?"

"Trudy. She used to call you Mr. Richer. Remember?"

You could almost see the cogs in his head turning. For a second, he appeared ready to slam the door in my face, then he appeared to think better of it.

"You with the police?"

"No. I'm working on Trudy's behalf."

"A private investigator?"

"Something like that." I put my hand on the door to let him know I wasn't about to budge. I sensed he was capable of violence. He struck me as one of those weak types who could lash out in a panic.

"And my wife? Do you have to talk to her, too?"

She was definitely his main concern. "Not if I get what I need from you."

He thought hard. He glanced across the street at Madelaine's house, then back at me with heavy-lidded, faraway eyes. "I never quite thought she'd vanish so simply."

"I don't understand."

His thin lips stretched. It was a sad painful smile. He opened the door wider. "Come in. We'll talk. I don't see what harm it can do now."

The interior of the house was much larger than it appeared from the street. The upper floors over the living room had been ripped out all the way to the roof and a skylight had been put in, opening the room to the blue evening sky. An alabaster sculpture of a reclining woman by Henry Moore stood in a corner. A Jasper Johns flag swallowed up the wall beside it. Opposite were two medium-sized Rauschenbergs and what looked like a small Chagall.

"Sit down, please," he beckoned. "Can I mix you a drink?"

I told him what I'd have. The room was sparsely but expensively furnished. I sat down on one of the two lemon yellow Italian couches in the center and watched as Richard Silliphant mixed a Johnny Walker Black for me and another martini for himself. He remained standing for a moment, staring out the front window at the unlighted house across the street. When he turned back he appeared ready to handle my questions. I wanted to open him up slowly, carefully. There were a few shadows hidden in dark corners of this guy's personality.

"You said you never thought she'd vanish so simply. What did you mean by that?"

He smiled ironically. "Did you know her, Mr. Paris?"

"No."

He rubbed the rim of his glass with one finger, carefully rounding the curve. "But you appear to be a man who knows women."

"I've had a few encounters."

"Yes." He held up his glass and examined the light critically through it, then glanced at me. "Madelaine Lucie was one of those creatures who complicates men's lives."

"Did she complicate yours?"

He wrinkled his nose defensively. "I suppose she did, but I meant in general." He touched the side of his jaw like he was soothing a wound.

"The police report said neither of you knew her."

"Yes, that's what Cathy told them, and she didn't. She never so much as said hello. I'm sure she thought I never had either."

"But you had."

He rested his free hand on top of the Henry Moore. "True,

but there was no point telling the police. Cathy had already told them neither of us knew Madelaine, and they had the killer. There was nothing to gain by upsetting my wife. You're the first person I've mentioned Madelaine to."

I believed him. I also had the feeling he needed to get a load off his mind.

"How well did you know her?"

He studied the fluid curves of the Moore sculpture. "Do you know who my wife is?"

"No, I don't think so."

"Cathy Belson? *The* Belsons?"

It registered. The Belsons were one of the richest families in California, with a fortune that went back to the Gold Rush days, compounded many times over since then by oil and publishing. Cathy Belson was one of the family eccentrics. She would be about sixty now. I seemed to recall she had had a very showy wedding to a much younger man around the time I was at Berkeley across the Bay.

"I know the name," I told him.

"Yes, everyone knows the name." He waved a hand around the room. "It's all hers. Even me. They usually call me *Mr.* Belson. I don't mind. Not much anyway." He knocked off half of his drink. "Cathy dug me out of the orchestra pit of the Milwaukee Symphony fifteen years ago. I was a second-rate trombonist. The papers called me the golddigger. The odd part is that after nearly fifteen years of marriage, we still actually *like* each other."

"Did you have an affair with Madelaine?"

He straightened. "No . . . and I wouldn't tell you if I did."

There was no coyness in his answer, just an old-fashioned gentlemanliness that was refreshing.

"But you knew her."

He nodded. "Yes, in a way I suppose I did, though I really never knew anything *about* her."

"I'm not sure I understand."

Silliphant scratched the side of his head and appeared to be trying to unravel the mystery himself. "She was like a painting, a modern Mona Lisa, a riddle . . . intriguing yet impenetrable . . . aloof. When we first moved here eighteen months ago, I couldn't get her to say so much as hello. I think the fact that she was so unapproachable excited me." He shook his head in self-reproach, then flopped onto the couch opposite me. "I even took up jogging to have an excuse to run into her whenever she'd come out of the house. I used to stop and talk to Trudy. Finally, Madelaine and I became friends. Sort of. There was always a reserve about her as if she were afraid to get too close to anyone." He examined his fingernails. "She made me feel young."

"What did you talk about?"

"Gardening, mostly. She could make anything grow. She was always experimenting with something new in the beds out in front. I used to watch her from my study upstairs. Sometimes I'd buy her books on flowers. Cathy never knew anything about that, of course."

"Did you know any of her friends?"

"No, but I saw her several times with other people. The first time must have been a few months after we moved in here. She came out of a hotel downtown with a much older man. Maybe that's what gave me the idea I might have a chance with her."

"Can you describe him?"

"Oh, I don't have to describe him. I know who he is. She was with Simon Greeves, the founder of TEK Industries."

More ghosts. I could feel the hair on the back of my neck prickling. "You're sure?"

"I wasn't at first. I'd only seen them for a couple of seconds. Besides, she denied it. Then, a couple of months later, I saw her with Amelia Greeves, Simon's exwife. I was coming home from a jog. It was raining. Madelaine was out on her front porch talking with someone. They went inside as soon as they spotted me, but I still got a good look at the other woman. I'm sure it was Amelia. She's a hard woman to forget. Quite tall with prominent cheekbones and lots of red hair. She and Cathy both went to Stanford and were in the same sorority. Their fathers had business connections, and the girls spent weekends together at the Belson ranch hunting quail. At one time they were both on some sort of college pistol team. Cathy has a whole batch of ribbons and pictures somewhere upstairs. It was definitely Amelia."

"How long did she stay?"

"Not long. A few minutes later, Amelia came out again, got in her car, and drove off."

"Did you ask Madelaine about her?"

"Yes, but she said I'd been mistaken. Said she'd been interviewing a new maid and she'd never heard of anyone named Greeves. There was no point arguing with her, so I let it drop. That was the only time I saw Amelia."

"But there were others."

"Yes. Madelaine's mother visited about a year ago. Then, about six months ago, two others showed up. A man and a woman. It was late, probably about one in the morning. I couldn't sleep. I was reading in the study. They drove up in an old station wagon. A Ford, I think, but I can't really remember. Madelaine was up and dressed as if she'd been expecting them. I don't know how long they stayed; I went to bed."

"Did you ask her about them?"

"No."

"Can you describe them?"

He rubbed his fingertips together and narrowed his eyes. "I didn't get a good look at their faces, but the man was small and thin. He was wearing a narrow-brimmed hat, I think. The woman was tiny with short dark hair. Sort of punkish. I had the impression she was young, around Madelaine's age."

I took out the pictures of Johnny Sylvester and handed them to Silliphant. "Was this the man?"

He studied the photos, then shrugged. "Maybe," he replied, handing them back to me, "but I can't say for sure."

"Did she tell you why she was moving back to Los Angeles?"

"No. She never said a thing. I didn't even know she was going. One day I just saw the moving truck outside. When I asked, I found out she'd already left."

"Did you ever see her afterward?"

"No." He paused and gazed cynically at me. "If you're wondering where I was the night Madelaine died, I was here in San Francisco with two hundred people at a fundraising ball for the Ballet that lasted all night."

"Was your wife with you?"

"Yes, of course. She was cochairman."

The words were barely out of his mouth when there was a rattling of keys in the front door lock. He looked askance at the sound of the door opening and closing.

A second later, a tall, elegant woman, dressed in a navy blue suit and long yellow scarf, swept into the living room pulling off a pair of yellow gloves. "Richard, darling—"

She stopped in the middle of the room when she saw me. Both Richard and I stood up.

Richard smiled sweetly. "Darling, this is Mr. Paris, Evan Paris. This is my wife, Cathy."

Cathy Belson Silliphant was a sharp-faced middle-aged woman with dark wavy hair, a long thin nose, and dark eyes that were set just a little too close together to be called pretty.

Coming toward me, she finished peeling off her gloves and extended a long thin hand with blood red nails. "Pleased to meet you, Mr. Paris. I'm sorry. I didn't mean to interrupt. Richard didn't tell me he was expecting visitors."

She looked me over curiously. I was right. Richard seldom had company.

"Can I fix you a drink, darling? Mr. Paris was just leaving." Richard shot me an isn't-that-right smile as he crossed to the liquor cabinet.

"Can you stay for one drink?" Cathy asked. Her smile bordered on flirtatious.

Richard had put me on the spot. I didn't want to make him look bad; on the other hand, I had a few questions I wanted to ask her.

"I'm sorry, Mrs. Silliphant. I do have to leave. I was just asking your husband about the woman who used to live across the street. I wanted to know if either of you ever saw any visitors coming or going from the Lucie residence?"

Her hand went to the yellow scarf and played with the ends. The enormous ruby on her finger sparkled. "I thought that awful business was all finished. Are you with the police?"

"No. I'm working for the family on behalf of the little girl, trying to find her father."

Richard brought over a martini with two green olives and handed it to his wife. "I told him that neither of us saw anyone else there except for the woman and her daughter," he said smoothly. Behind her back, he shot me a furious look. I was obviously on the verge of complicating his marital affairs.

What he couldn't see was her face and the peculiar look she gave me. It lasted only an instant, but for that moment I had the feeling she wanted to say something to me without his knowledge. She turned back to Richard. "I hope you did try to help. It was a terrible tragedy."

"Yes, yes, of course." He scratched at his chin absentmind-edly. "But I just couldn't think of a damned thing."

She turned back to me. "I'm sorry, Mr. Paris. I can't either. We hardly even knew she was there."

I waited a few seconds. The air was so charged with tension it felt like you could float a cork in it. Neither one offered any more information.

"Thanks, I guess that's it," I told them cheerfully.

Richard gave me a tart smile as I headed toward the door. Cathy walked beside me to let me out. Her perfume was complex, and I liked it.

"I hope you find what you're after." She spoke sincerely, petting the back of my left arm.

I stopped her at the front door. "I think there's more," I said, in a very low voice.

"No." She shook her head but her eyes said, yes.

I told her where I was staying and gave her my LA phone number.

Her lips were still mouthing the numbers as she closed the door.

I stood on the step for a moment. Three days ago, I hadn't been out of the house in months. Now I was poking my nose into some very deep shit.

It felt strangely good.

Eighteen

The home number for Jack Starch, the insurance man who'd handled the Joyce Lucie fire twenty-two years ago, was listed in the White Pages. I called him from a pay phone as soon as I left the Silliphants.

Starch agreed to see me and gave me good directions. In ten minutes I stood in front of a pleasant split-level in Seacliff with two pink iron flamingos on the front lawn.

Starch was a square, heavy-set, hairy fellow with a thick, curly gray beard and a brown mole the size of a half dollar on his left cheek. He was smoking a Meerschaum pipe carved in a bust of Abraham Lincoln.

He had no trouble remembering the Joyce Lucie case and seemed eager to talk about it.

"It was my very first case," he said, waggling the stem of his pipe at me. "There's something about a first case that you never forget, especially if it doesn't go just right. I've thought about it dozens of times since. If I knew then what I know now, I'm sure I'd have tripped up the husband." The thought bugged him even after all these years.

"Any evidence of arson?"

He answered without hesitating. "No. Nothing like that. I couldn't find one scrap of evidence, but there was something about Lucie I just didn't like. Ah, well, what can you do? I followed procedures; we paid out. Double indemnity. Thirty thousand dollars, a lot of money twenty-two years ago. For thirty grand, you could buy a nice house and a car and have enough left over to live on for a couple of years."

"Did you verify Joyce Lucie's identity with her family?"

"There was no family."

"But there was," I told him. I explained all the family connections.

He fumed while I talked, then exploded, slapping one hand against the side of his leg. "Damn, sonovabitch. I should have known. Lucie claimed his wife was from Chicago. He said she'd run away from home four or five years before and her parents had moved. I never did find any relatives, or friends, or anyone who knew her. I even checked FBI missing persons, hoping her parents might have put out a search on her, but there was nothing."

"When was the last time you saw him?"

"About two months after the fire. I had him come into the office to fill out some more papers. I was stalling on the payment, but we both knew I couldn't hold out much longer. He said he was moving to Reno and told me to forward the check there. I mailed it out to the address he gave me a couple of weeks later. About a month after that, I tried to trace him down just to see if I might be able to poke him with a few more questions, but he was gone. There was no forwarding address."

I took out the rap sheet on Johnny Sylvester and handed it to Starch.

"Do you recognize him?"

"That's him all right. He's a lot older, and he didn't have that scar on his face when I knew him, but that's Lucie. I never forget a face. If you got him and need someone to identify him, count on me. I wouldn't mind taking a few shots at that fellow." Visions of Lucie strung up by the neck definitely made his day.

"Somebody beat you to it," I told him. "Lucie was shot dead in LA early this morning."

He took his pipe out of his mouth again and thoughtfully scratched at his beard with the stem. "Does his murder have anything to do with the fire?"

"I don't know yet, but I'd appreciate it if you'd keep our little conversation private for the time being."

"Sure. I don't see why not."

I gave him my number in Los Angeles and told him if he remembered anything that might help or if anyone else came calling on him to let me know. He assured me he would.

I drove back to the hotel. When I arrived, I found an envelope at the desk with my name on it. Inside was a message that said, "I have information. Please meet me at nine-thirty." It was signed "Cathy," followed by a Fulton Street address that I guessed was somewhere opposite the Golden Gate Park. I asked the clerk if he'd seen the woman who'd left it. He said he hadn't. The note had been left on the counter during the past half hour.

I thought of phoning, but that might only complicate things. Besides, it was five after nine. She was probably on her way or already there. I went back to my car and drove out.

The night air was chilly and damp, and a thick fog was rapidly enveloping the city. Visibility was down to a block and a half, and the air had the aroma of a thick bouillabaisse. Typical San Francisco for any time of the year.

The address on Fulton Street was smack in the middle of a vacant strip of property where someone was putting up a new apartment complex. The street lamps along Fulton threw spots of light along the mud-spattered sidewalk and street. The lot itself was dark and ringed with a high plywood barricade running for a half a block in either direction. Someone had decorated the barricade with injunctions to love Jesus. On the opposite side of the street stretched the Golden Gate Park. The gray mist hung in between the trees like ghosts.

I parked, got out, and walked the twenty-five feet to the plywood barricade. A mesh-covered viewing hole had been cut in the wood. I looked through and could make out the outlines of several large pieces of earthmoving equipment sitting in the giant hole. The fog turned into a light drizzle. I could feel the water starting to bead in my hair. Pulling up the collar of my jacket to cut down the chill, I walked along the barricade for fifty feet in each direction. There was nothing else to see.

I turned and headed back to the car. It was nine-thirty-five. The street was empty. I figured I'd wait in the car and give it a few more minutes.

Just as I reached the car, another car went by. For a second, I thought I saw something or someone across the street in the park. Whatever it was, it vanished into the shadows again like a cat.

I opened the door and was just about to step in when I sensed something behind me again. I swung toward the park.

There was a flash of light, a bang, and something piercing the air by my head all in the same instant.

I reacted instinctively, throwing myself over the hood, smacking to the ground on the other side.

Two more shots followed me over. One went over the car and hit the plywood wall behind me with a dull thunk. The other hit the car and pinged as the bullet ricocheted off metal.

For what felt like eternity, I ate concrete. My heart felt like a rock'n'roll band. The adrenaline coursing through my arteries made all my senses twice as sharp. I could smell the gas under the car. I also thought I could see someone running off in the distance.

Male? Female? I couldn't tell. All I knew for sure was that I was wet and covered in construction dirt. I felt like a jerk. A scared jerk. A can of tunafish about to be opened and eaten.

Finally, I shrugged off my jacket, bunched it up and held it up over the hood. Silence. Either they knew I was trying to fool them, or target practice was over.

Two cars cruised by on Fulton Street. One from either direction.

When the third one passed, I crawled into the car on the passenger side and made my way to the driver's seat. Staying low, I started the engine, then popped off the brake and shot out of there like a space shuttle launch.

I drove back to my hotel. The shooting had occupied no more than two or three seconds. It was like it hadn't happened at all. But it had. My knees shook as I drove. I tasted bile in the back of my throat. The street lights bounced off the hood where one of the bullets had hit. It looked like someone had run a can opener across the surface for six inches.

I left the car with the attendant, brushed off his questions about the mud with a joke, and went up to my room. There were no messages.

I felt chilled to the bone, vulnerable, stupid. I forced myself to feel nothing, to keep my mind open and perfectly clear.

I called Liz.

She sounded soft and reflective. "Evan, where have you been? I've been trying to reach you all evening. I wanted to see you."

I wanted to see her, too, but for the moment, I had to convince her that her life might be in danger without panicking her. "We'll take a raincheck. Is Trudy with you?"

"Yes. She's right here. Evan, what's wrong?"

"I'm in San Francisco. It's a long story. I want you to do just as I say. Turn off all the lights and stay away from the windows. Sit tight for five minutes. I'll call you right back."

"Evan—"

"Trust me, Liz. I don't have time to explain. Now, hang up."

I waited until she'd put down the receiver, then called Matt Hecker in Los Angeles. My mind raced. If he wasn't in, there were three or four others I could call.

I was never so happy to hear his chipper greeting.

"Matt, it's Evan. I'm in San Francisco. I need a big favor. You still got your gun?"

"Sure, and licensed. You want me to fly up?"

I wanted to hug him. "No. I want you to look after Liz in LA."

"Anne's friend?"

"Yes."

I synopsized the situation as much as I dared over the hotel line, gave him Pete Blanche's number, and told him to call Pete if things got out of hand.

"You know, you're doing an old guy a favor. You're keeping me young," Matt remarked happily just before he hung up.

Liz was in good hands. With his roly-poly Buddha looks, Uncle Matt would be the most soothing person I could send to look after Liz and Trudy. He was also one of the toughest.

Despite the cream puff veneer, Matt had been an operative for the OSS behind enemy lines in World War Two.

Liz answered on the first ring.

"Matt Hecker will be at your place in fifteen minutes."

"Matt? I don't understand?"

"He'll explain everything."

"Please tell me what's going on—"

"Not on the phone."

"Evan, are you all right?"

"I'm fine. Don't worry about me. Now, hang up, and I'll speak to you tomorrow."

"I miss you."

"I miss you, too." I kissed her good night and hung up. Then, I looked up Richard Silliphant in the phone book and dialed.

His hello was slurred with alcohol.

"It's Evan Paris."

"Oh, Jesus. What d'ya want? Didn't you do enough damage already?" He was whispering into the phone.

"I don't understand."

"You don't understand," he mimicked sarcastically. "You had to come barging in here with Madelaine. Cathy didn't even *suspect* until you showed up. Then she began dragging them all out, throwing them all in my face, screaming at me."

"Is she there now? Maybe if I talked to her—"

"She's here, but you can't talk to her. She's taken some sleeping pills and gone to bed. Besides, I don't want you near her. Now, fuck off, Paris, and leave me the hell alone."

He hung up before I could say anything.

I didn't quite know what to do. I washed off the dirt from my hands and my face and stripped off my muddy clothes and exchanged them for my old ones. I thought about driving out to see Richard and was about to dial the number again when I heard a light rap on my door.

"Who is it?" I called through the door.

"Cathy Silliphant. I need to see you."

Nineteen

She was dressed in the same blue suit she'd been wearing earlier in the evening, but she looked somehow smaller, as if she'd shrunk in the last few hours.

Her small dark eyes were red and smeared with mascara—a sure sign she'd been wiping away tears and didn't care how she looked.

"May I sit down, please?" she asked in a low voice, eyes on the floor. Her skirt and her shoes were spotted with rain drops, but there was no mud on her anywhere.

"Yes, of course." I had the feeling she might fall down if she hadn't slid onto the couch beside the window.

"Would you like a drink . . . coffee . . . something else?"

She shook her head. She sat silently staring at her hands folded in her lap.

I fixed myself a Scotch and sat down opposite her in the armchair.

"You want to tell me about it?"

"Richard and I had a fight. A terrible fight." She looked up, her dark eyes searching mine for sympathy. "He walked out."

"When?"

"Twenty minutes after you left."

If Richard had left when she said, he could have made it to the hotel, left the note, taken his potshots at me, and been back home by the time I'd called. *If* she were telling the truth, that is.

"Did you come by here earlier?"

"No."

"Does Richard know you're here now?"

She shook her head. "No. I don't want him to know. I locked my bedroom door, left him a note saying I'd taken some sleeping pills and didn't want to be disturbed, and went out the back way. If he knew that I came to see you, we might never patch it over."

"But you risked coming here anyway."

She took a deep breath and let it out.

"Yes."

"Why?"

"I want you to tell me what he told you."

When I hesitated, she went on anxiously. "You don't have to keep it from me. I know he was involved with her. I lived with it every day for nearly a year and a half. I just never knew to what extent they were involved."

"Why do you need to know now?"

She looked at me like I was the dumbest man alive. "For peace of mind. When she was alive, it didn't really matter, did it? I could just pretend that everything would eventually get back to normal. Now that she's dead . . ." She paused and wiped at her eyes, smearing more mascara. "Do you have any idea what it's like for a woman my age to be competing with someone who's dead?"

She couldn't know it, but the question hit home. I thought of Liz—and Anne. I wanted to sympathize, comfort her, maybe even hold her hand, but I couldn't quite forget that I'd also been shot at less than an hour before and led there because of a note with her name on it. I decided to keep my cards close to my vest.

"What did he tell you?"

"Nothing. He denied it, but *I know*. If it wasn't true, why were *you* there?"

I explained again that I was looking for leads to Trudy's father.

"You don't think Richard . . . ?" She gave me a pathetic look.

"Not unless he and Madelaine go back more than three years."

She shook her head. "No. Impossible. He only met her when we moved to Vallejo Street. I'm sure of that. For the two years before that, it was the waitress in Sausilito. Richard's very faithful to his little tarts. He thought I didn't know about that one either." A sudden burst of anger seemed to restore some of her old poise. She yanked a tissue and a compact from one of her pockets, opened the compact to the mirror, and began repairing her makeup.

Exposed as she was, I sensed she regarded me now as an

ally of sorts and had accepted what I had said at face value. I sensed also that she was as ready to talk now as listen.

"What can you tell me about Madelaine?" I asked. "Did you know her?"

"No. As I said, I rarely saw the woman, and I never spoke with her."

"What about visitors?"

"I never saw any."

"But you had an impression of her?"

She snapped the compact shut and slipped it back in her pocket. "Yes, an impression." She twisted the tissue around her forefinger. "She was a little bitch in heat. The kind that dogs fight over. Poor Richard . . . I feel sorry for him. She must have driven him crazy."

"You figure she went after him?"

She laughed. "She didn't have to. She didn't have to go after anyone. All that woman had to do was walk down the street. She sprayed it into the air. And I don't think she was even aware of it. She was crude. She appealed to man's basic instincts."

She stopped and looked around the room in a way that suggested she'd just arrived, then threw me an embarrassed look. "I'm sorry, Mr. Paris. I'm being terribly boring. I really should go."

She stood abruptly, tucking the tissue into her pocket and straightening her skirt.

I stood up with her. "One more question if you don't mind."

"I don't mind." But she looked like she did. She was suddenly in a big hurry to leave.

"Is it possible that any of your friends were in any way involved with Madelaine Lucie, either personally or socially?"

I was thinking of what Richard had said about Simon and Amelia Greeves. It was possible Cathy hadn't seen Madelaine with them, and if she hadn't, I didn't want her to know in case she might say something to them.

She bristled at the suggestion or at least pretended to. Her lips pulled away from her teeth when she spoke. "That woman and I did not travel in the same circles, Mr. Paris." Hate dripped off of each syllable.

"Just thought I'd ask."

I smiled, but she didn't smile back. Cathy Silliphant was through with Evan Paris.

I let her out and went back into the room, poured myself a stiff shot, and sat down to think.

Jet lag. Being lied to. Followed. Shot at. I was drained and yet wide awake. I ached. I'd lost one of my cat lives. I thought about quitting. I could go to the police and tell them what I knew and hope that somehow, some way, someone else would make things better. Or I could stay in. If I stayed in, I just might get shot at again. If I stayed in, I had a hundred directions to go in and only one pair of legs.

Anne once said that things which are really meaningful are like *déjà vu*. There's always a feeling you've been there before. I had been. It had nothing to do with what I was going through now, not in the literal sense, but it was *déjà vu*. The choices for me were already laid down like some giant railroad track in the sky. Like it or not, we're all pretty much stuck with who we are.

Twenty

A year ago, I had come home late expecting to crawl into a warm bed next to my loving wife.

Nothing had prepared me for what I found. Nothing could have.

My dog was lying in the driveway with his throat cut like a second ugly mouth in his neck. Blood soaked into the gravel.

The front door was open. I raced through the house. Anne was gone. Covers were torn from the bed. A note was pinned to the headboard with one of her brooches.

A ransom note and a threat that they'd cut her throat if I went to the cops.

My brain was on fire, lungs filled with smoke. I couldn't breathe. I was choking.

I had to wait for the banks to open. All night. Endless night. I thought hard. Yes, I could put the money together. If I had to, I'd have stolen it.

Visions of Anne already dead ripped through my head. Throat cut like Zoot's. Somehow I'd failed her. My fault. I sleepwalked, ran, sleepwalked from room to room. I was a madman, raving, calling softly, flinging doors open, slamming them shut. Tearing my hair. Screaming into the empty house, "It can't be."

It was the night I saw into myself, deep down into everything I hated about me, into everything rotten. If I could have sliced myself open to change it, I'd have done it, traded my life for hers.

When the first rays of light came in the morning, I felt a sense of hope. It was short-lived. The police called at 6 A.M. to say she was dead. I was dead too. It was all a dream. I would wake up. Laugh.

It was no dream. Cops came in a steady stream of blue piss, swarming over the house and the grounds like ants at a picnic looking for filthy crumbs of evidence. A couple of plainclothes detectives from LAPD brought me downtown to identify the body.

She had spent the night in the ocean, smashing against rocks. A red, white, and blue corpse. Cold hands. Empty eyes.

I was the chief suspect. *Because* I hadn't reported her missing, *because* statistically the spouse is always the most likely killer. Jarrish and a couple of others grilled me for ten hours straight. All the most painful questions . . . Did we fight? . . . Did we have problems? . . . Did I love her? . . . Who else was I sleeping with? . . . Who else was she sleeping with?

On the surface, I took it all in like I was watching it all happen to somebody else. Inside I was smoking, cold smoke, dry ice. I wanted to kill someone. Anyone. Even the cops who were interrogating me. Worms swam in my brain.

I stayed awake in a stupor for days, waiting for some break in the case. When I did sleep, it was filled with blood, vomit, bloated corpses, knife wounds. Anne's screams. Me running down endless hallways, trying to reach her. I did anything I could to keep from closing my eyes.

A fingerprint on the ransom note positively linked Eddie. The police were combing LA for him. Jarrish warned me to stay out of it. He knew me. He knew if I found Eddie, I would kill him. I had no compassion, no understanding. I wanted nothing but revenge.

And yet, I stayed out. I did as I was told. Why? Because my confidence in myself was as dead as Zoot. I blamed myself. Like Jarrish said, if I'd come clean when I had the chance, none of it would have happened. My past had killed Anne.

For a miserable week, I waited for the phone to ring, for someone to tell me they'd found him. There were Jarrish's daily reports about leads that promised, always promised, and led nowhere. Then, one break. They found the scarecrow girl, the one who'd been shooting up with Eddie. She had turned up dead in an apartment in Gardena. The body had been there a week. They found maps and travel information on Mexico, and more specifically, Guadalajara.

They ordered me to wait. They had more leads. Another week passed. The trail grew colder. Doing nothing was rotting me out inside.

Eddie was going to get away with what he had done to Anne. I had to do something. Finally, I went to Mexico and crawled around Guadalajara for a couple of weeks. I found nothing.

When I came back, the trail in Los Angeles was an iceberg. The cops were still going through the motions, but the momentum was gone. Nothing new had turned up since I'd left. Two of the officers on the case had already been assigned to another case and hadn't been replaced.

Hate took over and sustained me—that and the fact that I had nothing else that I had to get back to. Anne had been the only part of my life that had mattered.

I haunted the Strip, Hollywood, and Venice and the beach bars where the drug-heads collected. I crisscrossed the Valley. I hit the barrios, ghettos, and Chinatowns from Anaheim to Ventura. I scored grass, coke, speed, and smack to make contacts. I asked questions, and more questions. Sometimes I'd get answers. I threw away the drugs, but I was still infected by the slimy underbelly of the world I crawled around in. If I died from a knife or a bullet in the back, I didn't care.

Maybe I'd have gone on like that forever. I can't imagine what would have made me stop if I hadn't finally stumbled on what I was looking for.

I ran into one of the women who used to come up to the house to visit Eddie. She was hooking in a bar in Reseda, earning money for a three-hundred-dollar-a-day smack habit.

She took my number and called the next day. For five hundred, she said she could take me to someone who'd seen Eddie after the murder.

The someone she delivered me to was Eddie himself. He was waiting for me with a revolver at the end of an old mining road in the middle of the desert north of Mohave.

He stood there with both hands on the gun to steady it.

I should have felt scared, but I wasn't. I was used to the numbness by then.

"I have to kill you," he insisted, in a quavering whisper. "If I don't, Evan, you won't stop until you get me. I know you. If you'd gotten the drop on me first, I'd already be dead."

He knew me all right. I had a gun, a 9mm Browning automatic, but I'd stopped carrying it, afraid I might shoot the wrong person.

I watched his finger tighten around the trigger, the gun trembling in his hand. Another dream, I thought. I was already dead. Eddie had fired and I just hadn't heard the gun go off.

But he hadn't fired. In the end, he couldn't. He lowered the gun to his side and dropped it in the dirt. Neither of us moved.

"Evan, I didn't kill her. I'm a thief, not a killer. Believe me, man, I'm sorry for what happened to Anne. I liked her. She was good to me."

It was strange hearing the words out of his mouth. *Déjà vu*. Something I already knew. From the moment he'd dropped the gun, I'd understood.

"Who?" I asked. I already knew that too. I just needed to hear it from him.

Eddie licked his lips and let out a whine. "Jarrish. He did it, man. He did it."

Yeah, Eddie, I thought, I know, I know. I've been here before.

Twenty-One

The sun came up strong and bright over the San Francisco Bay. The sky was clear. The bottle of Scotch was empty, and I was stone cold sober.

I took a cold shower and shaved. Then I went downstairs and drove out to Fulton Street.

I parked in the same spot I'd parked the night before and began looking for bullet holes in the wooden barricade. The site was crawling with workmen in yellow hard hats starting their day. No one paid any attention to me. I found one hole that went right through the plywood and out the other side. After ten minutes, I found a second hole. I was in luck on this one. The bullet had smacked into a four-by-four post that held the barrier wall in place. Fifteen minutes of digging with my pocket knife extracted the bullet without scarring it. It was a copper-jacketed .38 caliber slug. Pocketing it, I went back to the car and stood exactly where I had been when the first shot was fired. I fixed what I saw in my mind and sized it against the tree. My assailant probably was someone about my size. It was a crude guess, but the best I could do.

The mud around the base of the tree where the gunman had waited for me yielded a bit more. I measured the foot length against my own. Again, about my size. The man-sized imprints were waffled. Probably made by jogging shoes. The prints led through the mud for about fifty feet, then disappeared when the tracks hit the park lawn.

On my way back to the hotel, I couldn't decide whether whoever had fired at me had tried to hit me and had been unlucky or had simply intended to scare me off. The only thing I was sure of was that I'd been set up. Someone was on to what I was doing and didn't like it. Unfortunately, I had a list of names about a mile long.

I checked out of my hotel and had a quick meeting with Abel at a coffee shop on Market Street.

"I need you to check out a few things for me," I told him. "One, I want to know where Cathy Belson Silliphant and Richard Silliphant were on the night Madelaine Lucie was killed. They said they were at some fundraising ball for the Ballet. It shouldn't be hard to verify. I want to know if they were there and when they left. I'll also need a sample of their handwriting. A few words should do it, but a signature would be nice. Finally, I want to know if either of them owns a gun."

"Jesus, Paris, you know who these people are?"

"Yeah, and that should make it easy to check."

"Evan—"

"It'll have to wait, Abel." I stood up, paid the bill, patted him on the shoulder, and left him sitting there in front of his coffee with a very deep scowl on his face.

My gut feeling said the Silliphants were simply part of the blind. Someone had found out I'd visited them and used Cathy's name on the note. The answers weren't here in San Francisco. Not now, anyway.

I returned the car to the rental agency at the airport. I didn't mention the damaged hood. The insurance would cover it. Then I boarded my plane and slept until we started our descent.

Los Angeles lay below in a brown funk.

I phoned Liz from the airport, catching her between appointments at her office.

"You and Trudy okay?"

"We're fine. What about you?"

"I'm fine. Is Matt there?"

"Yes. He's with Trudy. He's teaching her to read. You want me to get him?"

"No. Tell him I'll call him later."

"Evan, what's going on? Please tell me. Matt seems to know almost nothing."

"He told you all I know."

"Will you call me later?"

I promised I would and hung up.

Then I dialed Elena Rachel. I got her answering machine.

I tried Jay's Exotic Dancers on Santa Monica. She was there, but she was dancing. I was ungraciously informed that she got off at three. I didn't leave a message. I wanted to see her face to face.

I drove up to my place to change clothes, then called Arla Coltrane at the hospital.

A young female voice I didn't recognize answered the phone with a stiff hello.

"This is Evan Paris. Can I speak with Arla, please?"

"This is Nurse Broydman. Mrs. Coltrane is resting. She can't be disturbed."

I could hear Arla's hoarse protests in the background. "I'm not resting. Give me that phone. I'll do my own deciding."

"Hello? Evan?" She sounded weak but better than the day before.

"I can call later if you want."

"I can talk," she insisted. "I hoped it was you. These people here have me dead and buried already. Don't pay any attention to them. What did you find out?"

"Not much," I said, not wanting to get her hopes up. "I have to ask you a few questions about Joyce. Background information. You don't mind, do you?"

"No, not at all. Not if you think it will help."

"It might. Can you tell me if Joyce ever broke her leg?"

"No. Broke her arm once. Her right arm. Fell off her bike. She wasn't supposed to be riding it because she hadn't done her homework. Vernon was so mad he refused to take her to the hospital. I finally took her when I got home. It was one of those funny breaks that never quite healed properly."

"What about drinking problems? Did Joyce drink a lot?"

"Oh, no. Absolutely not. Alcohol made her sick to her stomach."

"Did she have any serious problems with her teeth?"

"No. None. She had the same teeth as Vernon's. She never had a cavity in her life. The school used to send a dentist around every year. They said she had perfect teeth."

"So you can't think of any reason she might have had to have her teeth pulled while she was in San Francisco."

"Heavens, no. What a strange bunch of questions."

"Yes, I know."

She was silent a moment, then asked, "Are you going to tell me what they're all about?"

"Not just yet. I have a few more things to check out."

"Well, go to it," she urged. "Call me as soon as you know something good. And don't let these nurses push you around.

You just tell them I gave you orders to put you through to me."

"I will," I promised.

She was a tough old broad, I thought as I hung up. A real fighter. I was glad Liz had had the good sense to send her my way. Short of nearly getting myself killed, I hadn't felt so alive in a year.

Twenty-Two

I drove back down the coast and turned off on a side road opposite the cliffs. I kept an eye out for black-and-whites as I crossed the highway and walked up the service road to Professor Celli's cottage. I climbed over the chain blocking the driveway and walked straight out to the backyard, where I was hoping I might get a better idea of who might and might not be home at the Cliff House.

A haze had swallowed up the pale sun. The tide had coughed up a beach full of green and yellow seaweed. A salty, sour breeze blew in from the ocean.

Laura stood under the arbor, looking over the wall directly at me. She was alone. I waved but she didn't wave back. Instead, she turned and walked toward the wall until the high stone barrier hid her from view.

A moment later, the back gate in the wall opened and she ventured out. She closed the thick door behind her and headed down the path. I caught brief glimpses of her as she swiftly made her way toward me. Her long white-blond curls were tied back. She wore a loose white cotton blouse, white baggy slacks with the bottoms rolled up to her knees, and sandals. A colorful Mexican bag was slung over her shoulder.

When she reached me, she was out of breath and flushed from the climb.

"It's funny, but I knew you'd come by this morning."

As if to prove it, she dug in her bright bag and pulled out

two one-ounce bottles of liquor—one of Scotch and one of Campari—and held them up gleefully.

"See. I came prepared." She took my arm as if we were dear old friends and walked beside me as we moved back toward Celli's house. Her clothing was faintly scented with Joy, one of Anne's favorite perfumes.

Choosing a spot that couldn't be seen from either Mrs. Pinfield's or the Greeves's, we settled in the grass. Laura twisted off the two caps and handed the Scotch to me, then clinked her bottle against mine and said, "Cheers."

She laughed and drank straight from the tiny bottle. I did the same.

"Well," she declared when I'd finished, "I guess you have some more questions."

"I do."

"I thought you would. You know, you had everybody quite upset last time."

"Including you?"

"Excluding me. I thought you were interesting." She smiled meaningfully.

"Do you know what they were upset about?"

She shrugged. "Oh, probably that I'd say something."

"Like what?"

She shrugged again. "I don't know. I guess like what I told you, that I didn't think Arthur did it." She stuck her finger in the mouth of the Campari bottle and wiggled it.

"Do you think you know who did it?"

She hesitated a few seconds, then said, "No, not really."

"But there is something else, isn't there?"

She tilted her head to one side. "No, not really. I thought maybe you might just come back to talk with me." She looked faintly uneasy as if she feared I might leave.

"Let's talk about you, then," I suggested.

"All right," she replied more enthusiastically. "What would you like to know about me? Like when was I born? Things like that?"

"Sure. Why not?"

She was relishing the attention. "I was born in Portland, Oregon. September 13, 1963. Claudette Colbert's birthday."

And exactly six months after the San Francisco fire that killed Joyce Coltrane Lucie, I thought.

"What do you remember about Portland?"

"Not much. I was only five when my mother and I moved down to Los Angeles."

"What about your father?"

"Oh, he wasn't living with us by then."

"Do you remember him?"

"Not much, I'm afraid. His name was Sam."

"Patterson?"

"Yes, Sam Patterson. He was from Seattle, like mother. He looked a bit like Henry Fonda. Tall and light-haired and with a mustache. Like in *Once Upon a Time in the West*. He was in some sort of business; I think it had something to do with lumber. We lived in a big house. Not as big as the Cliff House or even the house that Tom and I had in Beverly Hills, but it was big, and nice. I had a cat named Princess and a swing in the backyard. Princess got run over by a car. Right after that I remember my mother and father having a terrible fight. I remember my father packing a suitcase and getting ready to leave. I asked him when he was going to come back, and he said he wouldn't be seeing me again for a long time. I always thought Princess's death had something to do with their fight. Isn't that funny? I kept telling him that it didn't matter, we'd get another cat, but he left. That was the last time I ever saw him."

"Is he still alive?"

She shook her head. "No. About a year later he died in a plane crash in Vancouver. We'd moved to Los Angeles by then. My mother didn't tell me he was dead until I was almost nine. She said when it first happened she was afraid it would upset me. I was a very emotional child." Laura laughed mirthlessly. "I guess I haven't changed much."

"Why did she tell you at nine?"

"We had a fight and I was threatening to run away from home. I used to pretend I was Cinderella and my mother was the wicked stepmother. I told her I was going to go find my father and live with him. I told her I had the address of Uncle Harry in Washington and was going to write to him and find out where my father was."

"Who's Uncle Harry? Your father's brother?"

"No. My great uncle. My father's uncle. My father was an only child. Uncle Harry was my father's only living relative. He was a widower and lived alone on his apple farm near Tacoma. We went up to visit him once when I was little. All I can remember is that he smelled of pipe tobacco and that he

looked a little like Walter Matthau. A lumpy-faced old guy.
Every Christmas he'd send us a card with ten dollars in it. I
took his address from the envelope. That's when Mother told
me about the accident and what happened to Daddy. I was so
angry, I told her I didn't believe her. I said I was going to
write anyway. She said that would be all right, and I guess
she was really trying to make it up to me because she even
helped me write the note. Uncle Harry wrote back a nice
long letter and sent me the newspaper article about the
accident. There was a little picture of my father with his
mustache. Uncle Harry said I could still come up and visit
him if I wanted to. I wrote back that I would, but I never
did. He died when I was twelve."

"You said your father was tall. Could you have been mistaken? You hadn't seen him since you were five. Most adults
look tall to children."

"He was very tall. I have a picture of him with my mother
and myself. My mother is over five seven. My father was at
least six or seven inches taller."

"What did your mother look like in the picture?"

"She was pretty. Maybe a little like Sharon Tate, only with
brown hair. . . . No that's not right. Maybe like Ann-
Margret. . . . No, that's not right either." She laughed and
tossed a pebble toward the ocean. "I don't know. It's tough to
describe your own mother."

"Was she heavier than she is now?"

"No. Thin. Like me. Like Mia Farrow in *Rosemary's Baby*."

"Do you ever remember her being heavy?"

"Mia Farrow?"

"Your mother."

"No, she's always been thin. She eats like a bird, never
gains any weight. Of course, in the last few years she's put on
a little weight, but she's still quite thin."

"Do you know much about her childhood?"

"Not much. She doesn't like to talk much about the past.
She grew up in Seattle. She told me once that her father was
a sailor during the war and that he died in the Pacific. Her
mother went crazy and had to be put in an institution and
died when Mother was in her teens. She was raised by her
grandfather and grandmother who had a little grocery store in
the city. They died before I was born."

"Do you know what her maiden name was?"

"Lee, with two Es, like in Bruce Lee, except it's English,

not Chinese. I think her grandparents originally came from Liverpool. There were no other relatives on my mother's side. When I was growing up, I always wanted to have grandparents and aunts and uncles and cousins and brothers and sisters like everyone else. That's why when I got married I wanted to have a lot of children. I guess I'm just not very lucky."

"You're still young," I reminded her.

"Yes, I suppose," she answered wistfully. "But I'm not sure I'll ever be able to have any. I was pregnant twice, but both times I lost the baby. But what I really meant was that Tom and I will never have children. Tom had a viral disease two years ago. He can't have any children of his own. Both Tom and his sister have had terrible luck that way."

"Nicki, too?"

"Yes. About ten years ago she had twin boys that were stillborn. Nicki tried to have another child at the time. She got pregnant but the fetus wasn't developing properly. The doctors did some tests. It would have been a Mongoloid. She had an abortion and she and Neil decided not to try again. For a while, I was the Greeves's great hope. Everyone was counting on me. Oh, well." She fiddled with her bottle again. "It would be nice. I do love children."

She'd make a good mother, I thought. A child would bring out the adult in her.

"Do you have any old pictures of your mother, say, before you were born or when she was a little girl?"

"No. The only one I have is the one with her and my father. Mother hates photos. I don't think she's had her picture taken in years. She says she just doesn't like what the camera does to her. I think she takes a very nice picture, but then, I don't particularly like my own pictures." She laughed softly.

"Your mother had her right arm in a bandage the other day. She said it was an old war wound. I take it, it's an old injury."

"Yes. She was a real tomboy when she was a little girl and loved to climb trees. One day she fell out of one and broke her arm. She's had problems with it ever since."

I took out the rap sheet on Johnny Sylvester. I had folded over the arrest record so only the photographs showed.

"Have you ever seen this man?"

She took only a second to look before answering. "Yes. As a matter of fact, twice before."

"Here at Professor Celli's?"

"No. Not here." She peered at the photos. "But I have seen him. The first time was about three or four months ago. I'd gone over to Beverly Hills to shop. I had parked on Rodeo when I noticed my mother standing beside her car across the street, talking to someone. I called out and waved. As soon as she saw me, she said something to the man. He looked directly over at me, then walked away. I got a good look at his face. It's not the kind of face I'd easily forget. My mother said he was just a panhandler. Then, about a month later, I was down in Malibu getting gas, and he pulled up in an old station wagon at the pump next to mine. He kept staring at me. I pretended I didn't see him and drove away before he finished. That night I had this terrible dream, like Jack Nicholson in *The Shining*. You know, where he's the ax murderer?" She shivered theatrically.

"Did you mention him to your mother?"

"Oh, yes. When I did, she seemed very upset. She asked me if he'd spoken to me. I told her no. She said there should be a law against people like that. Naturally, we ended up in an argument over it. I told her he couldn't help looking like he did. With a face like that, he probably couldn't get a decent job. She told me I didn't know what I was talking about. She said anyone who wants to work can get a job. She said I shouldn't be so sympathetic to the so-called underdogs, that they'd like nothing better than to have what we have. I don't know. Maybe she's right."

"Did you ever see him again?"

"No. But if I did and I had the nerve, I think I'd like to ask him what he was doing talking to my mother. Do you know him?"

"No, and I'm afraid you won't get to talk to him again. He was found shot to death yesterday."

She squeezed her eyes shut. "And it's all connected to what happened here, isn't it?"

"Yes, I think so, but I won't know for sure until I have all the facts."

Again, she looked as if she were about to say something, then changed her mind. "Well, I really hope you get them," she replied distractedly, pushing herself up on her feet and brushing off the white pants. "I should be getting back now.

Nicki or my mother will be home soon. They'll wonder where I am."

I stood up next to her. "There's something else, isn't there, Laura?"

She touched her head on both sides, following the hair back to the clip that held it in a thick braid.

"You can read minds, too, can't you?"

"Sometimes."

She started to walk toward the gate. I kept pace with her. "There is something else. I shouldn't really be telling you this, but I will. It might help. I saw Tom at Madelaine's the night she was killed."

"Are you sure?"

"Well, I wasn't at first. It was still early in the evening, but it was already dark. I'd just finished watching *Risky Business* on the VCR and was wandering around the backyard. I thought I saw him out on Professor Celli's back deck. I couldn't imagine what he was doing there. But I decided not to let it bother me. After all, we're separated and he's free to do what he wants. I went to bed without giving it another thought. The next morning the police came to tell us there'd been a murder. I didn't say anything about Tom because I really wasn't sure. I didn't want to start any trouble if I was wrong. So I waited until that evening and then drove over to our old house in Beverly Hills and told him what I'd seen. I knew then that he had been there."

"He admitted it?"

"No, no, he denied it. He said he'd been home all night and that I was mistaken, but I knew."

"How?"

"It's not hard to tell when Tom's lying."

"You could have said something to the police afterward. Why didn't you?"

She stopped at the gate and said matter-of-factly, "I didn't say anything because Tom asked me not to. Besides, I know he didn't do it."

"How do you know?"

"Because I asked him. If he'd been lying, I would have known it. I told you, I can tell when he's not telling the truth. I can even tell when he doesn't know whether he's telling the truth or not."

That threw me. "I'm not sure I understand. You mean he sometimes doesn't know whether he's lying?"

"Yes, exactly. There're times when he gets confused." She frowned. "Tom used to have a lot of problems with alcohol and drugs. He's been okay for the last few years, but when he was younger, he used to do things and not always remember what he'd done. That was years ago. He's different now. You'd probably like him." She smiled shyly.

"You still care for him, don't you?"

"Yes," she admitted. "But in a funny way. I've known Tom practically all my life. My mother began working for TEK when we first moved down to Los Angeles, and we somehow just ended up spending a lot of time with the Greeves, too. Tom and I've been friends practically forever. I guess maybe we identify with each other so much because I'm an only child and he's the baby of the family." She shrugged. "I don't know. My psychiatrist hasn't gotten to that yet in my analysis. Maybe in a couple of years," she reflected hopefully.

"One more question," I said.

"Sure."

"Does anyone in your family own a gun?"

She gave me a puzzled look, then said, "My mother-in-law does. I think she still does anyway. She once showed me a mahogany box with a pistol in it and told me she'd been a champion shooter when she was in college. But that was a long time ago."

"Do you know what kind of a gun it is?"

"No. Just that it was ugly."

"Does anyone else own one? Neil? Your mother? Nicki? Tom? Your father-in-law?"

She thought for a moment, then shook her head. "No. Just Amelia. But I could ask if you'd like. Discreetly, of course."

"I'd rather you didn't."

"Okay." She opened the gate, then paused. "Do you mind if I ask you a question?"

"No."

She glanced back at the cottage, then at me. "If a wife knew that another woman was destroying her marriage, would it be normal for that wife to think about killing the other woman?"

"You mean like Madelaine and Tom and you?"

"Like anyone," she said waving her hand in the air, presumably taking in the entire coast line. "Like you."

"I suppose it might be normal to think it," I said, reminding myself of what Liz had admitted to me when we'd talked about Anne, Claire, and myself. "I suppose we all think about things at times that we'd never do."

"Yes, that makes sense." She sounded relieved, then cocked her head to one side. "I did think it, you know."

I nodded. "Yes. I can imagine."

"You're sweet. Thanks for understanding." She took a short step forward, stood on tip-toes, and kissed me on the cheek, then whirled and went through the gate without looking back.

Twenty-Three

I called Shirley Bass at Don Claypole's office and asked her to an early lunch.

She was a secret writer of poetry and short stories. She took me to her place on Beverly Glen Boulevard to show me what she had written.

I read her poetry and two of her short stories and promised we could be friends, and she told me everything she could about Don Claypole. By the time I dropped her back on Melrose and headed off again, I had a fair idea where Claypole fit into the picture.

First, Shirley had been able to identify Don Claypole's new client, the one which was apparently keeping the doors open. It was TEK Industries. The deal had been set up by TEK's executive vice-president, Margaret Patterson, the same Maggie who had called when I had been in Claypole's office. The same Maggie who was Tom Greeves's mother-in-law and Laura's mother. The new client had come on board a week after Claypole had begun his search for Trudy's father. The TEK deal stipulated that Claypole and his associates would work exclusively for the corporation during the initial two years of the contract. It had been finalized in a week, and fat checks had begun coming in immediately afterward. As far as Shirley knew, no actual work had been done for TEK yet.

She speculated that Claypole might be mapping out strategy with Mrs. Patterson.

Second, she said, Claypole had gotten a phone call the previous day from someone she thought had said his name was Harold. I had asked her if it could have been Neil Harold, but she wasn't sure. Right after the call, Claypole had shot out the door, saying he'd be out until three today. He hadn't mentioned where he was going.

Third, she said Claypole kept a pistol in the safe in the office. She had seen it once, but she had no idea what kind of gun it was. She said she'd even offer to check it for me, but Claypole was the only one who had the combination to the safe. I told her to forget that we'd even had our little conversation. Grinning, she promised she would.

I drove along Santa Monica Boulevard, adding it all up. Most of the pieces still didn't fit, but at last the momentum was definitely on my side. There were still persons unknown, who might stoop to anything—even murder—to keep me from the truth. But I was pissed off enough to keep going.

Jay's Exotic Dancers sat on Santa Monica between a drug store and a Chinese fruit stand. I pulled up and parked in an empty spot out front. It was two-thirty and hot enough to refry beans on the sidewalk. I was hoping to catch the end of Elena's act.

Inside, a grinding disco beat pounded out through six speakers in the cavelike room. Air conditioning made the room cold but not cold enough to kill the stink of years of stale beer. A T-shaped stage stuck out in the middle of the floor. Under an amber spotlight, a platinum blonde undulated, more or less to the music. Her pink sequined bikini revealed fifteen more pounds than she needed. The only customer in sight was a beefy man wearing a Padres baseball cap and a yellow Hawaiian shirt. He was parked beside the stage, languidly waving a dollar bill at the blonde.

A bartender with a handlebar mustache stood behind the bar polishing glasses, occasionally shifting his broad shoulders. Two more ladies in sequined bikinis perched at the end of the bar. The thinner black one with reddish brown hair was fastidiously doing her nails. The heavier brunette nursed a pink drink through a straw.

The bartender told me Elena had just left but if I hurried I might catch her in the back parking lot.

I walked toward the rear exit. As I passed the stage, the man in the Hawaiian shirt slipped the dollar bill into the crotch of the blonde's bikini. She let his fingers linger there a second, then deftly moved back out of his reach.

I pushed down on the crash bar on the rear door and stepped back out into the bright light again. The hot air hit me like a mouthful of chili peppers.

At first glance, I thought Elena was necking with someone with her back pressed up against the side of a black Buick. The someone was a muscle-bound giant with a bald head, wearing a gray sweatsuit and running shoes.

At second glance, I realized this was no love match. He was trying to pin her arms behind her back. At the same time he was doing a little dance to try to protect himself from her knee which was trying very hard to connect with his groin. Her fingers grabbed for his goatee.

"Elena," I yelled. They both twisted in my direction, then he opened the car door with one hand and tried to shove her in with the other. As he moved to one side, I caught a glimpse of someone else on the driver's side through the dark tinted glass. Whoever it was started the car. As far as I could tell, there was no one else in the parking lot.

As I ran toward them, the muscle man hit Elena hard in the stomach, knocking the wind out of her and bending her double so she fell backward into the rear seat.

I grabbed him by the back of his shirt just as he moved to scramble after her. I yanked him back hard, knocking the back of his bald noggin against the frame of the door as the car jerked forward. It screeched to a stop as I pulled him back out of the door.

Elena came out with him, gasping for air but clinging tenaciously to the front of his sweatshirt. She sagged to the ground as he wheeled to face me.

"Run," I shouted, but she just lay there, her face pressed to the tarmac.

Muscle man came at me with a fist the size of a pineapple. It was destined for my chin. I moved quick enough so it missed my face and just grazed my shoulder. Even at that, it was enough to spin me backward a half step. I hit him hard on the side of the head with two fast lefts. It was like hitting cement. Elena was on her hands and knees, but it looked like a while before she'd get up.

He rocketed toward me again, throwing two punches that would have decapitated a bronze statue if they'd connected.

Neither did. I hit him on the side of the head. He shook it off with a chuckle that made my heart sink.

He lunged and missed again, giving me an easy shot at his nose. I took it. I felt the cartilage shatter under my fist and saw the rage in his eyes as the blood spurted out. I was hoping Elena would do me a favor and get up and run real soon before this gorilla got lucky.

But she just knelt there and wheezed.

I stooped to grab her and lift her to her feet, but I had to let go when he charged again like a bleeding warthog.

What neither of us saw was what ended it.

The lanky Chinaman from the fruit stand came out the back door of his shop and began hosing us all down, shrieking that he'd called the police.

And son of a bitch if there weren't sirens filling the air in the distance.

Muscle man heard them, too. One final furious glare at me, one last regretful look at Elena, then he dove into the back seat of the Buick. The car jerked away with a shriek of tires before he even had the back door closed.

I made a mental note of the license number, then grabbed Elena by the hand, picked up her purse, hung it over her shoulder, and quickly led her back into Jay's Exotic Dancers. She didn't resist, not even when we got inside. The fellow in the Hawaiian shirt was adding another bill to the platinum blonde's cache as we crossed the room. Elena kept her head down when we passed the bar. The other two dancers and the bartender pretended we were invisible.

I led her out front and helped her into the Jeep. I got in on the other side and was just pulling away from the curb as a black-and-white headed down the back alley toward the fruit stand.

Elena stared out the windshield as I made a couple of turns that put us on Sunset. The hot wind began drying us out. The spray from the Chinaman's hose had washed away the heavy makeup Elena had used to hide the bruise on her left cheek.

I drove for a couple of minutes, then pulled into a coffee shop just east of the Strip that I knew would be nearly empty at this time of day. I pulled around the back of the parking lot, fished a few towels out of a gym bag I had in the back, and handed a couple to Elena, and used the remaining one on myself to wipe the gorilla's blood off my hands. She dried off her hair and her face, then reached in her purse and pulled out a couple of jars of cream and powders and turned the side mirror around so she could see herself clearly.

A couple of minutes later, the bruise was covered up and her black hair was combed neatly into place—that is, slicked back on the sides and standing straight up on top in long black spikes.

When she was done, she turned and gave me a dull look and said, "Thanks. I guess I should get a taxi now and go back and get my car."

"Give it a half hour," I told her. I offered to buy her a drink while she waited.

She stopped and thought for a second, then agreed.

We went inside and set up shop in a nice quiet booth in the back where no one would hear us.

She ordered herb tea. Famished from all the exercise, I ordered a bottle of Coors and a plate of eggs, a bowl of chili and three grapefuits.

"I got the license number of the Buick," I told her after the waitress had left with our order.

"You didn't have to," she informed me. "I know who they are."

I was hoping she'd tell me, but she fell silent again. She took out a cigarette and lit it. The waitress made her way across the room to bring us our drinks. When she was out of earshot again, I asked, "Were they friends of Johnny Sylvester?"

She blew a stream of blue smoke over my head, then looked at me with a tough, cold frown. "Look, I'm glad you came along when you did. I'm glad you helped me out of a jam, but that doesn't give you the right to butt into my life." She grabbed her purse and started to get up.

"Sit down," I told her. I would have knocked her back down if I had to. I think she knew it.

She glared, but she sat.

"Now, you look. I didn't just happen to come along. I was there because I was looking for you. You lied to the police about giving my number to Johnny Sylvester. You lied about when you last saw Madelaine. I don't know what else you've lied about. I still haven't made up my mind whether you're part of the solution or part of the problem, and I'm not sure I care. What I do care about is a three-year-old girl who has no one else to look after her interests. With or without your help, I'm going to make sure she's taken care of. I'd prefer with, but if I don't get it, I'll take you head on, lady, or go around you, or right on over you if I have to. Do we understand each other?"

She tore off the top of a packet of sugar and poured it into her tea and stirred. She kept her inky black eyes on me the whole time, but the fight had gone out of them.

"All right. What do you want to know?"

"Let's start with Madelaine. How many times did you see her after she left for San Francisco?"

"Just a couple. Once in a while, she'd call and invite me up. She'd even send tickets if I didn't have the money. I'd go up and stay a couple of days, then fly back."

"You drove up once with Johnny Sylvester six months ago."

She shook her head. "I didn't drive up. I flew," she insisted.

"You showed up at Madelaine's door in an old station wagon, " I reminded her.

"How do you know that?"

"Never mind. Just tell me what happened."

"I didn't drive up with him," she corrected me primly. "He was already up there. He called and said Mad wanted to see me. Said it was important. He wired me the money for the tickets and then met me at the airport. It turned out she didn't even know I was coming. He and Mad had had a fight of some kind and he was just using me as an excuse to get to see her. I didn't care. It was a good break for me. I was ready to stay a few days when we got there. I'd taken a very late flight and was beat, so I went to sleep in Mad's room while the two of them talked. When I woke up it was the middle of the night. Mad was sitting beside me on the edge of the bed. She said she wasn't feeling so well. She didn't look so hot either. She asked me if I'd mind leaving, said she wanted to be alone. I told her sure, I didn't mind. Well, I minded, but I wasn't going to make a big deal out of it. If she didn't want me there, she didn't want me there. Johnny dropped me back at the airport and that was that."

"Do you know what the fight was about?"

"No. I asked him, but all he'd say was, 'It's business.' Those two had some sort of deal together, but I never understood it. I asked a couple of times, but no one ever told me anything."

The waitress brought my food.

After she'd gone, I asked, "Do you know when Madelaine first met Johnny?"

"Not for sure. I first started to see them together right after she moved into my place in Hollywood. He just started coming around. Like I told you, I was spending a lot of time at my boyfriend's place and was working crazy hours, so I wasn't around much, but Johnny showed up sometimes when I was there alone and just hung out.

"At first, I thought he was pretty creepy. I mean, like you saw his face. Right out of Frankenstein. But he'd kid around a lot and make me laugh, and sometimes he'd bring around a little coke or a little weed and lay it on me, so I figured he was okay. I don't mean like I liked him or anything. I mean, he was okay, like a friend. I couldn't figure out what was going on between him and Mad though. I'd ask, but all she'd say was he was looking after her interests and exposing her to culture. He used to take her to football games and the race track. A real culture nut, right? But then what do I know? Johnny used to say she was something real special, that she had what it takes to grab the brass ring and that he'd help her get it. Me, I thought it was all bullshit. Then, the next thing I knew, it was like she was a different person. She was reading books, talking different, and acting different. It was like she became somebody else."

Elena rolled her teacup between the palms of both hands and sipped the pallid brew. "Funny, when she moved out, I figured that was the last I'd ever see of her. You know, like she was on the fast track and I wasn't even on the train. Now, she's dead." Elena frowned distastefully. The thought of death made her nervous.

"Did you see her much after she moved out, before she left for San Francisco?" I asked, scraping the pulp out of one of my grapefruits.

"I didn't see her at all for four or five months. She'd call and ask how I was, and we'd bullshit about getting together, but we never did. She said she was modeling and was seeing a couple of guys, but she never said who they were. Then, one day, she called me at work. I was dancing days then and had just broken up with my boyfriend and was feeling kind of like rat shit. She asked me if she could drop by the apartment that night. I told her sure. She said she still had the key and would I mind if she just met me there. That was fine with me.

"When I got home, I found out she'd brought along a couple of suitcases. She said she had a little problem and

wanted to know if it was okay to stay for awhile. She said she
had money to pay half the rent. I told her to forget it, I had
plenty of room and I was glad to have her."

"Did she say where the money came from?"

"I didn't ask. I assumed it was from modeling. She'd been
working a lot. Done a couple of magazine covers, I think."

I scooped the last of the eggs from my plate. There was
nothing left but the thin orange slice garnishing. I ate that too
and washed it all down with the last of the beer. "Did she say
what kind of trouble she was in?"

"When I asked, she laughed and said I'd just worry if I
knew. I told her that made me worry more, but she played
like it was a game and wouldn't tell me. The strange thing
was that I really did start to worry. You know how you
sense something is really wrong? I mean, she never left the
apartment. She'd call me at work and ask me to make little
shopping trips for her. When I was there, she'd never answer
the telephone, even when I was in the shower. She started
putting on weight. I'm not stupid—I know a pregnant woman
when I see one. Finally she admitted she was four months
pregnant. I asked if that was the trouble. She said that was
the solution. She said the trouble was a woman with a gun
who'd shown up at her place and threatened to blow her
head off. She said the kid was her insurance policy. I thought
she was kidding around about the woman with the gun. I told
her she wasn't making sense. She said to forget it, that she'd
said too much already. I didn't know if she was kidding or
not, but everything seemed to work out okay."

"How do you mean 'okay'?"

"I mean like *okay*." She gestured to indicate something
big. "Like about a week after that she said her boat had come
in. She kissed me and said she was moving to San Francisco.
I asked her about the baby and money. She thought that was
funny. She said she'd never have to worry about money for
the rest of her life. She'd tell me all about it some other time.
Said she was leaving at the end of the week. Two days later, I
came home and found a note from her and an envelope with
hundred dollar bills in it, ten of them. It said, 'Sorry to put
you through all this. Go out and buy yourself something nice.
I'll call you when I get settled.' That was pretty damned
bitchin' of her. She didn't have to do that. Mad was special."

She lit another cigarette from the butt of the one she'd

been smoking and studied the end of the new cigarette while crushing out the old one in the ashtray.

"That was around the end of August '81. I remember 'cause my boyfriend and I split up just before that."

"When was the next time you heard from her?"

She took a puff and blew a jet of smoke over my head. "About eight months later. That's when she sent me the tickets to come up the first time. Trudy was only a few months old. They lived in this nice house on Russian Hill. Mad said it was hers. At first I thought she must still be modeling, but she said she'd retired. I tried to get her to talk about Trudy's father or boyfriends and stuff like that, but all she wanted to talk about was baby stuff and recipes and junk she was buying for the house. She never told me anything about the kid's father or the bread."

"When was the last time you saw her?"

"The time I went with Johnny. She called a couple of months after that and said she was down in LA looking for a place and we'd get together the next time she came back. After she moved to Malibu, she called and said she was trying to settle a few things and as soon as she did she'd call. A couple of weeks later, I read she was dead."

"Did she say what kind of things?"

"No. Just things. Look, I don't know what you're thinking, but I was pretty shook up by her death. I liked her a lot."

The waitress brought Elena more hot water for her tea and a second Coors for me.

"You never mentioned Johnny to the police. How come?"

She took a deep drag on her cigarette, then slowly let the smoke out, twirling the lit end against the side of the ashtray. "I guess I should have. I guess I was stupid. Johnny showed up the day I saw the article in the paper about Mad's murder. I was in a little trouble with the cops a few years ago. I got off pretty light, but I know what police are like. Johnny had his own problems with cops. He'd been in the can a few times. He said since they already had the killer, the best thing for us to do was to stay out of it. That made sense. Besides, when you come right down to it, I don't know very much."

"You know about him. You kept in touch after Mad went to San Francisco."

She studied her mug for a couple of seconds as if the answer might be on the bottom, then looked up at me. "Actually, it was the other way around. He kept in touch with me.

He'd ask me to pose for some photos once in a while. Nude shots, soft core fillers. He did a lot of real porn too, and he asked me to do it, but I told him it wasn't for me. A few times he had me working the car shows and conventions as a hostess. It was good quick money, so I didn't complain. Sometimes he tried to set me up on dates, but I told him no. I don't hook. I get plenty of chances for that sort of thing where I work. You're walking a pretty thin line when you do what I do. You either keep your head straight or your brain fries. That's how it is." She stopped, stubbed out the old cigarette, reached for a new one. The pack was empty. She crumpled it and scowled out the window. I could see the dull shadow of her bruise through her makeup.

"Johnny give you that mark?"

She touched her hand lightly to the spot. "Yeah," she admitted. "I called to warn him you'd come by. He came right over to see me. He acted real jittery, kept pumping me, wanting to know what I'd said. I told him none of his business. I was only telling him out of courtesy. He started screaming at me, calling me stupid, saying I didn't know anything. I told him to get stuffed. He hit me. He was sorry right away, kept apologizing, saying he didn't mean it, but that something was up, a big deal, and if I could just keep my mouth shut, he'd take care of me. He even tried to give me some money, a hundred bucks. He said he'd like to give me more but he owed a lot to the sharks. He kept saying he'd make it up to me. I told him to forget it. He wouldn't leave until I promised I wouldn't call you or say anything. The next time I saw him was in the morgue."

"Why didn't you tell the police what you just told me?"

"What for? You think the cops would believe me? Besides, whoever got him might decide to get me too if they thought I knew anything. Anyway, I don't know who killed him."

"But you know who the sharks are, don't you?"

"Sure. Zip Guzzo. Johnny was always into him for something. Somehow he'd always manage to pay it off. Those were Guzzo's boys in the parking lot. The big one's name is Satori. They call him the Shrimp. The driver is called Mooch. I don't know his real name."

"Do you think they might have killed him?"

She smiled grimly at my naïveté. "What for? Johnny was a good customer. He was worth more to them alive. They might beat him up a little if he got too far behind in his payments, but they wouldn't kill him. Besides, he only owed them around thirty grand. That's not exactly a fortune."

"What did they want with you?"

"Johnny used to give the impression that he had cash stashed away somewhere. Talked about money in the bank. I guess Guzzo figures I know where it is. If I did, I'd grab it and run, wouldn't I?"

"Would you?"

She gave me a sharp look but said nothing.

"Did Johnny own a gun?"

"No, not that I know of. Said guns were too hot, hotter than dope, with his record."

"Did he ever tell you his real name?"

"Sure. Johnny Sylvester."

"No," I told her. "His real name was Jimmy Lucie."

It took a couple of seconds for the penny to drop. Then, she gave me a puzzled look and asked, "You mean like in Madelaine *Lucie*?"

"Like in Madelaine Lucie."

"They were related?"

"Jimmy Lucie—or the man you knew as Johnny Sylvester— was married to Madelaine's mother."

"You mean Jimmy was like Mad's father?"

"Something like that."

She sat back. "You're bullshitting me, right?"

"No. I'm telling you the truth."

She stared at me with the smile frozen on her face until she convinced herself there was no reason for me to lie. Then she patted the black spikes on the top of her head. "That little gumball and Mad? . . ." She didn't bother to finish. "I don't believe it. That's the craziest thing I've ever heard."

"Believe it," I told her.

"Jesus, that's incredible," she breathed. "What else?"

"I was hoping you'd tell me. We're still missing a father for Trudy."

"Yeah. I can see where you're coming from, and I wish I could tell you something more, but I can't."

"You sure you've told me everything this time?"

She nodded. "Everything. I swear."

She looked me straight in the eyes. There was something that I liked about her, but I didn't believe her. She was holding back. But I'd gotten everything out of her that I was about to get for the moment.

"Okay," I said. "If you remember anything else, call me or come by." I wrote my name, address, and phone number on a napkin and gave it to her.

She read what I'd written, then chuckled, "Hey, same as last time."

"This time, don't give it away."

"Don't worry." She folded the napkin delicately and tucked it into her purse like a thousand dollar bill.

Twenty-Four

I drove her back to Jay's to pick up her car. The cops were gone, and there were no signs of the Shrimp, Mooch, or the black Buick. The fruit stand owner watched us nervously. Just to be on the safe side, I told her I'd follow her home.

"You don't have to."

I insisted. "Let's just make sure they're not waiting at your place."

"Whatever," she said with a shrug.

There was something endearing about her fatalistic attitude.

I followed her pink Honda over to Doheny and up to Butterfly Lane. She raced down the driveway as if eager to get home, or lose me, or both and was out of her car and halfway to her door by the time I parked. There were no other cars in the turnaround.

I figured everything was all right and I'd just tell her a quick goodbye.

Then, I heard Elena scream.

I ran to the house. The front door was open. A hurricane had ransacked the insides. Chairs lay smashed on the floor, her futon had been gutted, drawers had been pulled out and emptied. Even the molding along the floor had been torn out. Paintings lay heaped in the middle of the living room. Several had been ripped from their frames and slashed. A bag of cat litter was dumped over the floor of the sun porch. All the plants had been yanked out by their roots. There was dirt everywhere.

Elena stood on the edge of the chaos, just beyond the back door of the porch, mechanically calling, "Mustard. Here, baby, here. It's all right."

I went to her. Her face was pale white; her eyes, desperate.

She wouldn't look at me. She stared off into the woods as she spoke. "If anything's happened to him . . ." The cords of her neck pulsed like the strings of a musical instrument. Her fists were in knots clutching imaginary enemies. She raked the foliage with her eyes, straining to keep her voice under control as she crooned, "Here, Mustard. Come on, baby. It's me. No one's going to hurt you."

She walked forward a few steps and continued to implore the cat. Her lower lip quivered. Tears welled in those dark, impenetrable eyes. She sniffed them away and moved forward again a few feet, stopped and listened, then called out again, "Here, Mustard. Come here." She gave a short trilling whistle.

I remembered the hollowness I'd felt when I'd gone into my own house to look for Anne the night she'd been grabbed. I had gone from room to room, calling her name. It was like swimming through thick gauze.

"Here, Mustard. Here cat." The heat of Elena's fear radiated from her body like smoke off a brush fire.

Then, from somewhere deep in the thickets, came a forlorn mew.

We peered into the dense brush, then crept ahead cautiously, as if we both might have imagined it but dared not admit it. Elena continued to whistle. From somewhere overhead, there was another pitiful meow.

About thirty feet up in the high thin branches of a handsome green Pacific madrone, Mustard perched. As soon as he saw us, the mews changed to shrill petitions for aid.

Elena began to sob. "Oh, God, oh, my God. He's okay. How am I going to get him down? He's scared. He's stuck up there. My God."

Mustard's wails joined hers. He looked like he would enjoy nothing better than to crawl down but didn't know how. I remembered something Anne once told me about cats in trees. They always came down. No one had ever found a cat skeleton in one. I thought about telling Elena that but decided against it.

Instead I patted her shoulder and told her not to worry.

Meanwhile, Mustard was having a hard time. At each move, the branch he was on swung him out into the wide open spaces like some kid's ride at Disneyland.

"Come on, Mustard, jump," I called encouragingly, but Elena flashed me such a dirty look that I kept my mouth shut and simply stood by and waited for the inevitable.

In the end, it was impossible to determine whether he slipped or tried to jump and missed, but he plummeted a good halfway down to the ground before catching hold of a much larger branch that held his weight. He clung to his new perch without moving for a healthy period of time before he finally ventured the last leg of his descent.

Elena greeted him like a returning astronaut, hugging him to her bosom and weeping. She repeatedly kissed the top of his head. He repeatedly licked her face. Both acted like I wasn't there.

I could relate, but there were other considerations.

"Elena, I think it might be better if you had someone around for the next few days to keep an eye on you. If you'd like, I could arrange it."

She glared. "I don't want any help. I don't want anything." She said it so sharply that Mustard squirmed in her arms.

"Elena, I—"

"Just leave me alone, for God's sake," she snapped, cutting me off. "Just get the fuck out of my life. I don't want to talk right now. *Please*."

Okay, I thought, I understood how she felt. She'd been property raped. She needed to be alone. I wasn't about to get through to her by arguing. Whoever had searched her place either found what they were looking for or had decided it wasn't here. Otherwise, they'd still have been here when we'd arrived. So, for the moment she was probably safe.

I walked back past the devastation, wondering if they'd found Johnny Sylvester's stash or if there had even been one in the first place.

I wondered, too, what Elena knew that she wasn't telling me. And would she tell me before it was too late? Whatever it was, it would have to come from her. Anne used to say the hardest part about diagnosing wasn't chasing down what you suspected, but waiting for something to show that you *could* suspect.

The waiting, I thought as I drove out of there, was the worst part of any business or disease.

Twenty-Five

I found unexpected company when I arrived home. Don Claypole stood beside a gray Oldsmobile with a half-smoked cigar clenched between his teeth. He gave me a hard, unwavering look as I drove up and parked the Jeep beside him.

He stepped up to the door while I was getting out, giving me only a couple of feet to stand.

"You're making a damn mess of things," he said, without even so much as a hello. Gray bags hung like dirty laundry under his eyes.

"What things? I'm afraid I don't know what you're talking about."

"You know damned well what things, Paris," he growled, making an attempt to suck in his enormous belly when he spoke. I could see the slight bulge under his left arm where his gun holster stuck out. His fleshy face was purple. He jabbed a stubby finger at me. "You had lunch with my receptionist. Don't deny it. One of my men saw you dropping her off."

"What's the problem?" I asked coolly. "We're both adults." Claypole was a stick of dynamite looking for an excuse to go off.

"You grilled her about me. You used her. You're trying to bitch things up for me."

"She told you that?"

"She didn't have to. I've been in this business long enough to know when someone's lying to me. I fired her."

"Because she had lunch with me?"

"You sonovabitch."

I saw the punch coming in plenty of time to get out of the way.

"Take it easy, Don," I told him, putting up my hands to keep him off.

"You sonovabitch," he swore again, taking another swing at my face. He stumbled as I stepped out of the way. I could smell the liquor on his breath as he brushed by me.

He wheeled and faced me and spat the cigar out. "I'm going to teach you a lesson, hotshot."

He should have known better. Maybe it was age, maybe it was because he was a little drunk, and maybe it was simply that he'd been pushing people around most of his life and getting away with it that he thought he could pull it off. He came at me like a bull. He grabbed hold of my collar and tried to get in close to hit me.

I slipped a foot behind his leg and tipped him over easily. His back hit the gravel with a thud. His hair flopped away from his bald spot and hung in the air like a rooster's comb. The look on his face was a mixture of surprise and humiliation.

He went for his gun.

I dropped with both knees into his chest, flattening him back out again like an overgrown butterfly and yanking his hand away from his holster. I grabbed the gun. It was a .38 caliber Smith and Wesson Police Special.

Claypole's eyes bulged as I cocked the hammer in his face. I aimed over his head at my gate post, fired off two rounds into the wood, then opened the cylinder and emptied the spent shells and the remaining bullets into my palm.

He'd gone from purple to a mottled white. I tucked the empty gun back in his holster and pocketed the shells.

"I'll let you up now," I told him, "if you can keep your hands to yourself."

He didn't answer. His eyes bulged, but the fight had gone out of him.

I got off and stood back a few feet to make sure he wasn't about to try anything foolish. He struggled up on his haunches, then painfully lifted himself the rest of the way up.

"I don't know what you got against me," he wheezed. He rubbed his right hand over his chest—not where the gun had been, but where his heart was. "I don't know why you think you have to dig up dirt on me. I haven't done anything."

"If you really don't know, Don, then the only advice I can give you is get out now," I told him. At the very least, he knew—and he knew that I knew—that he had broken the unwritten code of the business when he'd dropped Mrs. Coltrane's case in favor of a sweeter deal. But that wasn't enough to hang him. "If you do know," I warned, "be prepared. You're coming down with the rest of them."

"That sounds like a threat," he grumbled. Some of the color had seeped back in his face. He seemed to be having an easier time breathing.

"I'm not vindictive. I'm just sensitive. I was in San Francisco last night. Someone tried to shoot me. They were using a .38. You wouldn't know anything about that, would you?"

He paled again. "You don't think it was me, do you?"

"If it was you, you wouldn't have come charging up here like you just did," I surmised. "But I wouldn't be surprised to discover you were up in San Francisco yesterday. I wouldn't be surprised if you carried your gun with you, and I wouldn't be surprised if you even had it checked with the crew on the flight up and back like the law demands. There's probably a record of it somewhere. So, if someone needed to, they could point a finger at you. Think about it."

"You're messing with things that you don't understand," he repeated under his breath.

"You're being used, Don."

"You're a fool, Paris. A fucking fool. You're going to pay for this."

He combed his hair back over his bald spot with his fingertips and stalked back to his car.

Mean as he was, I felt sorry for him. He wasn't smart enough to be who he thought he was. That, Anne used to say, was the worst way to get into trouble.

I went inside and made a quick call to Shirley Bass at home.

"Oh, hi," she chirped as soon as she heard my voice. "Guess what? I just got fired. I'm just on my way out to meet a girlfriend. We're going to celebrate. Want to join us?"

"Another time," I told her. "I just wanted to make sure you were okay."

"Thanks. Best thing that ever happened to me." She giggled.

I hung up and called Liz at home.

She filled me in on the latest.

"Arla seems to be holding her own. Matt's been great with Trudy. I'm just getting dinner ready for both of them now. There's plenty if you feel like coming by. If not, maybe I could leave Matt here to babysit and come up to see you."

"Dinner sounds nice, but I'll have to skip it. I have a few

more errands to run. Might take me a while. I'll call you when I'm back."

I spoke to Matt for a few seconds. Everything appeared okay on that end. I was reasonably sure I was the target, not Trudy, but, just to be on the safe side, I asked Matt to hang in.

I went back outside to the gate. It took me a good twenty minutes to pry out the slugs from Don Claypole's gun.

I went back inside and put the two slugs in a small envelope and marked it "B." I put the envelope next to the one I'd labeled "A," the envelope containing the slug I'd dug out of the wood in San Francisco.

I took all the pictures I had—Madelaine Lucie, Jimmy Lucie/Johnny Sylvester, Joyce Coltrane Lucie—and spread them out on the ledge over my desk and just stared. What it all added up to was three deadly nights spread out across twenty-two years.

Joyce, the misfit, the fat girl. Jimmy/Johnny, the Svengali, the freak. And Madelaine. The most haunting of all. Even in her photos, there was something about her that reached out and grabbed at a man's balls. Aloof. Unobtainable. Unpossessable. Like diamonds that melt in your hand or gold that vanishes under your breath.

Funny, I thought. She was around the same age as Anne when I'd fallen in love with her and married her. I stared at the pictures and told myself that I couldn't imagine falling for her, but I could. In a way, I had, though I'd seen no more than the pictures. She'd reached out, right from that very first day, reached out from the grave and grabbed at me.

I booted my computer, called up my word processing program, and began to type with the pictures staring down at me. I banged out everything I'd found out about Mrs. Coltrane, Trudy, Madelaine Lucie, Jimmy Lucie/Johnny Sylvester, Elena Rachel, Don Claypole, and the Greeves family, including Margaret Patterson. I made notes of my visits to Mrs. Pinfield, the old man in San Pedro, Fred Jessel, Matt Hecker, and my lawyer friend Marvin Feldman, who'd filled me in on Simon Greeves's paternity suit. I made a comprehensive report on my interviews with Colin Smythe, Richard and Cathy Silliphant, Jack Starch, and the others in San Francisco. It took an hour to get it all down. When I was done, I sealed it into an envelope and scribbled a note to Marvin Feldman, instructing him to hand-deliver it to Peter Blanche if anything should happen to me in the next few days. Then I sealed it into a second envelope and addressed it to Feldman. When I finished, I called Pete Blanche at home.

"I just walked in," he said. "What's up?"

I could hear him chewing on something as he spoke. "I need a favor. Can I buy you a drink?"

He hesitated for a fraction of a second, then agreed. "Sure. You know the Brass Monkey on Pico? It's right around the corner from my place."

"I've driven by it. I'll meet you there in forty-five minutes."

"I'll start without you."

I hung up, climbed back in the Jeep, and drove down to Beverly Hills. I dropped the envelope through the mail slot at Feldman's office, then drove back to Pete's bar.

The Brass Monkey was nearly empty. A couple of middle-aged beer drinkers in sweatshirts and jeans sat at one end of the joint watching the Dodgers and Giants on the television. The bartender stood behind the bar counting cash.

Pete was sitting in a dark corner at a table wolfing a plate of nachos and cheese. He was already ahead of me by two bourbons. He gave me a meager smile under his drooping mustache as I slid into the seat across from him.

A chubby waitress in a miniskirt came up and took my order and came back a minute later with another bourbon for Pete and a Scotch for me.

"Hobbish called me this afternoon from San Francisco," he informed me.

"What did he say?"

"Not much. Just that he's worried about you."

"Why?"

"Said he had a feeling."

"Hobbish likes to worry."

"Well, I don't, and I'm worried, too."

"About what?"

"You. You got something hanging over your head. I can see it in your eyes. You gonna tell me?"

"Can I trust you, Pete?"

He looked grim. "Yeah, you can trust me, Evan, but only so far. I'm a cop. I'm paid by the county. I gotta work within the rules. You know that."

"That's your answer, Pete. For the time being, I have to go it alone."

"You never were a group player, were you?" He yanked on the left side of his mustache.

"I guess not. But don't worry. If anything should happen, it's all down in writing. You'll be contacted."

He nodded. "Okay. Fair enough. Now, you did say you needed help. What kind?"

I slipped the two envelopes with the slugs out of my pocket and handed them across the table.

He opened the flaps and peered inside.

"Where'd you get these?"

"Crackerjacks."

"Funny man. I forgot. I'm not supposed to ask." He shook the envelopes once more and then added, "They're too big for the gun that killed Johnny Sylvester."

"I know. But run them through the lab anyway. See if the two in envelope B came from the same gun as A. I don't think they did, but just make sure."

"Okay. What else?"

I thought about having him check out gun registrations on the Greeves clan but decided against tipping my hand just yet.

"That's it."

"That's it?"

"That's it."

I left Pete sitting there nursing his fourth bourbon and a giant burrito with sour cream on top.

I started for home. I thought about Liz again but decided to stick to my original plan and not go near her for the time being. It was dark, and I had no idea what kind of trouble was trailing me now. There wasn't much I could do but sit and wait for something to happen. I'd shaken enough trees for one day.

Besides, I hadn't had much sleep in the last forty-eight hours. I'd be doing both Liz and myself a favor to crawl into bed alone.

It sounded like a good idea, but it didn't work out that way.

Once again, I had company. The night had gone foggy. The floodlights from the house dimly silhouetted a car at the top as I started up the driveway. I couldn't make out whose until I was almost there.

I was only a hundred feet away when I recognized Elena Rachel's pink Honda sitting there like a piece of virgin bubble gum. She was stretched out on the hood with her back resting against the windshield. Dressed in a heavy black trench coat with the collar pulled up, she puffed on a cigarette and gazed out into the fog.

As my brights passed through her window, Mustard's eyes caught the lights and gave off an eerie yellow-green glow from the top of the driver's seat.

I parked and got out. Elena didn't look up until I was practically beside her. Then she gave me a crooked smile.

"Thought maybe you'd moved," she said coolly. It was a studied coolness. Her hand trembled when she raised the cigarette to her lips.

"Do you want to come in?"

"Sure, why not," she said with the cigarette dangling precariously from her lower lip. She slid off the hood of the car. Mustard meowed and pressed his nose to the window. She gave him a sad, motherly look.

"You can bring him along," I told her.

"He's not big on dogs," she replied nodding toward the "vicious dog" sign Anne had put up.

"It's just a sign. There's no dog." Anyway, I thought, Zoot had never met a cat that he hadn't been able to charm.

I looked in the back seat of the car. There was a small suitcase, a bag of kitty litter, a plastic litter pan, two plastic bowls and six cans of gourmet cat food. She'd come prepared. "If you're planning to stay, he'd be more comfortable in the house."

She gave me a nod. "If you really wouldn't mind," she said.

"I really wouldn't," I told her.

She grinned, showing off her crooked tooth, then dropped her cigarette on the driveway and crushed it out with a pink plastic sandal. "You're okay. At least, I'm hoping you're okay."

"I'm okay," I assured her. "Let's get your gear inside."

She nodded gratefully, but the edge of fear was still there in her eyes.

I gathered up the suitcase, the bag of kitty litter and the plastic pan, the food, and the bowls while she took charge of the cat.

While she fixed up a spot on the back porch for Mustard, I made a quick call to Liz and told her I wouldn't be coming over. I promised to call again in the morning.

When I looked in on Elena, she was opening a can of cat tuna. She had already poured a bowl of water and fixed up the litter box. When she was sure he knew where everything was, she came back to the living room.

"You want something to eat?"

She shook her head.

"Relax," I told her. "I'll show you your room if you want."

She shook her head again. "I think you'd better take a look at these first," she insisted, reaching into her purse and pulling out a large manila envelope.

"What is it?"

"I'm not sure." Whatever it is, it wasn't making her very happy.

I opened the envelope and shook the contents out on the coffee table while Elena flopped down on the couch opposite me. A dozen eight-by-ten glossy photos spilled out. The compositions weren't much to write home about, but the subject matter was. Eight of the dozen photos showed Tom Greeves and Madelaine Lucie, naked and in various sexual acts. Neither seemed camera-shy. The remaining four shots were of Tom and Madelaine standing together on the back porch of the house Madelaine had rented from Professor Celli in Malibu. This time, they were both dressed, kissing or holding hands. A small yellow envelope contained the negatives for the twelve prints. Finally, there was a slip of paper with several scribbled notes and a phone number on it. One note said, "Tom = $$$$$." A second one said, "The bitch. Don't let her scare you." The last one said, "Make them pay." It was underlined three times. Someone had made a crude doodle of a woman with oversized breasts beside it.

"Where'd you get this?"

Her eyes fell sheepishly on her hands which were folded in a ten-finger pile on her lap. "It was buried out back of my place in a plastic envelope."

"How long have you had it?"

"I dug it up right after you left."

"Did you know it was there all the time?"

She looked up. "I didn't know it was there at all. It was only after I saw my place ripped apart that I got to thinking."

She stopped as if that was enough.

"Thinking about what? You better explain."

She nodded and pulled on one finger, tugging at an invisible ring. "About a week ago, I came home and found Johnny in the back, coming out of the woods with a shovel in his hand. I asked him what he'd been doing back there, and he said he'd come by and found a squirrel that Mustard must have killed and left on the back steps. Johnny knew how much I hate it when Mustard leaves dead things around." She grimaced squeamishly. "I didn't think much of it at the time. Johnny could be sweet when he wanted to. Then this afternoon, when we were back there trying to get Mustard out of the tree, I remembered it. After you left, I started to look around. I didn't even know what I was looking for. I only found the spot where he'd dug because I found a cigarette butt that Johnny had dropped. I got a shovel and started to dig. I was half expecting to find the squirrel. Instead, I found these in the plastic envelope."

"Do you recognize the guy in the picture with Madelaine?"

"No."

"Does the name Tom Greeves ring any bells?"

"It's one of the names you asked me about the first time you came to see me. That's the only time I ever heard it," she said, fidgeting with her purse and taking out a cigarette.

"Did you tell anyone else about the pictures?"

She nodded grimly as she struck a match to the end. Her hand trembled noticeably.

"Who?"

She hugged her arms around herself as if suddenly cold. "The guy on the other end of that number," she explained, pointing with the cigarette to the piece of paper with the phone number written on it.

"Who was that?"

"I don't know," she protested, "I didn't ask. I wasn't thinking. If I was thinking, I probably wouldn't have done what I did."

"I think we better start even farther back. I seem to be missing the opening chapters."

She paused and looked directly at me with frightened eyes. "Look, I didn't tell you everything this afternoon because I was scared. I don't even know what I was scared of Johnny mentioned something to me about two weeks ago that I figured was just bullshit, see. He was always bragging about something. I mean like he was always telling me how he knew big shots, like famous movie stars and stuff. He even said he had a pipeline to the governor and the White House if he wanted it. I'd laugh at him and say, If you got so much pull, how come you ain't rich? He'd laugh back and say I didn't understand real pull. Well, like I said, about two weeks ago, he came to me for some money. Said he needed a grand to tide him over. Lucky him, he just happened to know that I'd saved up nearly a grand to take some art classes. He said he only needed the money for a few days, he had something really big on the hook. He wouldn't tell me what at first, but when he saw I wouldn't give him the money otherwise, he said he had some photos of a very important celebrity. Nude ones. He was negotiating with a big magazine for the rights. He said they'd already offered him a hundred thou. My grand was just to keep Zip Guzzo off his back for a few more days. If I went along, he'd double my money. Stupid me, I went along."

"What happened?"

She took a long drag on the cigarette, burning it halfway down. "Nothing happened. I asked him about the photos, but he said it was better if I didn't know that part. I started having my doubts when he kept stalling and stalling. Finally, he told me he was having trouble with the first client but if he didn't come through, then he'd always be able to sell them to someone else."

"Any idea who he was talking to?"

"No, and I didn't hear anything from him for a couple of days. Then, you showed up, and I called him like I told you. He hit me just like I said he did, then offered me a hundred bucks to make up. *My* hundred bucks. I told him to keep it and give me back the whole thousand and pronto. He said not to worry, that things were going better than he'd planned. He said he thought he could sell the pictures twice, and when he did, there'd be a bonus in it for me. The next day he was dead." She crushed the cigarette in the ashtray like she was pushing in someone's face.

"What happened? Did anyone else try to contact you besides Guzzo and his boys?"

"No. Nothing happened except for the police. I just figured I was out of luck and my money was gone. I figured I got off easy compared to Johnny. The best thing I could do was forget the whole deal. I was doing just that when I got home this afternoon and saw what had happened to my paintings. I guess I flipped. My whole life has been trashed." She took out another cigarette but didn't light it. She just stared at the end. "If anything had happened to Mustard, I swear, I would have killed one of those turkeys."

"Guzzo's turkeys?"

"I don't know." She shook her head wearily. "It could have been him or some of his men looking for Johnny's secret stash, or it could have been someone looking for the photos. When I saw they were pictures of Mad, I knew the whole deal with the magazine had been bullshit. I mean, she wasn't a celebrity. It was something else, and whatever it was, it was the same something that had gotten Johnny killed. I was so mad, I wasn't even afraid. I wanted to fuck them over. I dialed the number on that sheet of paper. A man answered; I said I had the photos. I asked if he wanted them or not? He asked 'like what photos?' I told him not to play dumb. Either he wanted them or he didn't. He said, yes, he wanted them. He asked me how much. I told him the price was the same. He said, 'Look, I did what the other guy said. I got the hundred grand. I went to meet him, but he never showed. I want to get this over with.' I mean like he acted like he didn't even know Johnny was dead."

"Maybe he doesn't."

She looked at me queerly. "You want to run that by me again?"

"Later. I want to hear the rest first."

She toyed with her cigarette, looked like she was going to stick it in her mouth, and then opted for sticking it back in the pack. "He wanted to know where to meet me. I thought of a place in Griffith Park near the Municipal Golf Course. I used to go there on picnics with my old boyfriend. It just popped into my head. I figured I'd go up there and pick up the cash and get the hell out. I didn't even think about where I'd get out to. Then, I sat down, smoked a joint, and started to get real fucking scared. I got sick to my stomach. I decided I was maybe real nuts. I packed up a suitcase, dumped Mustard in the car, and drove over here . . . I guess because you said you wanted to help me."

"I do," I assured her. "When did you say you'd meet the guy in Griffith Park?"

"Ten-thirty."

It was twenty after nine. It would take just about an hour to get there. We didn't have much time.

Twenty-Six

She insisted on coming with me, pointing out that Madelaine had been her friend.

We were ten minutes early. I had dug out the pistol I'd kept around the house. I was licensed to carry it, but all I'd ever used it for in the past year was shooting tin cans on the hillside in back. Maybe I'd still be able to say the same after the night was over.

The fog was thinner over the park. The moon intermittently poked through the clouds, but the trees and the lingering wisps of fog created dozens of dark pockets all around the area Elena had selected. A couple of bats cruised overhead. Elena wanted to know what they were. I told her sparrows. She rubbed her arms with her hands, looking thoroughly miserable.

The picnic area itself contained a half dozen wooden tables and had been partially cleared of trees and brush. Footpaths from the north, west, east, and south crossed the small clearing, giving our man a wide choice of entrances.

I made Elena stand with her back up against the thick trunk of a shadowy sycamore tree, which protected her from the rear. A damp breeze rattled the leaves overhead.

I squatted down beside a smaller tree ten feet away, giving me the best view of the three most likely directions for anyone to come in—from the path down the hill, from the path up the hill, and straight across through the thin patch of woods at the edge of the picnic area.

Our man was prompt. As I suspected, it was Tom Greeves. He came by the lower path, dressed in slacks and a light windbreaker. In one hand, he carried an attaché case. The other hand appeared to be empty. I kept my hand on the gun in my pocket. I had a flashlight stuck in my back pocket, but I wasn't about to use it. I wanted to see without drawing attention to myself. Better if Tom thought Elena was alone, at least initially. On the other hand, I didn't want to put her into any unnecessary danger.

Elena saw him a moment after I did. She stared over at me, looking petrified and gripping the envelope in both hands. I signaled to her to stay put. She nodded that she understood.

The light was working in our favor. He hadn't seen either of us yet.

I watched him closely. Almost too closely. Something moved in the woods opposite me.

A shadow. The tiniest glint of light reflected off the barrel of a pistol.

Diving toward Elena, I knocked her flat beneath me just as the first shots blasted out. The bullets chewed into the tree trunk and spat dirt around us. I counted five shots. It might have been six.

"Stay down. Don't move," I whispered urgently to Elena as I spun up into a crouch behind the tree, straining to get a better look.

Tom lay flat on his face on the path with his hands over his head. I couldn't be sure he was breathing.

I peered back where the shots had come from. The shadow fled, crashing noisily through the brush. I checked out the woods behind me as best I could, but I couldn't see anything. Grabbing Elena's arm, I dragged her back behind the tree.

She was trembling all over, moaning softly. The envelope lay on the damp grass. Her hands reached up and gripped my arm fiercely.

"Stay down," I whispered. "I'll be right back."

I had to pry her fingers off of my arm.

"You'll be okay," I assured her, stopping to stroke her cheek. "Don't worry."

She nodded, but she looked terrified. The tough girl facade had gone out for coffee.

I scrambled to my feet and dodged from tree to tree in a wide arc, heading toward the edge of the woods where the shots had come from. Tom Greeves had disappeared in the shadows. The darkness curled around me like mourners at a funeral. A car just on the other side of the woods started up, stalled, then started again. Tires squealed, then silence. I stepped farther into the woods, moving from tree to tree, twigs and leaves crunching beneath my feet.

I took the flashlight out of my pocket. The ground was moist, covered with grass and leaves. I found only one small print, probably made by a small, narrow, low-heeled shoe, belonging to a short man or a medium-sized woman. A second car started up farther down the hill. This sound, too, quickly evaporated into the night.

I continued on to where Tom had dropped. There was no sign of him.

I went back to Elena. She was still on the ground, face down, hands folded neatly beneath her chin.

"You okay?"

"I think so. Can I get up now?"

I helped her up.

"Did you see who fired at us?"

"No. Just a shadow."

That's all I'd seen. As she brushed the dirt off her clothes, I picked up the envelope and handed it to her.

She leaned against me, gave me a weak smile, and asked, "Can we get out of here now?"

"In a couple of minutes." I searched the tree trunk with my fingers until I found where one of the slugs had ripped into it. Using my pocket knife, I dug out a .25 caliber slug— the same size bullet that had killed Johnny Sylvester.

I slipped the slug into my pocket and walked to where Tom had fallen. Elena stuck to me like Scotch tape.

Tom had made a short trail as he'd crawled off into the woods. I started to follow it down the hill when Elena gave a loud gasp.

I spun around. She was pointing to the ground beneath a thick bush. My flashlight beam gleamed off the brass on the attaché case.

She was on it in a second, snapping the clasps and lifting the top.

The inside was filled with neat bundles of new twenty and fifty dollar bills.

Elena's black eyes gleamed. "We could take off. They'd never find us," she whispered.

I must have given her a rotten look.

Her apology came quickly. "Sorry. I'm getting crazy again. This stuff makes my mouth water." She stared down longingly at the money. "Forget I said anything." She closed the lid on the attaché case, snapped the clasps shut, and held it out to me. "Here. *You* take the money. *I'll* take the flashlight."

We traded and wasted another ten minutes looking around. There were no more footprints and no tire tracks in the spots where the other two cars must have been parked. We walked back to the Jeep and got in.

"What do we do now?" she asked.

"We go home and get a good night's sleep."

She gave me a quizzical glance, but was silent. As we drove, she opened her purse, rooted around in it for a couple of seconds and pulled out a joint. She lit it and took a deep drag, then held it out to me while holding the smoke in her lungs.

I shook my head no.

She blew out an uneven stream of smoke. "You know, we almost got killed. I mean like we almost died."

"I know," I told her.

"We're fucking lucky," she murmured prophetically, then took another deep drag off the joint.

We drove the rest of the way without further conversation. I settled her in the guest bedroom, set the alarm system that would pick up a fly trying to enter the premises, then had a couple of stiff drinks and a long, hot shower.

Sleep was a recurrent bad dream. I kept thinking of Jarrish and the night I had gone after him, rerunning it in my head like a film loop that kept playing and replaying the same story.

Twenty-Seven

Eddie's story didn't take long to tell. He told it to me while we stood there in the desert that night. Jarrish had lost out on several promotions over the years because of the case I'd made against him. Somewhere along the line, he'd decided to get me. Jarrish had stumbled on Eddie during a drug investigation and caught him with enough dope to send him away for life. He blackmailed Eddie into showing up at my place. At first, Eddie didn't know what Jarrish was up to. Later, Jarrish convinced him he was just after money, that he planned to kidnap Anne and hold her for ransom, and then release her unharmed. After all, Jarrish argued, I was rolling in dough. He convinced Eddie that they could get away with it. Jarrish had given Eddie a gun—the same gun Eddie had pointed at me—then the two of them had gone to my place after making sure I wouldn't be home. Jarrish had killed Zoot, Eddie said, to make it look real. They'd worn masks so Anne wouldn't recognize them, then afterward, split up. Jarrish was supposed to put Anne someplace safe, then meet Eddie on the highway near Barstow. Jarrish had arrived first. When Eddie showed up, Jarrish opened fire. Somehow, Eddie managed to escape. He'd been living a hand-to-mouth existence ever since.

Crazy as it all sounded, I knew Eddie was telling the truth. Tying up him and his junky girlfriend, I stashed them in a safe place. Then, I took Eddie's gun and drove to Jarrish's bungalow in Westwood.

On the way, I thought of every way you could kill a man. A bullet in his brain. A bomb in his car. Hands around his throat. A blade to the jugular vein like he had done to Zoot. Ways of torturing him first, making his death slower, more horrible.

There were honorable ways—letting him go for his gun first and beating him to the draw. A fair fight, pitting right against wrong. Celluloid fantasies that had nothing to do with real death. Artistic crap about the justice of revenge.

Freud had once talked about murder in terms of pleasure. A high. There were no laws against sticking one's hand in a fire because it hurt. But to kill is to taste the power of God. Anne had talked about Freud, and God, and being alive.

Jarrish was home watching the late night movie. He wasn't particularly surprised to see me. I'd visited him a couple of times during the early part of the investigation.

The grin on his face was patronizing. I caught a glimpse of my own in the hall mirror on the way in. I looked like I'd just come from hell. My cheeks were hollow, dark rings encircled my eyes. My hair was a tangle of straw. Jarrish flopped back down on the couch and flicked off the tube with the remote control. I sat down stiffly opposite him, drew the gun out of my pocket and set it on the glass-topped coffee table in front of me.

He sat poised like a snake, waiting.

He knew that I knew.

"Where'd you get that?"

"Eddie," I said.

He looked surprised. Or maybe amused. "You found him?"

"I found him, and he told me."

Jarrish sat up and rested his forearms on his knees.

"What did he tell you?"

"Everything," I said, "Everything, except why. Why'd you hurt her? Me, I could understand, but why her?"

"Anne *was* you, Paris. She was everything good about you."

"You never intended to go for the ransom, did you?"

"No. That was just a cover. I could have killed you, but so what? I wanted you to know what it felt like to walk around dead. That's what you did to me, Paris. That investigation of yours . . . you killed me, then left me to walk around dead. Now, we're even."

His body shifted to the right. I sensed it, more than I saw it. Then, I saw him hurl the channel changer at me with his pitching arm. It caught me on the side of the jaw like a hard punch and knocked me back. He dove toward a cabinet and yanked open a drawer.

Going for a gun.

I grabbed up Eddie's. Aimed point blank at his chest. I can kid myself that it all happened so fast I didn't have time to think, but I knew I had planned it; I knew I had wanted it to happen just like it had. In a way, I was no better than he was; I knew and I didn't care. I could see into the future and understand that later I would hate a part of myself. But at that moment, I felt Godlike and good. I pulled the trigger just as his hand came out of the drawer clutching something black.

The world exploded. The concussion from that explosion jolted the whole room.

The gun had blown up in my hand. The gun Jarrish had given to Eddie had been tampered with to explode and kill the shooter. Only Eddie had never fired it, not even when Jarrish had shot at him.

Jarrish was holding a shoe. A woman's black shoe. Anne's. The surprise on his face was because I'd survived the explosion miraculously unscathed. He'd gambled with a stacked deck and lost.

He flung the shoe at me and moved for the door.

I dove for the sonovabitch and brought him crashing to the floor. He twisted and grabbed for my throat with both hands, trying to tear my windpipe out of my neck. I hit him so hard it felt like my fist sank an inch into his face.

The police found me beating an unconscious man. They said if they'd arrived a few minutes later, there might not have been enough left of him to put on trial.

Twenty-Eight

Something soft like spider's legs brushed against my face. Fur in my mouth. I woke with a start. Mustard was sharing the pillow. As I shot up, he yawned and stretched, then bounced off the edge of the bed with a thump.

It was just after six. The sun was already up. Three puffy white clouds stretched across the horizon like the three little pigs floating in an otherwise clear, pale sky.

I got up, shaved and got dressed, and walked down the hall toward the guest room. The door was open. Elena was gone. She'd made up the bed. Mustard had moved onto her pillow and was sunning himself in the wash of light that streamed through her window. His stare accused me of following him around. He gingerly crossed the bed, sinking in the duvet like he was crossing deep snow. When he reached me, he meowed and stretched his head out to be petted. I meowed back and scratched him behind the ears. Anne used to tease that I was the world's worst sucker for animals.

The scent of toast drifted my way from the kitchen.

Mustard followed me down the hall.

Elena was perched on a stool beside the counter with a cup of tea beside her, a sketch book in her lap, and a pencil in her hand. She was sketching the flower garden and fountain in the middle of the courtyard with remarkable sensitivity.

"Nice," I told her, reaching for the coffee.

"It's pretty up here," she remarked. "I was thinking about maybe painting a picture of the courtyard from this angle. That is, unless you want us to split. I don't want to be any trouble."

The look said it was okay to kick her out, or just kick her—she was used to both.

"You're no trouble, Elena, but you'll have to postpone your painting for a couple of days. I'll be gone for most of today. After what happened last night, I don't want you here alone. I know a place a few miles over where you two can stay. It's pretty there, too. The people are nice, and you'll be safe."

"What kind of place?" she asked suspiciously, not looking up from the sketch pad. She sounded a little edgy. "Maybe I should just go home."

"And do what? Wait until someone shows up again?"

"I'm going to have to get on with my life sometime."

"Take a break. A few days off won't hurt you. Take your sketch pad with you. There's a private lake, gardens, even a waterfall."

She pouted.

"Look," I said, "if you won't think of yourself, think of the feline here. You want him to end up an orphan?"

Her lips curled into a reluctant smile. "Okay, okay. You win. But I better like it, and it better be as nice as this place."

While she packed up her and Mustard's belongings I made a quick call to Liz. Everything was fine there. I hung up and called Pete Blanche at home. He was just getting up.

"I'll be there in an hour," I told him.

"What'd'ya got? Another goddamn bullet?" he grumped.

"Exactly."

"Funny guy. Why can't I ever get a straight answer out of you?"

"Have more faith in yourself. See you in an hour."

I really didn't expect anyone to come looking for us at the house, but just in case, I made a quick call to my gardener and told him to take the day off. Carmencita already had the day off so I didn't bother calling her.

I left Elena's car in my garage and drove her and Mustard to the meditation retreat in Topanga run by a Japanese scholar named Kunio Uyeno. Anne had studied painting with him for several years.

He was a bald little man with a happy smile that quietly

masked the fact that he had black belts in karate, kung fu, and judo. He agreed to look after the couple for a few days and asked no questions. A minute later, they had disappeared behind the thick walls of the retreat, and I knew they were safe until I returned.

I drove down to Westwood to Pete's place. I parked in the driveway and left the motor running.

It wasn't even eight o'clock yet, and the temperature was already topping eighty. Pete opened the front door before I even got to it. He was struggling with his tie in the hallway mirror. His sports coat hung from a peg on the wall behind him. There was a patina of doughnut sugar on his fat chin.

I waited until he finished grooming, then handed him the .25 caliber slug I'd dug from the tree in Griffith Park.

"You weren't kidding, were you?" he said, pulling at his lopsided mustache and rolling the slug in his palm.

"Nope."

"Is this what I think it is?"

"I'm not sure, Pete. But I'm willing to bet it came from the same gun that killed Johnny Sylvester. Give me another twenty-four hours, and I'll tell you for sure."

"Give you another twenty-four hours? Nuts, Paris. You're withholding evidence on a murder case."

"We don't know that yet. Besides, Pete, you're holding the evidence."

"Listen, you sonovabitch—"

"Save it, Pete. We both have a long day ahead of us. It's going to be a scorcher." I turned and headed back toward the Jeep.

He started after me, then stopped and went back for his jacket and came out again, scowling.

"Where can I find you?" he yelled after me, hastily locking the front door of his house.

"I'll call you. Don't worry," I yelled back as I hopped in the Jeep. I took off before he decided to come after me in earnest.

I made a fast stop at the home of a photographer friend of mine in Westwood who had a studio in his home and who had done work for me before. While I waited, he made a quick duplicate of the prints Elena had given me.

Then I drove over to Marvin Feldman's office and left him the originals, the negatives, and the hundred thousand in cash all wrapped up in a green plastic garbage bag. He didn't ask, and I didn't tell him what was inside.

I packed the dupes in the attaché case and drove to a pay phone and called the number on the sheet of paper.

The phone rang a half dozen times before Tom picked it up. His hello was slurred and sloppy.

"It's Evan Paris. I'd like to come see you."

There was an infinitesimal pause before he replied. "I'm busy right now. Maybe another time."

"I have your briefcase. I'm only a few blocks away."

The second pause was much longer. "I guess it'll be all right," he breathed softly. "Sure, why don't you come? I'll leave the front door open."

"I'll be there in ten minutes."

"Sure," he repeated dully. "Ten minutes will be fine."

Twenty-Nine

Tom Greeves lived on Carmelita Street in Beverly Hills in a white antebellum house with four columns in front. The avocado green Ferrari with the TEK-2 license was parked in the driveway.

As promised, the front door of the house was unlocked. I pushed it open and entered.

Inside it was cool and still. A sharp odor of gunpowder spiced the air. I made my way through the living room. The smell grew stronger as I headed down the hallway.

I stopped at the first door on my right and peered in. It opened into a small, booklined den with a massive mahogany desk in the middle. A half empty bottle of Southern Comfort stood on the blotter. Tom Greeves sat on the far side of the desk in a brown leather swivel chair with his head back and his eyes on the ceiling. He was looking at a small hole where a napkin-sized piece of plaster had been chipped out. A twisted grin ran across his face like a knife wound.

In his lap, resting under both hands, was a handgun.

The piece of plaster lay on an antique Karaman prayer kilim beside the desk. I circled the desk and took the gun from his hands. He straightened up and looked at me as if I were a doctor coming to check a patient.

I examined the weapon. It was a .22 caliber Remington single-shot bolt action target pistol. The one shell in the chamber had recently been fired. It was definitely not the gun that had killed Johnny Sylvester. Nor was it the one that had been fired at me and Elena in the park.

He shook his head.

"I'm a real fuck-up. Can't even hit my own head with a bullet." His garrulous laugh sounded very drunk. His small round chin and baffled eyes made me think of a cartoon chipmunk who'd just been caught stealing nuts.

"Are you ready to tell me about it now?"

He grinned stupidly. "Sure. Why not? I've been meaning to tell someone about it one of these days. You taking me down to police headquarters first?"

"I'm not a cop, Tom."

He tried to focus on me, but only one eye seemed to work. He slapped one hand over the nonfocusing eye and adjusted his head slightly. "Not a cop?"

"Right. How about a cup of coffee? Can you walk by yourself?"

He glanced down at his legs as if he were seeing them for the first time. "I don't know. I'll give it a try."

Bracing his hands on top of the desk, he pulled himself up to his feet.

I let him hold onto my arm as we stumbled toward the kitchen, where I sat him down in a chair and made two cups of instant coffee.

When he was on his second cup I showed him the photos. "Here's what a hundred thousand would have bought you."

He looked at them one at a time. It was hard to tell if the look in his eyes was one of love or hate. When he was done, he turned the photographs face down on the table and said, "What do you want to know?"

"Everything."

"Everything," he repeated. His voice was fuzzy; so were his eyes. The wounded smile was still on his face. He said simply: "I killed her." He laughed, then covered his mouth with both hands like the monkey who speaks no evil.

"Tom, what do you remember of that night?"

"I don't know. I was drunk; I was stoned. Fuck. I did it."

"Maybe you didn't."

He waved the idea away like he was shooing flies. But he was eager to talk. The close brush with death and the photos had opened him up like a knife in a ripe watermelon. "Oh, I know what you're thinking. You're thinking it was that handyman. Lannell. I thought maybe . . . Then, this other guy called. . . . He knew. . . . No sense pretending . . ."

"What other guy, Tom? What did he say?"

He looked up and mumbled. "He had proof I'd killed her. Said he had pictures, twelve of them. Said I could have them for a hundred thou. Ah, Christ, I don't wanna go to jail. I didn't mean to kill her." He covered his eyes with his hands. Sensitive hands, the hands of a musician.

I reached over and turned the photographs face up, spreading them out in front of him.

I told him, "Look at them, Tom. Look at them carefully."

He shook his head.

I pulled his hands away from his eyes and repeated, "Look at them. Tell me what you see?"

I had to shock him, but I had to do it carefully so I wouldn't lose him.

His eyes glazed as he looked at the pictures. Finally, he said, "Madelaine and me. Twelve pictures of Madelaine and me. What do you want from me?"

"Use your head, Tom. Think. They show you and Madelaine in bed. You and Madelaine on the back porch of her place. But nothing that even remotely suggests you killed her."

He struggled upright to take a closer look.

I tapped my finger on the one closest to him. "They show that you knew Madelaine, and that you were intimate with her. But they don't show who killed her."

"Then, it might not have been me?"

"That's right."

"It *was* Lannell?"

"No," I said. "Not him."

"Then who?"

"Someone else. I think you might be able to help me find out. You do want to help, don't you?"

He nodded slowly. "But what can I do?"

"Tell me everything you know. I mean everything, Tom."

He took another gulp of his coffee. "I don't know where to start."

"When did you first meet her?" I prompted.

"Four years ago. Laura and I were engaged to be married. The wedding was all set. I think it had been set for ten years." He laughed mockingly. "You met Laura?"

I nodded.

"She's just a kid. But a good kid. I'm the rotten one. She was supposed to keep me off the ropes."

"I think she cares for you a lot," I told him.

He shook his head. "There's nothing to care for. I'm a loser."

"Tell me about it."

He seemed surprised that anyone could be interested. He started to ramble. I let him go, hoping to get a handle on how he'd been set up.

Life before Madelaine had been nothing to write home about. He'd been kicked out of six different schools despite substantial donations by the old man. He'd wrecked eight cars and been a heavy user of acid, 'ludes, alcohol, barbituates, speed, coke, and heroin. A seizure that almost cost him his life precipitated an eighteen-month stay in a Swiss dryout clinic when he was twenty-one. Fifteen-year-old Laura began corresponding with him and quickly developed a crush. When he came back, the family closed ranks around him and kept him home most of the time. Laura became his constant companion. They became lovers a year later.

"She was only seventeen when we decided to get married. I was almost twenty-five. I remember thinking, I'm nearly a quarter of a century old, and I've done just about everything except get married, so why not? I guess that's a stupid reason."

"A lot of people marry for less."

"Yeah, I guess so. Anyway, my life was just rolling along," he said sarcastically. "I was slated for death in suburbia. Then, out of nowhere, Madelaine hits me like a car crash. I was working for Neil then. Laura had gone away on a trip with her mother to Hawaii for a month. I was feeling a little down, so I asked Neil for a couple of days off. He gave it to me and also let me borrow his speedboat. I went down to Marina Del Rey the next day. Madelaine was there on the end of the dock. Just there. I can't tell you what she was like. You ever meet her?"

His face was glowing; his eyes bright, lost.

Pure vixen, I thought. Even now, even dead.

"I never had the pleasure," I told him.

"She was something else. I just can't describe it." He started to finger the pictures on the table in front of him. "I can't believe she's gone. She was more alive than anyone I've ever known."

"Go on. What happened? Did you speak to her? Did she speak to you?"

He shook his head despondently. "I was afraid to even look at her. I kept sneaking glances out of the corner of my eye while I got the boat ready. I mean she was *that* good-looking. Then, just as I was about to go, she came up and asked me about some people she said she was supposed to meet at the marina. She wasn't even sure she was waiting in the right spot. I suggested maybe they'd already gone out, then asked her to join me. Can't say she exactly jumped at the idea. I had to talk her into it.

"I practically flipped out when she agreed. I mean she was so beautiful, and she seemed to *like* me. I drove across to Catalina and docked. I told her I'd drive her to Mexico if she felt like it. I was laughing, man. I was happy."

The more he talked, the more he was reliving it, detail by detail.

"And she laughed. She thought I was *funny*. I drove with her cuddled up beside me with the spray flying over our heads. It felt weird. I was in love. I guess I didn't try anything because I kept remembering I was engaged." He rubbed his hand over his face and looked at me blearily.

"You kept seeing her after that?"

"Not right away. She wouldn't let me have her phone number. She said she'd just broken up with her boyfriend and didn't feel like seeing anyone. I told her we could just be friends, platonic buddies. I would have told her anything to see her again. She knew it. I was so obvious. She finally took my work number and promised to call if she changed her mind. I let her go. I could have kicked myself afterward. I didn't know anything about her. Just her first name.

"The next couple of days I went nuts. I hung around the marina figuring she'd show up again, but she didn't. I kept calling in to work to see if she'd phoned, but she hadn't. Finally, I went back to TEK. I was a wreck. I was hooked on her. She was like a drug. I could feel the same restlessness eating away at me. I started calling around, digging up old contacts, trying to score a little coke. You know, just to get myself straight again. I was so miserable."

"But she called?"

"Yes. She sounded so strange. She wouldn't tell me what was wrong, just that she'd been thinking about me. I practically begged her to see me. We met on the pier in Santa Monica. She started to cry. At first, she wouldn't tell me what was wrong. She didn't want to involve me. I insisted. She said she'd just moved out on her old boyfriend—the one she had mentioned the first day. She'd been thinking about breaking up with him for a long time—before she met me— but just hadn't. Then, she'd gone out with me and she knew it was over. She'd just left . . . left the apartment, left the car, left all her clothes. She said she'd go back eventually and pick up her things, but she couldn't go back that night because he would be there. She said she had enough money to get by for a couple of months. She said she was sure she could find a place and pick up a job as a waitress. I told her she could be a model, but she just laughed and said you had to be pretty to do that.

"You wouldn't believe what she was like. She was so shy, so lonely, so helpless. She made me feel strong. She made me want to take care of her, to protect her. I was a man with her.

"I drove us to a hotel down the beach. It was . . . it was the best night I had ever had in my life. I called in at work the next morning and left word that I'd be late. I took Madelaine apartment hunting. By noon, we'd found a small furnished house in Laurel Canyon that she said was perfect. I rented it in my name. I insisted on paying. I even rented her a small car. It felt good.

"Then, every night for almost a month, I'd arrive at her place—our place—and she'd be there waiting with dinner and wine and candles. It was almost perfect."

"Almost?"

"Yes, almost," he said uncomfortably. "All that time, in the back of my mind, I kept thinking, Laura's coming home soon. I'd have to do something about it, but I didn't know what."

"Did you tell Madelaine about Laura?"

"No. After that first day in Santa Monica, neither of us spoke about our pasts. She insisted what we had depended on how we felt toward each other, not who we had been before we met. It was wildly romantic, and for me it was the first time I'd ever escaped being Simon Greeves's son. Somehow, even my problem with Laura didn't matter anymore. Nothing mattered but being with Madelaine."

"But Madelaine did leave you."

"Yes. One day I went there, and she was gone. Her things were gone. The car I'd rented was parked out in front. Her note said simply that she cared very much for me, but that there were things she hadn't been able to tell me. She said it would be best not to try to find her, but to just forget and let time take care of everything. She would always remember the kindness I had shown her. That was it.

"I blamed myself. I told myself she'd come back. I paid the rent on the place for another month and kept going there every day. But she was gone. I suppose I might have hired a detective or something, but Laura arrived a few days after Madelaine disappeared. She knew something was wrong. I was miserable, and she'd been there before when I'd been miserable. If she hadn't been there, I'd have gone over the edge completely. I flipped out a little, but the family did their thing again. Until the wedding, there was someone with me almost all the time. I just went along. Madelaine was gone, and whatever I'd had with her was gone." He stopped talking and hung his head.

"When was the next time you heard from her?"

When he began talking again, his voice was awash in self-pity. "About five months later. She phoned me at the office. I couldn't believe it was her. I begged her to meet me. She said that was impossible. She just called to find out how I was.

"I told her how miserable I'd been. I told her how much I missed her. She said she missed me, too, but things had changed. She told me she'd made a mistake, that she had gone back to see her old boyfriend . . . because there had been so much anger. They went to bed. After that, she felt as if she couldn't come back. She was sure I'd hate her.

"I pleaded with her to leave the guy, to come back. I was begging her. I made her cry. She said she was pregnant, that she wanted the baby, and that meant that she would stay with the relationship.

"I tried to convince her that that was a really fucked up reason to stick with someone, but she said her mind was made up. She wouldn't be calling again."

'But she did call you, didn't she?"

He nodded sullenly. "Yes. She'd call every few months just to say hello. Each time she'd call, I'd get wired. Crazy wired. Just like a coke fever. Cold sweats. After a couple of months, I'd tell myself she was gone and I was over it. Then, she'd phone. Maybe if I'd had the guts to tell her to stop, she would have." His fists clenched on the table.

"What did she talk about?"

He opened his hands and looked at his palms. "Nothing really. The weather. About her daughter and what a good kid she was."

"The boyfriend?"

"No. Never."

"Did you ever mention any of this to Laura?"

"No. When I finally realized how unfair I was being to her, I told her I wanted a separation. That was six months ago. It took me three years to tell her, because I couldn't stand hurting her. The funny thing was that I'd been so obsessed with myself, I hadn't even noticed that she'd grown up. She said a separation would be fine, that she'd been thinking about one for a long time but hadn't said anything because she hadn't wanted to hurt me. We actually had a good laugh over that. This might sound crazy, but Laura's probably the only friend I've ever had in the world."

I refilled his cup. "When did you first see Madelaine again?"

"About four months ago."

"In San Francisco?"

"No. I never knew she'd been in San Francisco until I read it in the newspaper. I saw her here in town. She called me and asked me to lunch. She was staying in the Bel-Air Hotel. She told me she was here to look after business and had left her daughter with friends. She wanted to know how my wife was. I told her we'd separated. She said she'd separated from her husband and was thinking about moving back down to LA. She invited me over. We ended up in bed. But when I tried to make a date to see her again, she said to be patient, that there were problems she had to work out first. I thought she meant money. I offered to help, but she said that wasn't it. She had to be careful because of custody problems with her daughter. What she needed most was a friend, a friend who wouldn't put any pressure on her.

"I agreed to do whatever she wanted. She said she'd call.

She left that night. I tried to find out where she lived through the hotel, but she'd paid in cash and left no address. I'd lost her again.

"I started drinking and doing coke. I was sure she was just playing with me. I started to imagine all kinds of things. I started hating myself. I even started to hate her.

"Then she phoned and said she'd found a place in Malibu. She asked if I still wanted to see her. I begged her to tell me where she was. Only if I came when she said, she insisted. The husband might be having her watched. I promised to do whatever she asked. She told me where she was living. I couldn't believe it. She was practically next door to the Cliff House."

"Didn't you think it was strange that she'd moved in so close to your family?"

"*Strange?* I thought it was fucking bizarre." He laughed, but he'd obviously missed my point. "Everything about Madelaine was strange. When I got there that night and told her we were next door neighbors, she freaked. She made me swear not to say anything to anyone."

"Was Trudy there?"

"No. She'd left her with friends. She said that way it would be safer when we were together, that we'd have more time alone together. It sounded logical, but I think there was another reason."

"Such as?"

"I don't know. Something about her had changed. Something about her made me feel uncomfortable. For one thing, there were all kinds of drugs around. It was almost as if she had them there to tempt me."

"Maybe she did."

He shook his head. "No. That doesn't make sense." He was still struggling with the two Madelaine's—the woman he wanted to see and the one that he had seen.

"Those photos were taken by someone who intended to blackmail you. They could have been taken by someone trying to get evidence on her for some reason and without her consent. On the other hand, they could have been taken *with* Madelaine's consent."

"But why? If it was money she was after, I would have given her anything she wanted."

Money, yes, I thought, but not money *and* freedom.

"How many times did you see her?"

He closed his eyes for a second and counted with his lips. "Six or seven. Each time it got worse. I mean, I got worse. I wanted to see her all the time, but she was pulling the strings. I could only see her when she said it was okay. In between, I started hating her. I hated the power she had over me. I hated myself. That last night, I was drunk, like a sloppy animal. I grabbed her. She pushed me away. I fell on the floor. She told me to leave, that she never wanted to see me again. I passed out, then I remember being awake, sitting in front of the fireplace staring at the flames. I . . . I remember we were arguing. I remember picking up the firepoker and hitting her. I remember strangling her. . . ." He lowered his head like he was waiting for someone to chop it off.

"You remember hitting her and strangling her?"

"Yes. I remember it," he said quietly. "Like a dream, like watching myself do it. I was a dark shadow. I don't remember anything after that. I must have passed out."

He stopped and cradled his face in his hands.

"Maybe you *were* watching it," I said gently.

He needed to believe he was guilty. "Oh, no, it was me. When I woke up, she was dead. I was scared. I didn't know what to do. There was nothing I could do to bring her back. I got in my car and drove back here. I decided to kill myself. I took a bottle of sleeping pills. I got sick and threw up and passed out again. I woke up with the worst hangover I'd ever had. To tell you the truth, I thought maybe I'd dreamed the whole thing. Then my old man phoned to tell me there'd been a murder up the beach. I was just about to tell him that I'd done it when he said they'd caught the killer.

"I didn't know what to say. My father said to sit tight. He drove over here. The reporters had been hovering around the Cliff House all morning, trying to make the murder into a celebrity event by pulling us into it. My father said we had to stay out of it. I wanted to know more about the killer. He told me that they had him down at police headquarters. There was no question the man had done it.

"I didn't say anything. I knew it was possible that I hadn't killed her, but I still thought I should go to the police. Then, Lannell hung himself. I figured that's what I would have done if I'd done it. I told myself the police know their business. I tried to forget the whole thing.

"I was doing just that when I got a call about the photos."

"When did he call?"

"Sunday night. He knew I'd killed Madelaine and he didn't care about that. All he wanted was a little money to leave town. A hundred grand. I told him I'd need a few days to put it together without attracting anyone's attention. He gave me two. He called back on Tuesday. We set up a meeting in Venice, near the pier, after midnight. He never showed. Then last night this woman called. I went to Griffith Park with the money. Someone started shooting. I dropped the money and crawled back to the car. I can't take this anymore. When you called this morning I decided I'd had it." His face sagged hopelessly.

"It would have been a waste, Tom."

"Why are you so sure I didn't kill her?"

"You'll just have to trust me." I took out Johnny Sylvester's pictures and handed them to him. "Have you ever seen this man before?"

He shook his head. "No. Never. Who is he?"

"The photographer who took the pictures of you and Madelaine. He was killed sometime late Tuesday night."

Tom was silent.

"He was probably killed by someone else who knew about these pictures."

"Who?"

I didn't give him a direct answer. "The police are investigating the murder," I replied vaguely. "Who knew you were putting the money together?"

He licked his lips. "Nicki, I guess, but she wouldn't say anything."

"She gave you the whole bundle?"

"Not exactly." He shifted uncomfortably. "Look, I really didn't want to involve her, but I was in a bind. Any withdrawals over a thousand from any of my accounts have to be checked by someone in the family. It's a holdover from my drug years. Fortunately, I've got a few accounts they don't know about, and I was able to get a quick loan on the car. All told, I put together nearly ninety thousand by myself. I had to go to Nicki for the rest."

"That's a sizable chunk of cash. Wasn't she suspicious?"

"A little, but I told her I wanted to put down some money on a stock I'd heard about. A real long shot. I didn't want to go to the old man, because I wanted to do it on my own, and he's always putting me down. She understood."

"Where'd you get the gun?"

"It's an old target pistol of my mother's. She doesn't even know I have it. I had it with me last night. I'm such an ass I forgot all about it when the shooting started. I only remembered it when I was halfway home."

"Did you see who was doing the shooting?"

"No. I didn't see anyone. I just heard the shooting and ran."

"Does your mother have any other guns?"

He shook his head. "Not anymore. She used to have a whole collection, but she got rid of them about ten years ago. She kept this one because she'd won a couple of prizes with it."

"What about your father? Does he own a gun?"

"Not that I know of."

"Your sister or Neil or your mother-in-law?"

"No, I don't think so." He stopped and stared. "You don't think any of them are involved in this, do you?"

"Guns have a way of ending up in the wrong hands sometimes."

"Yeah, I guess so." He unconsciously pulled at his lower lip with thumb and forefinger.

"Did it ever occur to you that you might be the father of Madelaine's little girl?"

He let go of his lip and looked more certain. "Sure. In the beginning I thought the kid had to be mine. I even told Madelaine I hoped it was, but she said her daughter was born in April, a year after we'd slept together."

"When were you with her, Tom? Do you remember?"

"April. Madelaine disappeared on May 1," he said without hesitating. "I know that for sure because it was the day before Nicki's birthday."

I did some quick calculations in my head. Trudy's birth certificate said she'd been born in January, nine months—not twelve—after Madelaine and Tom had had their little fling. I didn't tell him.

"What about Madelaine's friends and family? Did she ever say anything at all about her background, even in passing? She must have said something."

He rubbed his face wearily, then shook his head. "No, nothing really. Once when we were riding around in my car I was fiddling with the radio station and hit the baseball game. I started to change it, but she said she wanted to hear the

score. I thought she was kidding. I asked her if she really
liked baseball. She said, yes, but she liked football best. She
said her father was a football player, said it was in her blood."

"Her father *was* a football player or he *liked* football?" It
was hard to keep the excitement from my voice.

"She said he was a star at UCLA many years ago. She
wouldn't tell me any more. He was dead and she didn't like
talking about it. I never brought it up again. I don't know
why, but I think she was probably just making it up."

"Probably," I agreed, but that isn't what I was thinking. I
was reasonably sure she wasn't making it up, and I was
almost as sure I knew why. Something the senile old man in
San Pedro had said suddenly made sense.

Thirty

I asked Tom if he really would like to prove his innocence.

"I'll do anything."

"Good." I told him he had to gather everyone in his
family—his father, his mother, his sister, Nicki, his brother-in-
law, Neil, Laura, and his mother-in-law, Maggie—at the Cliff
House that night. I told him to tell them all that he had
something to tell them about Madelaine, but to say nothing
more.

"Why?"

"Because one of them has information that will help prove
your innocence. You'll just have to trust me."

After I left Tom, I drove to the UCLA alumni house and
picked up a copy of the 1965 yearbook, then drove down to
San Pedro to pay one more visit to Fred Jessel on Eleventh
Street.

He was sitting on the rocking chair with the blanket tucked
around his legs just as I'd left him two days before, wearing
the same T-shirt with both sleeves rolled up and the same

Nike jogging shoes with the laces undone. The *Playboy* he was reading was still open to Miss May.

There was a flicker of recognition in his crossed eyes.

"Do I know you?" he asked.

"Yes. I was here the other day. I'm a friend of Arla Coltrane's. My name's Evan Paris. I was asking you about Jimmy Lucie and Joyce Coltrane."

"Must have been a long time ago, or I'd remember," he said testily.

I didn't argue. I opened the yearbook to the football team and pointed to one of the players. "Do you recognize him?" I asked.

He studied the picture out of the corner of his eye and said, "Sure I recognize him. That's that fellow Jimmy. He used to come by here to visit all the time."

"Jimmy Lucie lived here," I reminded him.

He shot me an angry look. "Now, don't tell me, young fellow. That's Jimmy Lucie," he repeated, hammering his forefinger on the picture. That's the one that went off and played for the Bruins."

"Was he the one who used to take Joyce upstairs?"

He looked up at me, and shook his head. "I don't know. I just don't remember," he replied meekly.

I tried using his logic. "Do you remember the name of the fellow that Jimmy Lucie used to visit when he came here?"

"No. Can't think of it. Ratty-looking little shrimp. Never did like him."

I tried a couple of names on Fred, but he wasn't able to remember anything more. It didn't matter. I had enough.

I thanked him and drove to the County General and had a quick visit with Arla Coltrane. She was feeling better, but she wasn't out of danger. She was breathing at only fifty percent of her lung capacity.

"I'll hang on until you find something," she informed me sternly. Bless her heart, I thought. "You're going to find something, aren't you?"

"I'll find something," I assured her. "You up to looking at another picture?"

"Sure." She gave me a cheerful smile, but the shortness of breath had bled most of the light out of her eyes.

I showed her the pictures I'd shown to Fred Jessel, but Mrs. Coltrane didn't recognize him.

"His name is Neil Harold," I told her. "Ever hear of him?"

She shook her head. "No, don't think so. You think this fellow Neil Harold went to high school with Joyce?"

"As a matter of fact, he didn't. He went to high school in Palos Verdes on the other side of the peninsula. But he went there at the same time as Joyce went to high school in San Pedro. They're the same age."

"What does this have to do with Joyce?"

Everything, I thought, but told her simply, "I'll know more tonight. I'm meeting with a few people."

"Will you find Trudy's father?"

"We'll see."

"You know more than you're telling me, don't you?"

"Are you reading my mind?"

She smiled. "Well, when you do find out more, you'll know where to find me," she said sweetly. "I'm not going anywhere."

I squeezed her hand and left, then went across the hospital to Liz's office. She was out giving a seminar to a group of residents. Trudy and Matt were sitting under Liz's desk. They both wore large, boat-shaped hats made out of newspaper. Trudy was reading a Dr. Seuss book to Matt. The book was upside down in her lap. Both looked slightly perturbed when I interrupted.

Matt said everything was okay. Trudy said everything was okay.

They definitely didn't need me. I left and drove home.

I called Pete Blanche. The bullets that I'd pulled out of the plywood in San Francisco hadn't come from Don Claypole's gun. On the other hand, the shots that had been fired at Elena and me in Griffith Park had come from the same gun that had killed Johnny Sylvester.

"I want you down here in an hour, Paris. If you're not, I'm putting out an all points bulletin. I'll have you dragged in if I have to."

"I'm at home, Pete. If you want me that badly, come and get me, but if you do come, I promise you I'll do my very best to make sure you come out looking like shit."

The line crackled with silence.

"I wish to Christ I knew what the hell you were up to. I can't keep a lid on this forever."

"I need until midnight tonight."

I could hear heavier breathing on the other end. "All right. Ten hours, but that's it. You got until midnight to call me. I'll be here until six. After seven, I'll be home. Call me by twelve, win, lose, or draw."

"By midnight. I promise."

Seconds after I hung up, Tom called, sounding exhilarated. They'd all agreed to meet at the Cliff House—Amelia, Simon, Margaret Patterson, Nicki, Neil, and Laura.

"Maggie has a business meeting she couldn't get out of, so she won't get there until eight. She'll be the last one."

"Good. You come up here at eight, and we'll go together. I gave him directions and told him to check himself into a hotel for the rest of the afternoon so no one could get to him.

Then, I went out to the backyard and spent the rest of the afternoon evicting a nest of gophers that had taken up residence in the rose garden.

Thirty-One

Tom and I arrived at the Cliff House at nine. The others were gathered in the living room that overlooked the ocean. The moon was just coming up. There was a pale orange halo around it.

My arrival caused a stir of uneasiness among everyone except Laura. "I had a feeling I'd see you tonight," she mused with a warm smile.

The others wore frozen, somber expressions. No one asked me to leave, though, which was noteworthy, considering that most of them had shown me the door in the last few days.

Simon Greeves took charge, not surprisingly. I figured he'd probably been among the most deceived and therefore, ironically, thought he knew the most. Begrudgingly, he acknowledged my presence with a nod, but he addressed his son, not me.

"Well, Tom, you called us all here tonight. I'd like to know why."

Laura looked as if she were about to say something, but I

caught her eye, and she stopped before the words were out of her mouth.

Tom struggled in silence for a few moments before he finally said, "Madelaine." He said it so softly no one would have heard him under normal circumstances. But everyone in this room had. "Madelaine Lucie," he went on unsteadily. It wasn't his story that shook him, but the faces around him that had run every move in his life for as long as he could remember. Every move that is, except the one that had brought him right to the brink—Madelaine. "I was with her the night she died. I was there." He clenched his fists, fighting against himself, fighting against them. "I should have gone to the police and told them what I knew, but I was afraid. I thought . . . I thought I even had killed her. Now . . ."

He paused and looked at me for help. The others looked like they wanted to eat my face.

It was Amelia who made a half-hearted attempt to come to her son's rescue.

"I'm sure whatever you did wasn't as bad as you think, dear. We can have our lawyers look into it, and you know you can count on the support of your family." She spoke gently to him. Then, she shifted her focus on me. Her eyes glared at me like a chicken hawk's ready to sink its talons into a rat. "You must be a very twisted person, Mr. Paris, to take advantage of people to get your stories. I don't know what hold you think you have over my son, or what you expect to get out of the rest of us, but I can tell you now that you'll be hearing from our attorneys. We're a very tight family. We don't like outsiders interfering."

"That's exactly why I'm here, Mrs. Greeves, on a family matter," I corrected her. "There's one member of this family who isn't present tonight—a little girl you all seem to be forgetting about."

"I'm afraid I don't know what's going on," Laura piped up innocently.

I smiled at her. "I know, Laura. You're about the only one who really is in the dark."

"But it has to do with Madelaine, doesn't it?"

"Yes," I said.

Amelia's eyes blazed. "You're certainly not accusing one of us of killing that woman, are you?"

"No, though of all the people in this room, you came the

closest to killing her. But all of you are involved in some way in the three murders."

"Three murders?" Tom's face was stricken.

"Three. Madelaine; a man by the name of Jimmy Lucie who more recently went by the name of Johnny Sylvester; and Madelaine's mother, Joyce Coltrane Lucie, who died in a San Francisco fire twenty-two years ago."

The air crackled. Nicki stole a quick look at Neil. Neil glanced at Simon. Simon missed that look but shot a suspicious look at Amelia, who gave him one back. Maggie Patterson stared with unconcealed concern at her daughter Laura.

"Suppose you explain yourself, young man," Simon Greeves demanded. The look I got was business-only, but the eyes were no longer on the offense.

"All right." I directed my aim at the family patriarch. "First of all, Simon, you lied to the police about Madelaine. Not only did you know the woman who lived in Professor Celli's cottage, but you had known her for the past five years. You had an affair with her."

Simon didn't deny it. Tom's jaw dropped open. Laura sat with her hands folded on her lap, nodding thoughtfully.

"I don't know how you first met, but I suspect she just happened to be somewhere where you were. A party, or a convention, or something. It doesn't matter. She was there. You fell for her, or rather, she made you fall for her. You see, Simon, what you thought was spontaneous was part of a well-constructed plan. In a word, you were set up."

Greeves's lips curled away from his teeth slightly. He was fighting it, but I think he knew he was going down for the count.

"Madelaine didn't just happen into your life. She was deliberately placed there by a man who knew that he was pushing her into the middle of an explosive situation that ironically had very little to do with you in the beginning. If you had, for whatever reason, failed to fall for Madelaine's charms, he would have tried some other way to meet his objectives. His motives were simple. In you, in your family and extended family, he saw the chance to score big. But there were pitfalls, so he had to be clever, and he had to be lucky. For a while, his luck held. Then, about a year ago, everything went wrong. The irony is that your own run of bad luck precipitated the fall."

Simon sat like a statue. Nostrils flared, eyes narrowed.

"Let's go back for a second to five years ago. You grabbed at Madelaine—at her youth, her beauty—and for a while, she held your interest. That suited her, but it wasn't enough. She needed something more to make your commitment permanent. The obvious way would have been to become pregnant by you, but you had had a vasectomy. You'd probably even told her about that. But there was a way around that. Tom. If he made her pregnant, she would be set for life. Callous? Yes, but we're talking about a girl who had grown up with practically nothing, an ugly duckling who'd spent her formative years as a shy repressed thing who'd suddenly been set free by a monster called Johnny Sylvester. Besides, I have a feeling she may have been very much in love with you, Simon, at least for a time."

Simon brushed at the front of his suit as if checking to see if he hadn't been stripped naked. Tom was hunched down like a turtle pulling into its shell, his mouth half open as if wanting to ask his father *the* question but not daring to.

I answered it for him. "Madelaine got pregnant by Tom." I turned to him and said, "Tom, you're Trudy's father. She was born exactly nine months after you and Madelaine had your affair. Blood tests will confirm it within a reasonable margin of error, if you have doubts. Your mother and father can also confirm it. Trudy is the only Greeves heir. Madelaine's daughter is the continuation of your line."

Tom's head moved as if a pulley were swinging it around in an arc. "Is this true?" he asked everyone.

Amelia sucked in her lips. "We wanted to tell you, Tom, but we thought it would be better if you didn't know."

"But why?" he cried.

She shifted uneasily but remained silent.

I gave it a shot. "Because Madelaine never loved you, and because you loved her too much. Madelaine had a very good side to her, Tom. Trudy is proof of that. Madelaine was a good and loving mother, but there was another side to her also, a bad side that had been made worse by Johnny Sylvester. Your parents both recognized it. She would have eaten you alive. Your mother—even more than your father, I think—understood that." I turned to Amelia and said, "It was you who went to Madelaine with the gun and threatened to kill her just before she went to San Francisco four years ago, wasn't it?"

"I wanted to scare her," she admitted stiffly, stroking her

great mane of reddish hair back away from her face. "I hated her. Simon had had little flings before, but he'd always come back. Madelaine destroyed our marriage. Through Simon I found out that Madelaine had gone after Tom. I couldn't stand by while she wrecked my son's life as well. I told her to leave town or I'd kill her. She screamed in my face that I'd never touch her because she was carrying my grandchild, my own flesh and blood. She was right. But I had to keep her away from Tom. Simon and I talked it over. We agreed to send her away and give her whatever she needed to look after herself and the child. It was the only way."

"You went up to San Francisco to visit Trudy, didn't you?"

"I tried to. Yes. She's my only grandchild. But Madelaine wouldn't let me see the baby. She said all she wanted from us was money."

"So you let her alone."

She nodded, twisting the emerald brooch on her blouse.

"And after the murder, you were afraid that if you did anything it might trigger a new investigation. You knew Tom had been seeing Madelaine, didn't you?"

"Yes."

I turned to Simon and said, "It made perfect sense to keep Trudy in San Francisco with her natural mother and to support both of them by feeding Madelaine inside information on the company so she could make money off TEK stock. It might have worked forever if you hadn't lost your touch in the last year. You began losing money for both yourself and her."

Greeves interjected. "The markets just weren't reacting the way they should. I told her to be patient, but she wouldn't. I would have made it up to her, but she began to panic."

"You could have gone to jail if she'd blown the whistle on you for giving her inside information," I pressed him. "Is that what she did? Threaten you? Is that why you cut her off?"

"Yes. I tried to bring her under control. When she wouldn't listen, I had to protect myself. I was protecting her, too. Hell, I was protecting all of us. If she'd dragged us into court, she would have killed the stock. It would have taken years to recover. Everything I did, I did for her own good."

"But Madelaine didn't see it that way," I pointed out. "She saw it as a personal affront. She moved here, into Professor Celli's cottage to take you head on. When you wouldn't budge, she moved in on Tom."

"We had an agreement. She'd promised she'd never go near my son again. She went back on her word."

"Did you kill her?" Tom nearly choked on the words.

The room was oppressively silent as father and son measured each other.

Simon's eyes were damp. "I never laid a hand on her, son. I was very fond of her."

Tom swung toward me to confirm or deny it.

"He didn't kill her, Tom."

"Then who did?"

I ignored his question and turned back to Simon. "Did you know she was being egged on by Johnny Sylvester?"

"No. I'm not even sure I know who he is. You said his name was originally Jimmy Lucie. Was he some kind of relative?"

"Yes and no," I replied. "I guess I should explain who he is, or rather was. He was shot to death two days ago."

"The man with the one eye lower than the other," Laura interjected. "He was the man I saw."

I nodded. "Jimmy Lucie didn't just stumble on Madelaine five years ago. He'd been around from the beginning. Madelaine's mother, Joyce Coltrane, became pregnant in her last year of high school. Jimmy Lucie was one of the kids she'd hung around with."

"Then he was Madelaine's father," Laura cut in.

"Not exactly," I corrected her. "But that's what everyone assumed at the time. Lucie married Joyce Coltrane, Madelaine's mother, about six months after Madelaine was born. Shortly after that, they left Madelaine with Joyce's parents and moved to San Francisco. A few months later, Joyce died in a fire. Jimmy scooped up the insurance money and vanished. Years later, when Madelaine was eighteen, Jimmy, who had changed his name to Johnny Sylvester, decided that it was time to play his one trump card. The trump card he'd been carrying all these years was that he knew the true identity of Madelaine's father."

I turned to Neil, then explained to the others. "Neil is Madelaine's natural father."

Neil remained silent. He was probably watching the Presidency of the United States slip through his fingers.

Nicki tried to come to her husband's rescue. "If Madelaine was his illegitimate child, so what? Surely you're not suggest-

ing that Neil would go to any great lengths or do anything
illegal to try to cover it up? That's absurd!"

"That's just the tip of the iceberg," I corrected her.

Tom cut in. "If Neil's Madelaine's father, then, he's my
daughter's grandfather."

"That's right," I agreed. "But there's more."

Nicki made another feeble attempt. "If as you say, Neil was
Madelaine's father, than it's inconceivable that he'd have had
anything to do with the death of his own daughter," she
insisted. By the way she said it, I knew the Neil–Madelaine
relationship had been no surprise for her.

"Neil didn't kill Madelaine," I assured her. "I'm quite
certain that no one in this room did."

"Then, does it really concern us?" Amelia asked hopefully.

"I'm afraid it does. You see, when Johnny Sylvester began
to worm his way into Simon's life, he had an accomplice,
someone who knew Simon and how he could be gotten to."

Simon looked at me, than at Neil. Neil had gone gray.
Simon looked back at me and asked, "Neil?"

"No," I said. "Someone much more vulnerable. Someone
who had as much or more to lose as Johnny Sylvester. I'm
talking about Madelaine's mother, Joyce."

Laura sat forward on the edge of her chair and waved her
hand like a schoolgirl. "But you said Madelaine's mother had
been killed in a fire in San Francisco," she insisted. "You said
Jimmy Lucie collected the insurance money."

"That's what the police and the insurance company thought.
Two days ago, I flew up to San Francisco and checked the old
files on that case. I found a curious thing. Joyce Coltrane
Lucie had had a very serious break in her right arm as a
child. The X-rays of her remains showed no breaks in the arm
of the woman who died in that fire. The woman who died in
that fire wasn't Joyce Coltrane Lucie."

"Then, who was it?" Laura asked.

"I don't know," I said. "The only two who knew that were
Jimmy Lucie and Joyce. They murdered her."

I stopped and looked straight at Maggie Patterson. She was
stroking her bandaged arm, looking more dead than alive.
Her lips were trembling as if she were trying to speak but
couldn't find the words. The others turned to where I was
looking and tried to comprehend.

Finally, Maggie found her voice. It was a cracked unsteady
voice, but the words came out like shards of glass.

"I'm Joyce Coltrane," she said. Then, she turned and looked directly at Laura. "Madelaine was my daughter. Madelaine was your half-sister, Laura."

Laura kept shaking her head. "Mother, . . ." she said softly and started to get up, but Maggie held her good hand up to stop her.

"I want to explain. For you, Laura. For all of you, and also for my granddaughter Trudy. Try to make her understand someday." Maggie turned and addressed me. "Mr. Paris, you were right about most of what you've said, but not quite right about the other woman in San Francisco. She was murdered as you said, but I didn't know anything about it until afterward."

She paused and asked for a glass of water. Simon rose mechanically and brought it to her. The others watched as she drank it.

Laura moved to her side and held her hand. "Were you and Neil really lovers? Were you really married to that awful-looking man I saw you with?"

Maggie nodded.

She continued to address me. Maybe I was the easiest one in the room to face. "We were in San Francisco. I was already pregnant with Laura, but I hadn't told Jimmy. One day, he picked me up at work and drove me out to a cabin in the Sierras and left me there. Three days later, he came back and showed me the newspaper clipping about the fire and my death. I thought at first it was some kind of joke—a gag newspaper like the ones they print in amusement parks."

Jimmy, she explained, had enticed a wino up to their room and set it on fire. He told Joyce he wouldn't hesitate to kill her if she crossed him. "He said if I ever did try to turn him in, he'd swear the whole idea was mine. We'd both go to the gas chamber. He swore if anything every happened to him he'd make sure that Madelaine was killed. He meant it. If I didn't agree, he'd get her."

Jimmy left her in a hotel in Reno while he waited for the insurance payout. She escaped to Seattle, gave birth to Laura, and resolved to put the past behind her. She lost weight, had minor plastic surgery, and eventually married Sam Patterson, a businessman who adopted Laura and never pried into their past. But Sam left her holding a bank note for forty grand on his business and skipped out.

She drifted down to LA, where she got in touch with Neil. She broke down and told him the whole story. Neil tried to make up for his treatment of her years ago when he had refused to have anything to do with her after she'd become pregnant. He helped her pay off the debt, then found her a job with his father-in-law's company.

When Jimmy Lucie showed up six years ago and tried to blackmail Joyce, Neil ran him off.

But Jimmy wasn't through with them.

"He came back," Maggie said softly, avoiding her daughter's eyes. "He used Madelaine to get to us. I hated what he was doing to her, but I didn't dare interfere. In a way, I was happy. Madelaine had money; Trudy was well looked after.

"Everything fell apart when the stock market threw us a curve. Madelaine panicked. Jimmy played on her fears, convincing her Simon was cheating her. They both were so greedy. She could have ruined it all for everyone."

"So you killed her," Tom said.

She looked up in surprise.

"No," she replied softly. "No, Tom. She was my daughter. I loved her. I could never have hurt her."

"Then who?"

She wiped at her lips with a tissue. "Jimmy did. He tried to make me believe that it was her fault. He had come by to show her the pictures he'd taken without her knowledge. She was furious—because of the pictures and because Tom was there—dead drunk—but there. When she threatened to call the police and have him thrown off the property, he'd tried to control her by telling her the truth about San Francisco. It was when she went for the phone the second time that he hit her. He told me it was her fault."

She choked.

"That's enough," Laura said decisively. "You don't have to say any more."

Maggie shook her head. "No, let me finish," she said quietly. She straightened and seemed to recover some of her dignity. "I didn't know this until several days after Madelaine's death. I believed Arthur Lannell had killed her, just as the police said he had. There was nothing anyone could do. Then Jimmy phoned and told me what had really happened. He said he'd done it for both of us. He needed money to get out of town. I wanted to kill him. I think he knew what I was thinking. He jeered and said he had photos that could wreck not only my life but would destroy the whole Greeves family.

If I didn't come up with the money he wanted, he'd tell Laura the truth."

"So you killed him," I said.

"Yes. I killed him. I don't regret it. I'm glad that it's over." She paused and looked directly at me. "I'm glad I didn't kill you. I wanted to, you know."

"Yes," I told her. "I know."

"I'm sorry," she repeated to me, then turned to the others. "I'm sorry."

Thirty-Two

Neil Harold said he had only meant to scare me when he had fired the shots at me in San Francisco. The gun he had used was an unregistered World War Two service revolver belonging to his father. He claimed he fired over my head. I decided to give him the benefit of the doubt and not add to the charges against him.

Since Maggie had confided in him, he was charged with complicity in the murder of Johnny Sylvester and with withholding information in the murder of his daughter, Madelaine Lucie. He was given a one-year probation. He withdrew from active politics.

Several senior police officials in Los Angeles were shuffled, and one requested early retirement, but no charges were ever brought against any officers with regard to the original investigation into Madelaine Lucie's death.

Pete Blanche got the credit for cracking the homicide and was promoted a grade.

Joyce Coltrane Lucie Patterson was indicted for the murder of Jimmy Lucie. Her gun, which had killed Jimmy Lucie and fired on Elena and me, had been obtained, ironically, from Jimmy Lucie after her house had been burglarized. She admitted that at the time she had thought of using it on Jimmy, but hadn't been able to bring herself to do so until after he'd murdered Madelaine. While on bail during the pretrial hearings, she was reunited with her mother Arla Coltrane. In the end, Joyce was given a one-year sentence for manslaughter after considerable strings were pulled on her behalf.

Arla Coltrane met her second granddaughter, Laura Patterson Greeves, for the first time at a tearful get well party that Liz arranged.

Tom, his father, mother, and sister Nicki were all charged with withholding evidence in the Madelaine Lucie slaying. All charges were eventually dropped.

Tom and Laura went to a good marriage counselor who helped them get back together. Trudy went to live with her natural father and Laura who, as Madelaine's half sister, was also Trudy's aunt.

It was concluded that Arthur Lannell's suicide was the result of his drug disorientation. Maybe he died believing he'd killed Madelaine.

No identity was established for the wino burned to death in the fire Jimmy Lucie set in San Francisco in 1963.

No charges were brought against Don Claypole, the detective Maggie Patterson had hired to keep an eye on Tom.

Through a contact of mine, Claypole's former secretary Shirley Bass found a new job as a production trainee at one of the television studios. It wasn't difficult to arrange a loan for Elena Rachel to study art at UC Santa Barbara.

Mrs. Coltrane died a week after her daughter Joyce began her prison term. She passed away knowing that Trudy now had four living grandparents—Simon, Amelia, Neil, and Joyce; two living aunts—Nicki and Laura; and a father—Tom, and a stepmother, Laura, if you counted her twice. Trudy would be well taken care of.

A couple of months after that, Liz came to tell me she'd begun dating an old friend of hers from Seattle. I was out in the garden removing the braces from Anne's favorite orange tree. It had made a spectacular recovery and looked as if it would live another lifetime.

"He wants me to marry him and move up there." Liz stroked the trunk of the tree where the dark tar had hardened into a black shiny vein.

"Do you love him?"

The noon sun beat down mercilessly. She fingered the string of pearls around her neck and nodded. "Yes."

"Then, go. There's nothing wrong with making yourself happy."

She smiled. That had been one of Anne's favorite lines. She said seriously, "Evan, I love him, but I think I'll always love you more. I just don't think it will ever work. I just don't think you'll ever forgive me for what happened that night and . . . and I can't blame you."

What happened was that Liz had asked me to meet her after work for a drink that night. She was upset. She told me that she was beginning to fall in love with me. She just wanted to talk it out. She didn't know what to do. The only thing she could think of was to stop seeing Anne and me. I didn't know what to tell her except that I was in love with my wife. We left it at that. We finished dinner late. When I arrived home, Anne was gone. If I'd come home earlier, they'd only have come back for her another night. I was sure of that. I never blamed Liz, but no one could keep her from continuing to blame herself.

Even now, I could see that she wanted me to talk her out of Seattle, to say something that would change her mind and make it all right.

The truth was, it never would be all right. Anne would always be there between us.

I remembered something Anne had once told me about what it was like being a doctor. Most of the time you just psyched yourself up to be strong and kept up that sensitive detachment that allowed you to see what's happening without letting it get to you. You see people dying, day after day, without letting it inside. Then, every once in a while, someone dies on you—a baby, a teenager, an old man, it didn't matter. It just happened, and it was like a kick to the stomach. That was the time when you had nothing to hang on to. It wasn't good or bad or right or wrong. "It just is," she would say. "It just is."

In the end, I didn't say anything to Liz to talk her out of Seattle. There was nothing to say. As Anne would have said, "It just is."

A month after that, Liz moved up north and got married.